She lifted the rifle into the crook of her arm.

Brad's first impulse was to smile. "Look, Catherine, let's be reasonable—"

"Stay right where you are."

Brad let the seconds sizzle hotly between them. "You know, I've lived in New York for years and have never once been mugged."

Her look could have given him second-degree burns.

"Then I come down here to this godforsaken place," he added sullenly, "and get held at gunpoint. Figure that one out."

"Be quiet so I can think."

Despite his better judgment, Brad laughed, and she flushed so prettily and so sumptuously that a door that had been closed for a long time opened inside him.

Hadn't anyone ever told her that if she'd stop fighting the world for a few minutes, she could have it in the palm of her hand? She could have *him* in the palm of her hand. She might already, God help him....

Dear Reader,

Each and every month, to meet your sophisticated standards, to satisfy your taste for substantial, memorable, emotion-packed stories of life and love, of dreams and possibilities, Silhouette brings you six extremely **Special Editions**.

Now these exclusive editions are wearing a brand-new wrapper, a more sophisticated look—our way of marking Silhouette **Special Editions'** continually renewed commitment to bring you the very best, the brightest and the most up-to-date in romance writing.

Reach for all six freshly packaged Silhouette **Special Editions** each month—the insides are every bit as delicious as the outsides—and savor a bounty of meaty, soul-satisfying romantic novels by authors who are already your favorites and those who are about to become so.

And don't forget the two Silhouette *Classics* at your bookseller's every month—the most beloved Silhouette **Special Editions** and Silhouette *Intimate Moments* of yesteryear, reissued by popular demand.

Today's bestsellers, tomorrow's *Classics*—that's Silhouette **Special Edition**. And now, we're looking more special than ever!

From all the authors and editors of Silhouette **Special Edition**,

Warmest wishes,

Leslie Kazanjian,
Senior Editor

LINDA SHAW
Thunder High

Silhouette Special Edition

Published by Silhouette Books New York

America's Publisher of Contemporary Romance

SILHOUETTE BOOKS
300 East 42nd St., New York, N.Y. 10017

ISBN: 0-373-09492-2

First Silhouette Books printing November 1988

Printed in the U.S.A.

LINDA SHAW,

the mother of three, lives with her husband in Keene, Texas. A prolific author of both contemporary and historical fiction, when Linda isn't writing romantic novels, she's practicing or teaching the piano, violin or viola.

Española

Los Alamos

Valle Grande

Santa Fe

Running Wolf Ranch

Bernalillo

Albuquerque

NEW MEXICO

N

Underlined places are fictitious.

Prologue

When she was fifteen, Babe Polansky began her first romance novel. It wasn't an easy decision, but Babe bravely resigned herself to the risks of authoring love stories—all the heckling and elbowed ribs and what-have-you from her critics.

"Do you plan to research your books firsthand, Babe?"

"Read something to us, Babe. Skip the description and go straight to the good part."

"Do you plan to branch into movies, Babe? What about a screenplay for Patrick Swayze? Oo-o-o, would you get me his autograph, *ple-e-ease*?"

At the beginning, Babe had thought to draw upon her own experiences for the novel. But who wanted to read about a nice, too-plump, freckle-faced girl who'd run away from home at thirteen to escape a sadistic stepbrother?

To Babe the solution was obvious. She must write through the eyes of another person. But who? Or was it whom? No matter. She knew from the outset that her heroine would be Catherine Holmes.

Besides being the most extraordinary person Babe knew—like a drill sergeant, a lion tamer and a nun all rolled into one—Cat Holmes was the novelist's dream-come-true. At twenty-five, Cat reached halfway between five and six feet and was as willowy as a starlet. She wore her explosive, Cher-black hair long, to her shoulders, and her almond-shaped violet eyes would be absolutely *gorgeous* on a book cover. Her breasts were nice and full, too; breasts were very important in romance novels.

Cat wasn't just another pretty face. When times got really bad, which was to say when they reached the starvation stage, she would go out and buy a few yards of jersey, spend an evening with a chattering sewing machine and the next day walk into some of the most influential homes in Los Alamos or Santa Fe. After an evening of very sophisticated fund-raising, she would come back to the ranch with a thousand dollars for the abused children who lived with her. Then she would hang up her new clothes, pull a scruffy poncho over some jeans and chaps, drive out into the desert and restretch the fence where it was down.

Cat's secret was that she had survived hell. At sixteen, she, too, had run away from home. Out of the whole drug scene she had emerged intact; not only intact but better, wiser. Was it any wonder that she was tough sometimes? That she could handle junkies and punks who were in trouble with the law? Los Alamos County social workers sent their hardest cases to Cat. She, Babe, had been one of them.

And, just to set the record straight, it simply wasn't true—that rumor about Cat being cold and unfriendly. Sometimes, late at night when the New Mexico sky was filled with stars, and coyotes were yipping in the Jemez foothills, Cat would gather Diana into her arms when the girl was having one of her nightmares. At times like that, with her face softening and the lines at her eyes growing tender with love, Cat was the most gentle, beautiful woman in the world.

As she was now, at this moment, seated across the bed on the second-floor men's ward of St. Jude's Hospital, all her masks and facades peeled away as she held her father's hand. Now Cat was vulnerable and sweet and very touchable.

Babe's problem was how to make such a complicated woman the heroine of her book: Cat Holmes and her kids— nervous, frightened T. John with his needle-scarred arms; pretty Diana with her lovely lips that never talked; lovable Scooter, who talked all the time; Tucker and Steamboat, the ten-year-old black twins Cat had spotted one rainy night behind a laundromat in Santa Fe; plus Bingo, who was so afraid of being caught without clothes that he would wind up at the end of the day wearing three of everything.

Then there was the problem of Crowe. Babe had never liked the brooding Apache Indian who'd wandered in from nowhere and terrified her with his stormy moods and warrior's eyes. Crowe was definitely not hero material, not even if he was Cat's age and a magnificent pagan secretly in love with Cat. No, her hero must be a smoldering man with arrogant brows and rippling muscles and sinewy thighs, a giant, a monument of manhood, a virile champion capable of taming the fiery Catherine with a passionate kiss!

A certain lustful sensuality was necessary, too, for the love affair must be torrid from the outset. She wanted to write the love scenes first.

She had already begun. Before all that contempt-of-court business between Cat and Judge Constanza had turned their lives upside down, Babe started waking before dawn to get in some quiet writing time. At this very moment, folded safely in her bag, was a clean sheet of yellow paper with the beginning paragraph.

Chapter One, it said with an important sense of destiny. *Catherine knew from the moment she fell into the laughing pools of his eyes that she would belong to him.*

Though Babe wasn't exactly sure who ''he'' was, she was certain she would know him when she saw him.

Chapter One

Every morning, precisely at six, Bradley Zacharias hit the sidewalk, running.

Without variation he made for Central Park and followed the cinder bridle path from Tavern-on-the-Green to the track around the reservoir. One lap around the lake, he knew, was a mile and six-tenths. On a good day he circled it twice. When he was concerned, three. When he was upset, he lapped it four times. Today he was on his fifth.

Left, right, left, right. Feeling the impact deep in his spine, Brad clenched his teeth until his jaws ached. *Left, right.*

Through the shrubbery he could see the metallic glacier of buses, taxis, trucks and private cars as they spewed early-morning pollution upon New York City. Some of the world's most sought-after apartment buildings rose majestically beyond them—multiple towers that appeared distant and aloof in the pale morning of the last day of May.

The trees were in bloom. In the east, clouds were banking, their bellies burgeoning with the promise of showers.

A woman ran past. She was a good five years older than his own thirty-seven. Damn!

Stretching, Brad's muscles drove him forward and his breath began to labor. He was into the pain of endurance now. His feet hammered the ground while droplets of sweat escaped the headband circling his crew cut and drizzled down into the stubble of his jaws.

He swore under his breath. What was he doing here? Running around Central Park like some blond-haired windup machine? Around and around and around he went, and where he would stop only God knew. From the day he'd enrolled in Princeton and graduated from Harvard a George Baker Scholar, he hadn't slowed down or taken a deep breath.

Had it really been a dozen years ago? Now he *couldn't* slow down. People's whole lives would be wrecked if he slipped by so much as one tiny detail. He hadn't bargained for that.

And the fancy title, Consultant, which was printed in gold on his office door. What the hell did that mean? That he could work miracles and walk on water? People said he could.

Left, right, left, right. His legs were streaming sweat now, and his socks were clumped about his ankles. His bare, sweat-ribboned chest was on fire. A spot between his shoulder blades was racked with pain.

He veered off the moist earth of the bridle path and headed toward the solitude of his apartment on West Seventieth Street, his Reeboks continuing to gobble up the miles. When the silver-gray Rolls-Royce nosed alongside the curb, purring like a well-fed cat, he swore under his breath for he knew exactly who it was, and why.

A smoked-glass window slid neatly downward, and a chauffeur's capped head leaned briskly over the seat to poke out the passenger window. A voice said with just the right blend of condescension and self-effacement, "Miss Hessing would like a word with you if you don't mind, Mr. Zacharias."

Brad swiped at his face with an arm. Donna Hessing was so beautiful, it made him half blind to look at her. She was also one of the most respected attorneys in the snobbish firm of Hirshfeld, Kraus & Girard—a friend only, not a lover, though that was his fault, not hers.

"Jason," he gasped as he pivoted and jogged backward, his arms and legs churning like pistons, "would you be so kind as to tell Miss Hessing I'm not in a talking frame of mind right now?"

The chauffeur's look was one of genuine pity. "I understand, sir. Forgive me, sir, but I think she'd like a word with you anyway, sir."

With a whispered spurt the Rolls shot ahead and came to an elegant stop beyond him. By the time Brad reached it, the rear door had opened. Donna Hessing had extended a long, stockinged leg whose foot was shod with a superb Fendi shoe.

A body followed, a superb body, even if it was older than his own. It wore a silk suit made in French heaven, and its swanlike throat was circled with a 24-karat gold choker. Its hair was a profusion of luscious, nectar waves, its cheekbones high and Nordic, its eyes as gold as resin. Donna Hessing was the golden WASP incarnate.

"I know I've said this before, Bradley Zacharias," she declared, as she straightened to a height of five feet six inches and surveyed his half-naked body with interest. "This time I really mean it. I'm going to murder you with my bare hands." She smiled mutinously. "I'm going to tear you apart, limb from limb. And then I'm going to feed you to those cannibals in Washington you associate with. But first I'm going to have one night with you all to myself. For history."

Brad closed his eyes and wished he'd become a mechanic instead of Lowell's gofer.

"This isn't my scene, sir," he'd told the Old Man at the beginning, long before he'd been seduced by the six digits he earned every year. And by the plush suite of offices. And the four-man staff and the fancy breakfasts and dinners, the balls, the White House parties, the fawning respect he was paid by reporters and other media, all because he worked for the Old Man.

Joseph Lowell didn't build houses or banks or monopolies of trade. Joseph Lowell built men. He created governors and senators and placed them into strategic positions as some men would play an ongoing game of chess. Lowell made presidents and crafted policy behind closed doors, and when he needed things done he called upon his main man: Bradley Ardane Zacharias.

By the time Brad realized his mistake, he'd become too good. He'd become the Courier Par Excellence, the Divine Fixer, the Supreme Lobbyist. He'd become indispensable. So, for the past five years he'd been trying to write his letter of resignation. He'd been searching for the right moment to walk into the offices on the thirty-second floor of the Lowell Tower.

"Sir," he would say, "you've done more for me than any man alive. I respect you like I respect my own father. Thank you very much, sir, but I quit."

Now he forced himself to grin. He hitched up his sweatpants that had drooped low upon his pelvic bones. "Donna, do the words *bad sport* mean anything to you?"

Donna's brows blunted as she stared boldly at the line of sweat-glistening hair striping the center of his belly. "Everything would be simple, you said."

"Well, if you'd done what I told you—"

"I did *exactly* as you said, you blond Hitler. I went to New Mexico with a smile on my face, my papers neatly in my case. I unencumbered your Senator Johnson, the next president of our fair land, of his small financial troubles. That was *your* word, as I recall—'unencumber.'"

Brad turned his head and told the sky with more honesty than irony, "I hate this job."

"I wrapped up the deal for the loan company and the software packagers," she continued smoothly. "Then I played kamikaze, Brad. I found a buyer for those ten sections of land that DevCorp didn't know what to do with. Damn it, why didn't you warn me about Catherine Holmes?"

Feeling stupid as only Donna could make him feel, Brad stopped dancing around like a punch-drunk boxer. His smile was a grimace. "You were wonderful, Donna. Mr. Lowell is grateful. McGrath Johnson is grateful. I'm grateful. The whole world is grateful. Hey, take the whole universe."

She was momentarily distracted from her tirade. "Really?" she purred with kittenish sensuality as she watched a drizzle of sweat slide into his navel. "How grateful is that, Mr. Zacharias?"

Not liking at all what he was about to do, Brad gave her the full voltage of his old killer smile and peered deep into her eyes. "You're in a strange mood today," he drawled in his best man-eating voice. "Tell me, darling, have you and Trav had a wee tiff?"

At the mention of Travis Tanner, a second sputtered between them. They both stood as still as statues, he sweating, she cool as a marble. It was at times like this when he earned more than Lowell could pay in *seven* digits, Brad thought.

Anger serrated Donna's voice. "I have asked myself a thousand times why I take cheap shots like that from you, Zacharias."

"Oh, come on, Donna," he cajoled. "It wasn't meant to be a cheap shot. Anyway, you're supposed to take cheap shots from your friends, haven't you heard? Travis really is all right, isn't he?"

"I should think you'd know everything about Travis. You're the one who foisted him off on me."

"You love the man, Donna, you know you do."

"I love—"

"Hey..."

For a moment Brad thought he saw the bright sparkle of a tear in Donna's eye, but if it were really there it was gone in an instant. Donna was much too worldly to let anyone see her cry. Her voice, when she spoke again, was very low, very professional.

"Okay, Mr. Zacharias, let me tell you a thing or two about your good Senator McGrath Johnson. The man has a vicious mouth, which hardly speaks well of a potential president, do you think? He told me after I cleaned up his financial shambles that when this Holmes woman got through with him, he'd be lucky to get a job drilling oil wells in Midland, Texas. What could I say? The newspapers and television are having a field day because of what I did."

"How could I have known about Catherine Holmes?"

"Now the opposition is accusing the man of kicking homeless children out into the streets. Lovely, isn't it? If you'd warned me what I was getting into by selling that ranch, I could have saved myself a lot of grief by simply putting a gun to my head."

What puzzled Brad was why no one on his staff had known up front about Thomas Holmes and his daughter living on the ranch. It was McGrath's own idea to sell the corporation that owned it. He *had* to have known that his own father had told Holmes they could live there indefinitely, and that Catherine Holmes, counting on that, had seemingly begun a sort of mecca for abused children and runaways.

"There's been a misunderstanding," he told Donna in his most soothing Washingtonese, when what he really wanted to do was kick a three-inch dent into the side of her car.

"Yes." Leaning forward, Donna poked him in the ribs like a side of prime beef. "Yours. What're you going to do about it?"

Brad was painfully conscious of the stench of his sweats. When Donna got home tonight, an expensive bouquet of flowers would be waiting for her, plus a bonus check as a token of his apology. And later, when he nursed a drink in his own lonely apartment, he would take out his letter of resignation and finish it, by God!

Until then, he curved his arm loosely about her waist. "I'll take care of everything, darling." Like a hungry tiger, he growled and dipped his face into her neck for a pretended bite.

Donna smilingly detached herself, but deep in her woman's heart she wished she could hate the man. If she could find that one fatal flaw in Brad Zacharias, her life would be much simpler. It was no comfort to know that she wasn't alone; every woman she knew adored him.

Not because of his looks, obviously. Brad's nose was a mess, having been fractured in a car wreck when he was a boy. Time lines were tracking their way alongside his mouth. The crow's-feet beside his torpedo-gray eyes were the permanent kind. His blond crew cut was beginning to thin at his temples, a thing he was sensitive about. He was an inch shy of six feet and a bit too lean; what the stress of working for Lowell didn't burn off, his running did. His muscles were the consistency of granite, his arms beautiful, his buttocks the kind that would turn a woman's head until he was out of sight. His tan was simply, wonderfully there, like the Pony Express, come rain, sleet or snow. If anyone knew what was beneath his Jockey shorts, though, they weren't telling.

The intelligence and charm went much deeper. Brad Zacharias was "the most elegant, eloquent bachelor" on Washington's invitation lists. "An honest-to-God cavalier, darling," Kitty Diebaud, the capital's current ten-star hostess had been known to gush, "and the most sublime dancer."

Fast-lane power brokers liked Brad, too. Even the Georgetown snobs agreed that he wasn't too bad for a Seattle man. He wasn't only a "tennis player beautiful to behold," but one "smart enough to know when to lose."

Donna would come closer to finding someone who would bad-mouth Joseph Lowell than Bradley Zacharias, and everyone knew what a paragon of virtue *Lowell* was. But Lowell, like everyone else, was growing old. He was in a wheelchair now, and no matter how badly Brad wanted to leave the man, he was too honorable. He was stuck.

Well, wasn't everyone? She'd been living with Travis Tanner, Brad's public relations man, for months, and she didn't even love him.

Donna placed her hand upon the door of the car as Jason prepared to help her in. Turning, she said, "I have one question before I leave."

"Shoot." Brad grinned crookedly and held up his palms. "Not really."

"Are McGrath and his father having a falling-out?"

"Not to my knowledge." Brad was genuinely surprised.

"Then why didn't McGrath honor the agreement his father made with Holmes?"

Brad rubbed a palm over the damp spikes of his crew cut. "A good question, but from what I hear, Holmes won't live out the week."

"McGrath is a savvy politician, Brad. A man of his ilk wouldn't miss an opportunity to capitalize on Catherine Holmes."

"Maybe he thought capitalizing was beneath him."

Donna's laughter rang musically in the morning air. "Sweetie, *no* politician misses Brownie points like that. Miss Holmes has hired herself a two-bit lawyer, you know, and the creep's getting some free publicity at McGrath's expense. She's also got an angry judge on her back who says he's going to hold her in contempt of court if she's not moved off the ranch by the first of June, which will also make for fantastic headlines. I'll tell you, Brad, you'd better take McGrath in hand before he doesn't have any career left to jeopardize."

Brad's mind was far ahead of Donna's. "It'll be all right. People get confused. Verbal understandings get mixed up. I'm sure there's a logical explanation."

Donna waved his words aside. "Then you find it. And when you go down to New Mexico, tell the next president of these United States that I, at least, had my head on straight."

"Tell him yourself."

Donna was already ducking into the car. At Brad's words, she froze, then spun around to confront him. "Oh, no, you don't, Bradley Zacharias."

Brad wondered why he kept subjecting himself to guilt trips as sordid as the one he was about to take. He was thirty-seven years old, for pity's sake. And alone. Why hadn't he found a nice woman somewhere and given marriage a try? Why hadn't he fallen in love with Donna?

He leaned toward her, brushed the side of her mouth and drew the wonderful scent of her deep into his lungs. He sighed and despaired of ever feeling that raw, primal hunger for a woman again.

"I need you down there with me, Donna," he said persuasively, which was completely true. "Hell, I *want* you down there. I want someone to help me take the heat, bandage up my wounds, rub my throbbing temples. Come on, Donna."

Lowering her lashes to a battle angle, Donna mutely accused him of unspeakable crimes. "Have you no shame?"

He flashed his most charming, sheepish grin.

In a low voice, she said, "Joseph Lowell ought to endorse *you* for president, Brad. You could drag this country down to ruination a whole lot faster than a mere senator from New Mexico."

Turning, she disappeared into the burgundy confines of the Rolls-Royce.

Draping himself in the open space of the door, Brad compounded his guilt by bending until he could see inside. "Darling, I'm sorry."

"I hate you, Brad."

"I know. Will you come?"

"Someday—" her voice was heavy with battered dreams "—you're going to go meet someone, and she's going to break your heart into a million pieces. I'm going to be there on the sidelines, cheering her on."

Brad had no answer for such pain. He hated himself. "Don't worry about a thing." He stepped back and moved his hand briefly over his jaws.

"Go to hell," she hissed.

As the Rolls swept away from the curb in a whisper of tire rubber, Brad stood hugging himself. Donna would come with him to New Mexico, but in her heart she would hope that something might change and he would fall in love with her.

With a shake of his head, he turned and walked wearily back to his apartment. Maybe, he thought, just maybe her parting remark was a prophecy. Tonight when he got home he would get a little drunk and finish his letter of resignation. When this thing with Catherine Holmes was done, he swore he would stop pretending that a job could fill up the holes in his life. He would stop standing on the patio in the darkness, wondering if someone was out there, searching for him. When it was over, he would accept the inevitable; that he was alone and that he was miserable. He would make some changes in his life.

All day, as Cat had sat beside her father's hospital bed, she'd been telling herself that if she had to go to jail, the first day of June was as good as any. If a person applied a bit of sick logic, the first day of June was perfect. Her father's death and jail on the same day. Very tidy, very neat. She was a neatness freak anyway. She should be delirious with happiness. She should be ecstatic!

Cool it, Cat, she told herself, shaking. Keep your head. No hysterics. Not tonight. Tom is gone.

Now that it was all over, she realized that she'd never truly believed any of it. "It's okay," she whispered to Babe Polansky, as she reached across the bed and took the girl's hand to draw her into the hall outside. "It's all right to cry, sweetie. I just didn't want to upset any of the other patients. That's why I shushed you."

Shaking her head, Babe swiped a sleeved arm across her streaming eyes. She sniffed and swallowed and snapped to attention and presented a round, plain face bravely un-stained by tears.

"I'm not going to cry, Cat," she stoutly declared. "I'm fine. See? No tears." She blinked manfully. "Anyway, it's you who needs taking care of. You've been here three days now. Just leave everything to me, Cat. I'm in charge now. I'll take you home and make hot tea and peanut-butter cookies. You'll feel better right away."

Cat had no choice but to smile. "Cookies? At mid-night?"

"Just what the doctor ordered."

As usual, Babe's problem solving meant eating her ob-stacles. Cat took the girl into her arms and was amazed at the young, hard body that was already that of a woman. Yet inside, Babe was still very much a girl.

"Lean on me, Cat," Babe whispered with an important maternity and repeated pats on the back. "Just lean on me."

"I'm all right, Babe," Cat lied. "Having you here with me helps." Leaning back, she tenderly smoothed a strand of straight brown hair behind Babe's ear. "There's some things I have to do, though. Are you sure you don't want to wait downstairs?"

Babe's reply was to reach into the huge, striped canvas tote bag that was draped over her shoulder. No one knew exactly what Babe carried in the bag, but she was plunder-ing through her stash of paperback books and yellow pads and plastic Baggies and rattling bottles and secret sundry items. She produced a crumpled, tasteless red beret and crammed it onto her head so that sprigs of her hair spiked from beneath the edges like broken buggy springs. "I'm ready for anything," she announced with queenly fervor. "I'm with you till the well dries up, Cat. I'm with you till the wheels come off."

Tears of affection banked behind Cat's own eyes, tears she wished she could shed; but since she hadn't cried since she was sixteen years old, she smiled instead and said, "I know you are, honey."

"It's just that..." Babe's lower lip betrayed her by quivering as she stood so proudly, a valiant, top-heavy little trooper in baggy fatigue pants and an out-of-shape T-shirt that made her comically resemble a Hell's Angel.

"What?" Cat prompted.

"Now Tom is gone. I don't know what I'll do if you die too, Cat. Please don't die. Promise me you won't die, Cat."

How could she grieve over Tom? Cat asked herself. The living needed all she could give them and more, always more. Over the girl's shoulder, she gazed across the distance into the men's ward and offered her own private eulogy: *Rest well, Tom. Rest well.* As the page of a book is turned, then she let out her breath in acceptance and let it go. Tom had been the best father he knew how to be. He hadn't given her what she needed, but maybe no one alive could do that.

"I'm going to live a long, long time, Babe," she promised.

Satisfied, Babe bravely lifted her chin and gave her T-shirt a yank, ready to take on the world.

Cat looped her arm about Babe's shoulders as they walked down the hall together. She might just do some of that living in a jail cell, but really, she doubted it. No judge in his right mind would actually hold her to that contempt-of-court charge, not even Constanza, the ogre. Not when she'd been doing everything humanly possible to move herself and seven other people off the ranch as quickly as possible. Wasn't death considered an extenuating circumstance?

Anyway, her lawyer had filed a petition. The great arm of the law was in motion.

Their footsteps were noisy on the pale green floor whose tile gleamed from a recent buffing. Located in front of the twin elevators, the nurses' station was a paneled oasis of desks and drawers and telephones and monitors.

"I have to get the nurse now, Babe," Cat said. "She'll call the doctor. Papers have to be filled out, and all kinds of things like that."

"What about the funeral home? Do you want me to make the arrangements?"

Dear Babe. "I've already done that, honey." Cat's stomach made a rumbling noise, and, pressing it, she realized she hadn't eaten since breakfast.

At the sound of their talking, the nurse at the station looked up. Cat suspected they had been waiting all day for her to take this walk down the hall. Tom's death had been a mercy much too long in coming. The question was in the nurse's tipped-up chin; in Cat's own faint nod, the reply.

The response came instantly. In the eerie silence of midnight, the squish, squish of the rubber-soled shoes carried like machine-gun chatter.

Lenore Ames was printed on the woman's nameplate. Cat said quietly to her, "I guess you should call the doctor now."

No other words were necessary. "Yes, dear. It's for the best, you know."

"Yes, I know. I wonder if you..."

Turning, Cat searched for Babe's support, but she was suddenly disoriented, unable to remember what she was looking for. Hesitating, she touched a knuckle to her lips and looked at the nurse. She opened her mouth to explain, but no words came.

"Cat?" Babe whispered with wide-eyed apprehension, touching her arm.

Cat snapped into focus and brushed off her lapse with a smile. "For a moment I felt as if it were raining all over the world."

Knowing a bad case of battle fatigue when she saw it, Lenore Ames pushed past Babe and gripped Cat's hands very hard, shaking them. "You'll be all right," she declared gruffly, one woman to another. "You're very strong."

Cat nodded, but she didn't want to be strong. She was so very, very tired. She wished there were someone, somewhere, who would open his arms and hold her for a change.

Gently detaching herself, noticing again how clean the floor was even at the edges where the rubber flashing butted against the seam of the wall, Cat shaped her mouth into another smile.

"I have to use the telephone now, Babe," she said. "Would you mind staying here at the nurses' station?"

"I'll go with you."

"You can use this telephone if it's a local call, hon." Lenore Ames pursed her mouth in generosity. "We can make an exception just this once."

"I need a pay phone."

"Of course. I understand."

No, you don't. You couldn't possibly understand. Even I don't understand why I have to call him.

"Around the corner, dear. By the rest room."

Cat was struck by how civilly it was all going. How discreetly, how...decently.

A man was using the phone when she found it. Locating a bench, she sat but didn't touch the wall with her spine. She waited with her fingers laced like chain mail. Now that she wasn't forced to be brave for Babe, the past three days with almost no sleep had her head swollen like a balloon. Her eyes were gritty with sand.

She blinked and tried not to think about returning to the ranch. The sun would be coming up by the time they got there—no rest for the weary this day, either. And, horror of horrors, if Judge Constanza held to his promise, the National Guard would probably come with bazookas and flamethrowers to evict them all from the premises.

The caller was finished now. Rising, moving as calmly as a sleepwalker, Cat walked to the phone and lifted the receiver.

She pinched it between her jaw and shoulder while she fished for a coin. For four years she had known she would make this call—four years of having her life on hold, not knowing the love of any man except her father, not doing anything but taking care of him and the children and waiting, waiting, because Wrather had told her to wait. Wanting Wrather Johnson was as much a part of her existence as breathing. If not for Wrather, she probably wouldn't even *be* breathing.

"I'm going to die," she'd told him so desperately in the ambulance that night long ago when Tom had still been the overseer of Wrather's multimillion-dollar estate.

She sighed. Another lifetime. McGrath had been running for the Senate then. She had run away from her mother and, after a nightmarish year of roaming all over the country, she'd let Wrather bring her home to her father who lived in the apartment over Wrather's garage in Santa Fe.

"You will not die," Wrather had said.

He'd been summoned from one of his many important fund-raising dinners that night. He still wore his tuxedo and smelled so good that she hardly cared if she did die. Wrather Johnson—her handsome silver king, the age of her own father, his silver hair his crown, his voice a music that, at seventeen, she lived for. She worshiped him.

"I deserve to die," she grieved, and turned her head so he would not see her ugliness.

"You're a dumb, stupid kid—" Wrather never coddled her "—but you don't deserve to die. You promised you wouldn't take that junk anymore."

"I didn't want to."

"Breathe the oxygen." Wrather placed the mask on her face. "Deeply, deeply. That stuff is going to kill you one day, you know."

"I won't do it ever again. I mean it this time. I swear."

"I've invested a lot in you, Catherine, and how do you repay me?"

"I hate my life."

"Well, change it. Reach out and take what you want."

"I want you."

He had leaned over and kissed her lightly and had smoothed the riot of hair from her face. "You're a seventeen-year-old girl. I'm a fifty-five-year-old man. Be sensible."

"I'm a woman, Wrather."

"You're a junkie. Tell me why I should want a junkie. Hmm, Catherine? Get yourself straight, then come to me. We'll have this conversation again."

She *had* gotten herself straight. For him. And he had wanted her, too; she hadn't imagined that. No man could kiss a woman as Wrather had kissed her and not have desired her as he watched her grow from a girl into a woman.

Cat located a quarter and watched with dull disinterest as a woman, mirrored in the reflection of the night-darkened window, dropped it into the telephone. The woman was pretty, if one noticed, but she was nondescript in the faded men's Levi's and old sneakers and ancient A-line swing jacket that was nowhere near its original color. She displayed no breasts, no waist, no mysteries of womankind.

But she knew how to be a lady when she wanted to be. Oh, yes, Wrather had seen to that. When she was eighteen, he'd badgered her beyond bearing.

"Do you go out of your way to look like that?" he nagged. "Fix your hair, Catherine. Buy some new clothes. Stop chewing your nails. Get a degree. I'll pay for it myself. You can't even carry on a decent conversation. Do you plan to be a social dropout all your life?"

But Wrather hadn't really believed she could acquire her own chic. She knew that now. While Tom had been waxing Wrather's cars and mowing his lawns and Wrather had been going to his elaborate parties with stunning, glitzy women on his arm, even bringing some of them home, Cat had been buried in books and was learning everything she could in order to fit into his world.

She picked up other things along the way, poring over fashion magazines. She clipped newspapers and drank in style like a thirsty sponge. She didn't have the money to buy clothes, so she made them. She learned about living. She learned interior decorating. She studied piano and became expert at tennis. She pursued everything with a vengeance and mastered it. Every waking minute she worked. All because of Wrather.

"Hello," a female voice said brusquely on the other end of the receiver.

The voice wasn't one Cat recognized. The old familiar fear made her swallow convulsively. "Is Wrather...there?"

"I beg your pardon. Who is this?"

"Ahh, is this the Johnson residence?"

"Whom did you wish—"

"Wrather Johnson. Is he there?"

An annoyed sigh. "He's in Washington. I can give you a number, but—"

"Please."

Then, tiredly: "Do you have a pencil?"

"Yes," Cat lied, and memorized the number as the woman fired out the digits. Thanking her, she repeated the number over and over until it was dialed.

It had never been enough, any of it. The agony she suffered trying to compete with Wrather's women! No matter how she tried, it was never enough. The rules kept changing. Then there had been Tom. Tom had crawled into one bottle too many, and after twenty years of tending Wrather's estate, his body stopped fighting what he was doing to it.

Wrather had insisted they go to the ranch where Tom could convalesce. With a snap of his fingers he had placed himself beyond her reach one more time. Except now he said he loved her and wanted her. He had filled her head with crystal dreams and made her promise to call when it was all over. He would be waiting, he said.

Well, it was over, and she was calling. But she wasn't the same woman now. In those long, lonely years she had learned how to hate. Now she despised all the tuxedos and airs and sophisticated talk and panache and power cliques that excluded her. She hated the talk that never got anything done, the pretense and the glorious, white-collar lies.

After what seemed an interminable wait, a receiver lifted. That silky, Dorian Gray voice that could always melt her said, "This is Wrather Johnson."

Chapter Two

Time was a vacuum. Cat was lifted from the planet Earth and placed in a foreign sphere where the gravity was different and nothing was connected or made sense. Watching the stranger in the window's reflection, she saw not a woman, but a small, frail girl peering up at other men who had backed her into corners; strange, brutal stepfathers who had taken pleasure in watching her cower. She saw a backward girl with nails bitten to the quick, who, at sixteen, had finally found the courage to run away from a mother who would never believe what her husbands did. And she saw herself sinking into addiction until a man named Wrather Johnson had found her wandering the ruthless streets of Las Vegas.

"Hello?" The same impatience edged his voice.

Cat's hand was poised over the telephone connection as if hovering over the neck of an unwilling victim.

He clipped his words tersely. "Who is this? What do you want? McGrath?"

Cat's flesh was raised in goose bumps and her heart was racing, blood thrumming in her skull like a taut wire. The woman reflected in the hospital window had disintegrated into the darkness.

More gently, almost tenderly, he said, "Ah, Catherine. It's you, isn't it? It's over? Yes, of course, it's over."

He was hypnotizing her with his familiar eloquence. She owed him everything. *Oh, Wrather.*

"You've done right to call me, Catherine. Come home to me, darling."

Cat shrank against the wall. What was the matter with her? Didn't she still want to be Wrather's darling? If she didn't, she could at least bargain with him so she could stay on at the ranch, at least until she could find another place.

But Wrather had taught her too well, hadn't he? She was her own person now, too proud. No man, no money, no gifts, not even kind words, could equal that self-belief she'd earned. If she went to him, Wrather would swallow her *whole*!

Her finger pressed the chrome-plated switch. Gasping—for independence had its price—she covered her mouth, her eyes flared with disbelief. It was gone—just like that, her ace that she'd treasured and kept palmed all these years, her one light at the end of the tunnel that had kept her driving and churning and fighting was now gone. She'd flicked her life away like a smoked cigarette.

A horrible mistake! Should she call him back and repent?

No! With a sense of loss almost too heavy to be borne, she turned from the phone. Tom was dead, she thought in a daze. She must bury the dead. If there was no one meant for her, at least she had the children. Her love for them was vast and strong, and she believed in it with her whole heart; for them she would work and worry and hurt and want to keep on living. She would get on with her life, whatever that was. But she would never look for a man's love again.

Turning, the last glimpse she had was a woman walking away from the telephone with her head held at a proud, rigid angle. Raindrops were spattering upon the window.

Catherine Holmes. *Cath-e-rine Holmes. Another day of good old C.H.* Brad thought he was either growing to hate the sound of her name or falling in love.

Well now, C.H., it seems you've succeeded in screwing up my plans well enough. I could be at the Met tonight with Alicia Frazier. Madam Butterfly, *no less. At the least I could have my feet up in my easy chair at home, reading Robert Penn Warren or daydreaming of some sweet young thing. Why do you have to be such a hard case, C.H.?*

Brad had caught the late flight from Kennedy. With him was an attaché case full of work. Beside him sat Donna, her eyes closed, a Westlake thriller spilling from her lap and her fashionable gold-rimmed reading glasses having slid to half-mast upon her nose.

Farther up the aisle in first class, Lawrence Goodyear, his media expert, was repeatedly snapping a ballpoint pen and trying to make a date with the flight attendant. Travis Tanner, Donna's lover, who was another old friend and the PR man he usually hired in such emergencies, was on standby in Manhattan just in case this incident wasn't as cut-and-dried as they expected it to be.

"Ladies and gentlemen, welcome to flight six-nineteen," droned the uniformed attendant as she smiled slyly at Brad. "Would you please make sure your seats are in the upright position at this time and that all luggage is stored securely..."

Returning her come-on with a smile and a sigh, Brad removed a hefty file and pushed his case beneath the seat in front. Outside, big jets were winding up. Flight attendants were walking up and down the aisle, shutting overhead compartments.

In his lap was a statement he'd been preparing for Mc-Grath to issue to the papers to defuse the situation. So, C.H. took care of abused children, did she? Strange that she should be such a troublemaker.

He scribbled down some possible questions McGrath might be asked: Was Miss Holmes's lawsuit an indication that McGrath's political platform was shifting? Could they now expect pressure from HEW? Could this incident with Miss Holmes alienate financial support from the liberals?

"Please place the mask securely over your mouth and breath in a normal way," the attendant droned.

Brad sorted through possible scenarios. A press conference, perhaps? Some highly publicized bash with one of the local state homes for children? A simple "I'm sorry, Miss Holmes, I wasn't on top of it," from McGrath?

Personally, he preferred the latter. He pictured Sally Field—aka good old C.H.—walking out on the porch in *Places in the Heart*, her maternal breast curving sweetly beneath her pretty ruffled apron as she held her fatherless children poignantly to her sides and swore they would never, never leave the land, God bless them everyone.

Burnout, he thought with disgust. He'd finally done it. *Thanks, C.H., you've finally pushed me over the line*. Succumbing to his one, surefire sleeping tonic, that of his letter of resignation to Lowell, he leaned his head to the seat and closed his eyes.

"Ladies and gentlemen, there will be a short delay in takeoff. Please observe that the captain has turned off the No Smoking sign . . ."

Beside him, Donna roused and pulled off her glasses. "Wouldn't you know it?"

From his up-front seat, Lawrence strained to peer back at them, grimacing. "Hey, Zacharias, they've come to carry you away, brother."

Brad pried open his eyes in time to see two ominous-looking men entering first class and making a survey of the passengers. In precise James Bond fashion, one of them fastened his recognition upon Brad, signaled his companion and moved forward to stop beside Brad's chair.

Leaning over, he said politely, "Mr. Zacharias?"

The second man, Brad saw, was as dark-suited and as nondescript as the first. His face was perfectly forgettable. A dead giveaway; they had to be bodyguards. Whose?

"What do you want?" he growled.

The first man produced a badge that identified him as Secret Service: James Murphy.

"Charming, James," Brad said wryly, and wondered if this wouldn't be a good time to begin worrying. About what, he wasn't sure.

"We have to ask you to disembark, Mr. Zacharias," the man said politely.

"Why?"

"Briefly, sir, then you may resume your flight."

Yes, he should worry. Definitely. Brad had a startling vision of Joseph Lowell having died. Or an emergency having arisen with his parents in Seattle. Or McGrath having done something rash like putting out a contract on Catherine Holmes.

"What've you done, Brad?" Donna demanded in her usual attack mode.

"If I'm not back in two days, call Lowell," he mumbled, and heaved to his feet. Everyone in the coach was glaring at him as he walked down the aisle.

"Very funny," Donna called to his back.

"Watch your step, Mr. Zacharias," the flight attendant warned, no longer propositioning him with her smile.

A black limousine was waiting for him at the bottom of the steps, the driver of which, Brad saw as he stooped and peered inside, was as forgettable as his partners.

"I'm supposed to talk to you?" he quizzed, as the door opened and the smell of plush leather seats and expensive cigars blended with the acrid stench of kerosene from the jets shrieking overhead.

"Please get inside, Mr. Zacharias," urged Murphy.

Begrudging the humid night air and New York's skyline, a spatter of diamonds behind it, Brad got in and allowed himself to be driven along the fringes of the terminal, away from the lights and traffic to where the darkness was more peaceful, and more menacing.

No one spoke. The headlights captured the luridly irides- cent oil stains on the asphalt. Brad spotted another car fol- lowing close behind, its running lights turned off. He had no idea where it had joined them and felt increasingly uneasy with all the cloak-and-dagger shenanigans. In that car would be either a very important person or someone he definitely didn't want to know.

When they came to a rocking stop, the doors of both cars swept open as if they were sprouting wings and would now flap away into never-never land. *We're off to see the Wiz- ard.*

Brad's shoulders went back in his suit. Approximately five minutes had passed. "I'm getting a bad feeling about this, guys."

"Patience, Mr. Zacharias."

"Patience, hell." His impulse was to reach up and grab the man by his tie, but James Murphy and his companion were already outside. He followed them.

The damp wind whipped at the legs of his trousers. For no other reason than that it seemed appropriate, he struck the at-ease position and, keeping his face a mask, waited. *Why do I feel like Oliver North about to get court-martialed?*

Four men stepped from the other car and formed a loose quadrant of guards. A man emerged, a white silk scarf fluttering becomingly about his neck and forming a perfect frame for the glamorous silver of his hair—a tall man in his late fifties, stunningly charismatic, still very much in his prime, more fit than most younger men. His glasses were framed with silver, his features as cleanly hewn as if a sculptor had taken chisel and hammer in hand and created them. He moved forward, power radiating from him as if he were a walking nuclear device.

"Mr. Zacharias," he said in a voice with an edge of finely polished steel.

"Mr. Johnson." Surprised, Brad accepted McGrath's father's handshake.

Wrather Johnson was retired from the bar, a man now in private enterprise and one of the superelite contemporaries of Joseph Lowell. McGrath was his eldest son, but Wrather had sired five children in all. A man of driving ambition, he was the very epitome of Establishment mystique.

"You're a long way from home, sir," Brad said, for Wrather's retirement home was in the sleepy, clear-skied town of Santa Fe.

Wrather bestowed another of his magnificent, heart-stopping smiles. "Please forgive the drama, Brad. There're some matters I don't trust even to the telephone."

The handshake threatened to crack the bones of Brad's hand. Gratefully extricating it, he jammed it into the pocket of his trousers. "I understand, sir."

Smiling, Wrather Johnson peered up at a jet shrieking its way across the sky. When the noise had abated, he said, "The only way I know to keep a matter private is to *be* private. I won't keep you waiting. It is imperative that I speak to you about Catherine Holmes before you go to New Mexico."

If Brad hadn't spent the past twenty-four hours dwelling on that identical subject himself, he wouldn't have felt the prick of futility in the older man's announcement.

"These days," Wrather was saying, "it's a little hard for presidential candidates to have secrets."

Secrets? *Secrets?* A cold premonition of disaster struck the back of Brad's neck. He hardly knew how to reply.

"Especially when they pertain to a woman," Wrather added.

Brad closed his eyes. Not a woman. Not McGrath and a woman. "I'd say that depends upon the woman," he said evasively as anger kindled inside him. He'd kill McGrath. With his own two hands, he'd kill the man.

"And the candidate."

Brad didn't blink. "Of course."

"He died, you know."

"Miss Holmes's father?" Unable to make a connection, Brad shook his head. "I hadn't heard."

"It's been coming for a long time. Earlier tonight, I believe. A few hours ago."

Wrather Johnson's information gathering was impressive. "I'm sorry," Brad mumbled, still thinking about McGrath. "He must have been a good friend of the family."

Wrather fastidiously plucked a piece of lint from his sleeve and shook his head. "*My* friend, actually. There was nothing I couldn't trust with Tom, and his daughter—well, let's just say that before Tom got sick, I helped Catherine through a bit of difficulty. And then..."

The pause was all part of the drama. Wrather Johnson was too intelligent to hold up a major airline flight with wasted words. Without interrupting, Brad stood stone-still and waited.

"And therein lies the problem," Wrather said. "One so highly delicate that it had to be discussed—" he gestured at the surroundings "—in this manner. I'm depending on you to protect my son, Brad. In this one, singular case—from himself."

Brad didn't move a muscle, and Wrather sighed an elegant sigh, pressing his heart. "It all happened before McGrath ever planned a single political move. If you believe nothing else, you must believe that. The affair was quite brief. I know that McGrath regrets it more than he can ever say. Monique is the perfect wife for him, and he would never willingly jeopardize that for a mere caretaker's daughter. And now—" again he sighed beautifully "—we have a situation."

Brad stood torturing a muscle in his jaw and wondered if he could resurrect his old killer smile in the face of this latest development. How in the name of sweet sanity had it happened? He'd checked McGrath so closely—looking for that one human frailty, no matter how small, that could be traced or could pop up unexpectedly and bring everything crashing down. He'd picked McGrath's past to pieces with a pair of tweezers, put it under a microscope. He had never found evidence of the slightest breath of scandal. No affairs, no liaisons. And certainly not with Catherine Holmes, of all people!

"I'll take care of it, sir," he said, and smiled tightly.

"Good man."

"I just don't see—"

"There was no way you could have, son." Wrather shook his silvery head. "I didn't know myself until quite recently."

Well, well, well, C.H., Brad thought bitterly. *It seems I underestimated you.* Drawing the smell of burned-rubber smog into his lungs, he pinched the top of his nose. "Then all this contempt-of-court stuff—"

"Is perfectly true. The girl's gotten herself in a real mess. In all fairness, however, that was not her fault."

"And the verbal arrangement you had with Thomas Holmes—"

"Is also perfectly true. I told Tom he could live on the ranch for the services he had performed for me. McGrath had no hidden motives to hurt Catherine when he decided to sell it. He probably didn't realize that by putting Dev-Corp up for sale he would be putting Tom and Catherine out of a home."

Brad was still too stunned by his misconceptions of the woman he was fast coming to think of as the kiss of death. A petite, *Places in the Heart* kind of lady with a pretty frilly apron? Forget that! Catherine Holmes was a six-foot bottle blonde with brilliant red fingernails and a model's long legs and nipples that could bring a man to his knees and a mouth that could do *anything*! What a mess!

Wrather was removing a cigarette from a silver case. He didn't light it, but tapped the end upon a manicured thumbnail and placed it between his lips.

Removing it, holding it as if he were smoking, he said, "Every move is critical now, of course. As you undoubtedly know, Catherine feels as if she had been dealt a bad hand. Now she's filed a lawsuit against McGrath, and we both have horrors that every morning the headlines will be right off the front page of the *Inquirer.*"

McGrath was in more political danger than even Wrather could imagine, Brad could have told him. If Joseph Lowell found out about the affair, he would withdraw his support. That would mean certain death to the younger Johnson's career.

Well, Mr. Big-Shot Fix-It. Can you fix this? "My first order is to squelch the publicity," he told Wrather. "I've brought a man with me."

"Who?"

"Lawrence Goodyear."

"He's a good man. Now, what I want to do, Brad, is present Catherine with an attractive alternative. You have the reputation of being discreet. Well, this will prove your mettle, son."

"Do you think it's wise to be so closely involved with her?"

"Perhaps your staff could handle the matter. We, the family, would be willing to obtain another property where she could operate her little orphanage, or whatever it is she operates."

"I'll talk it over with my people."

"As far as the contempt-of-court thing goes—"

"That won't be much of a problem. Donna Hessing is with me."

Wrather hesitated. "I swear, Brad, I don't know how such a simple thing got blown out of all proportion as it has."

Brad smiled grimly. "The American public has been lied to too much these past years, Mr. Johnson. They're overly paranoid."

The older man sighed, then assumed a posture of satisfaction that he had done the best thing possible by dumping it all into Brad's lap. "You know, Catherine is actually a fine young woman. When she came back into Tom's life after such a troubled adolescence, I took quite a liking to her. I really don't think she'll give you any trouble. I also think it would be well if McGrath doesn't know we had this conversation, don't you agree?''

"You surely don't mean that he thinks he's kept this a secret from you?" Brad coughed into his fist.

"You find that hard to believe?" Wrather laughed. "Do you think your father knows all the personal details of your life, Brad?"

A smile reluctantly curved Brad's lips. "Okay. But I don't have to warn you about how fragile this situation could turn out to be—"

"Why do you think I interrupted a plane in midflight? Which reminds me . . ."

With a parting shake of the older man's hand, Brad gloomily returned to the limo that had brought him. Turning, he called, "One thing more, Mr. Johnson."

Wrather was bending, preparing to get into his car. As he looked back, his silver brows lifted in a stately way. "Yes?"

Not wanting anyone to overhear, Brad returned swiftly to Wrather. He spoke quietly. "As a matter of background information, sir, this difficulty you helped Miss Holmes with—was that financial difficulty?"

Wrather flicked the unsmoked cigarette into the darkness and, taking Brad's arm, walked him out onto the edge of the asphalt.

"That was part of it," he confided. "But Catherine never asked for help. You'll see that in her if you meet, that fierce pride—a most admirable quality, naturally. When she left home to get away from the string of lousy stepfathers she inherited, she wound up on the West Coast as part of that whole drug culture. At the time, I advised Tom to forget about her. Frankly, I didn't hold out hope that she would be worth a dime. She came to Tom and said she wanted to put her life in order. Who could resist that? When Tom became too ill to work, I sent them both to the ranch, never suspecting, of course, what had happened with McGrath.''

Brad studied Wrather with all the skills he'd developed over the years of working for Lowell. "And she did put her life in order? Except for McGrath?''

"Splendidly so. To tell you the truth, Brad, I thought she would simply move on when Tom died.''

"I understand.''

The engine of Wrather's limousine purred as Brad returned to his own car. As he looked back it was already disappearing into the darkness—two ruby dots like serpent's eyes, growing smaller and smaller.

Later, on the plane, telling Donna about the conversation, he skirted the part about McGrath's involvement with Catherine Holmes.

"You mean all Wrather wanted to do was talk to you about the publicity McGrath's getting?'' she asked, and patted a sleepy yawn.

"He doesn't want McGrath to know how worried he is.''

Donna snuggled down beside him for a snooze. "I'll try to get the judge off her,'' she said drowsily. "Give me your wallet for a minute, Brad.''

Tired, irritable, Brad scowled at her. "What?''

"Your wallet, Bradley Zee. Let me see it.''

Not in the mood to make a fuss, Brad proffered the folded leather. She flipped through the cards and pockets, then returned it.

Puzzled, Brad opened it up before returning it to his pocket. There, beneath his American Express card, was a neat foil packet. He looked across at Donna with a sharp snap, but she had closed her eyes. A smile was on her pretty lips.

Closing his own eyes, Brad pushed his seat back as far as it would go. The jet backed out onto the runway. The thrusters kicked in. *Dear Mr. Lowell, you've done more for me than any man alive....*

Nothing would ever be the same again. Deep in her bones, Cat knew it the way wise old dogs know when the weather will change long before the first frigid wind sweeps down from the North.

At six o'clock in the evening of the next day she was mounted on one of Running Wolf Ranch's two stock horses atop a plateau dozens of feet above the ranch house. From her vantage she could look out and see the road stretching into infinity. Like jet streams, pennons of dust floated across the desert from behind three cars as they drove nearer and nearer. She'd been watching them for a half hour.

Their coming had been inevitable, so now she must wait for a bomb to go off. She hated it—this situation that forced her to react to life. Was anyone truly a master of her own fate?

Exasperated, she glared at the cattle that had come to a stop some distance beyond her. She'd found them, two steers and one heifer, in a thicket, and she was herding them back to the catch pen at the ranch.

"Get your lazy hides to the house before I shoot you with this .22," she called. "I hope they make suitcases out of all three of you!"

The stock looked back as if to say, Dear lady, would you please not be a worse fool than you already are?

"Heaven hates me, Sal," she grumbled, as the cars grew larger and larger in the valley and her time to herd the cattle lessened every time their wheels came around. "What did I ever do to deserve this?"

With customary patience Sal picked her way along the plateau toward the arroyo, her hooves clicking daintily upon the sandstone. The canter of the stock stirred up copper-colored dust that irritated the lining of Cat's nose. She sniffed. Sal, poor thing, knew that she hated and despised all cows, which meant that horses rated only one notch above.

"With the exception of yourself, dear," she said with a cluck of apology, for what Cat didn't know about riding would have filled a large book, and Sal paid dearly for that ignorance.

Tom was at the funeral home now. Cat knew she should be making preparations instead of scrambling for a few more dollars. Somewhere out in the desert, T. John and Crowe were also looking for stock.

Cat wiped her face on the sleeve of Tom's plaid shirt. The most depressing thing about Running Wolf Ranch, she had always said, was its lack of mystery—ten sections of land and not really good sections at that. It *could* have been part of Valle Grande, the twenty-five-thousand-acre mountain meadow that was part of a collapsed volcanic crater, a huge, fertile, grassy bowl.

It could have been, but it wasn't; it only skirted it. And not one nugget of gold was buried in Running Wolf's canyons and arroyos. Not one drop of oil floated beneath its mesas and sandstone plateaus. Not one legendary name lingered in its past that was worth a few dollars in a museum someplace. Or a book. Or the rights to a movie.

Oh, it was beautiful, yes. Even the blue-hazed deserts could take a person's breath away as they hurled their stunning alkali flats toward the mountains. The elevations changed endlessly—grass in the small valleys guarded by rocky sentinels, gullies eroded by water sluicing off the hills.

But the herd, mostly cattle belonging to McGrath, was pathetic—not Black Angus or Jersey or Charolais, but a mangy cross between wild-eyed longhorn descendants from the Mexican border country and slow-witted, stodgy Here-fords brought in by the Anglos.

When the eviction notice had come, Tom was in the hospital for the last time. Not one complaint had he uttered about McGrath's treachery. "Round up our part of the herd, Catherine," he'd told her from his bed. "They'll give you and the kids something to trade on so you can move somewhere else and start over. Crowe will know what to do. When I get home, I'll have Eagen come with his truck."

She had pretended to go along. With a tease, she cocked her head. "I don't like cows, Tom."

"I'm not asking you to take one to dinner, hon."

"You miss the point. I don't want anything to do with cows. I don't want to eat 'em, I don't want to feed 'em. I don't want to see 'em, and I certainly don't want to argue with one about a catch pen."

As sick as he was, Tom chuckled. "Learn, daughter."

So, that was what she was doing now—having a "learning experience" with this heifer and two steers while cars sped along the valley floor, bringing people who would hang her life out to dry.

Suddenly, in a way that only cattle knew how to do, the two steers veered off in another direction. With a quick rein Cat urged Sal around in a deep circle to head them off. Once separated from the heifer, however, the steers headed straight for a clump of scrub trees protected by thick underbrush.

"That's just great!" Cat yelled as she was forced to come to a skidding stop. "I hate and despise you."

Left to her own resources, Sal, an excellent stock horse, whirled gracefully beneath Cat, spinning on her haunches and darting back to prevent the heifer from traipsing into the thicket on her own side. But once the steers had crashed through, the heifer—females were such idiots, really, Cat thought, blindly following males!—raced across to plunge in after them.

Cat pushed back her hat and blotted her face in the bend of her sleeve. "You're not good enough for suitcases," she told them fervently. "I hope they make pencil holders out of you."

They not only understood her perfectly, they insulted her by blandly chomping the tidbits of grass that were hidden succulently within the brush. Nibbling her lip, Cat would have considered her options, had she possessed any.

She muttered the most vile word she knew. Sal rolled a reproachful eye, and Cat, disheartened and weary, dismounted. Picking up a rock, she hurled it petulantly into the thicket at the heifer. She missed. The steers gazed at Sal as if they sympathized with the horse's plight.

"To hell with this." Taking a last futile look at the nearing automobiles, Cat fetched her .22 from the scabbard on the saddle, stepped into the clearing, cocked it, braced herself and squinched her eyes tightly shut. She winced with every shot. *One, two, three.* Her last three shells gone in an attempt to frighten cattle out of hiding.

Presently from the top of a slope a good mile away, the Jeep drew up and parked. From so far away it looked like a rusty Tonka toy. T. John was doing his part of the roundup on wheels—a necessity since Crowe had the other horse, and he was nowhere in sight.

Cat removed her hat. With it in one hand and the .22 in the other, she waved her arms back and forth over her head.

Across the dry gulches T. John drove toward her, a cyclone of red dust boiling out behind him. The cars were so near the house now that Cat could almost distinguish their color. The one in the lead was blue and white, the second a light-colored compact, the third a town car or limousine— dark, menacing.

"Come and get me, Constanza," she dared angrily, picturing the official lumbering out of the big car, his judicial robes trailing in the dust. "But you'll have to stand in line for a pound of *this* flesh."

Fetching her canteen, Cat tipped back her head and drank deeply. She swiped her mouth with the back of her hand and poured some water into her palm. Stepping to the horse, she held it beneath Sal's velvet nose.

Sal snuffled noisily. Laughing, Cat repeated the process. "We'd get along fine, you and I," she said, and replaced the cap on the canteen, "if I were more of a horsewoman and you were less of a horse."

As T. John crested the last rise, he braked and, standing in the Jeep, cupped his hands to yell across the valley. "Where's Crowe?"

"Don't you know?" Cat yelled back.

The cars had reached the perimeter of the yard now and were turning in to park. Cat pointed to them, and the boy rotated, shading his eyes to see.

The first words out of her mouth when T. John drove up and came to a screeching halt where she waited were, "I thought you were supposed to keep up with Crowe."

Like a too-fragile sapling in a hot wind, T. John wilted. Cat instantly regretted her impatience. Sighing, she walked over and pulled off the boy's hat and plucked the lanky strands of rust-colored hair that were glued to his forehead with sweat. He was just a child. They all were, and she was ramroding them as if they were men and could work the miracle she so desperately needed.

"I'm sorry, Johnny," she said with a tender cupping of his chin. "I'm going a little crazy right now."

A shy, fragile smile curved his thin lips. "It's all right."

She shook her head. "No one has the right to take another person's head off, T. John. I'm kicking the faithful dog."

Reddening, T. John grabbed his hat from her hands and crammed it onto his head until his eyebrows were hidden. "I ain't no dog."

"Well, you look like one." Cat took a playful swing at him.

"You don't look so great yourself," he said, and ducked.

Cat didn't have to look down to know her jeans and chaps and boots were caked with crusted layers of dust. Her hands were dirt-stained where holes were worn in her gloves. Her feet hurt, her back hurt, and the insides of her legs felt as if they'd been scraped with a dull blade.

From far across the plateau to their left drifted a shout. Both Cat and T. John looked up. Mounted, his back as straight as the long shank of raven-black hair streaming down his back, sat Crowe on the other horse. He, too, was empty-handed.

Cat considered the three head of stock who stared smugly at her from the brush. Then she pondered the cars waiting for them at the ranch. What good would a few dollars at a cattle auction do her now? She waved a hand before her face as if erasing everything she'd hoped to gain.

"Let's get out of here," she said.

Chapter Three

Holy Road Warrior," T. John mumbled, when they had driven so near that the windshield of the Los Alamos County sheriff's car ricocheted the rays of the setting sun into their faces. "They're really here. They're gonna take me back. I can't take bein' handcuffed, Cat. I swear t'God, I can't."

He had parked the Jeep. With a trembling that either was due to the excitement of the challenge or was the forerunner of disaster, Cat had given Sal's reins to Crowe when he rode up. Her hands were shaking so badly as she looked through the binoculars, she could hardly see.

Two men were climbing out of the county sheriff's car. Cat recognized the driver as Jim Lobos with his ponderous lawman's belly, but the deputy with him was a stranger. The second car, a meek, splotchy compact, spilled its lone occupant—Elenie Sepulvada from Social Services, a sweet, honest woman, but one whose rule-book brows rose whenever a new person came to live at the ranch. Elenie's wasn't a consolation call, Cat figured bleakly, but a body count.

The color had drained from T. John's face, bringing his freckles into fearful prominence. "What'll we do?" He shook like a leaf in a high wind. "I can't go back home, Cat. I'll die there."

Not for a moment did Cat doubt him. The scars on his wrists hadn't been inflicted by a spoiled child wanting attention but a desperate young man who saw absolutely no way out. Lowering the binoculars and taking him into her arms, she held him tightly.

"Hush, now!" she scolded with raspy toughness, and rocked him back and forth. "No one's going to cuff you, Johnny. Dry those tears right now. Don't you ever cry again. I'm here. Are you listening t'me?"

She released him only when he snuffled his promise to be brave. Taking up the glasses again, she focused and refocused, searching for the one magnetic force that was drawing her irresistibly into its field.

Lady, the dog, had rushed out to protest the intrusion, and she was barking frenziedly at the wheels of the cars. None of the children had shown themselves, despite the ruckus. Cat imagined them huddling behind the doors, wondering where she was and terrified by the sight of the uniforms.

The deputy was climbing over yucca plants and olives bordering the house. He rudely cupped his hands upon the windowpanes to peer inside.

"You're both wrong," Crowe exclaimed in his stoic monotone from horseback as his angry black eyes missed nothing of what was going on. "They've come for me."

With a chiding glance for the handsome Indian, Cat returned to her surveillance. "Don't be ridiculous," she said, and focused on the limousine.

The doors of the big car swung open. A man and a woman stepped out, the woman shading her eyes as the wind lifted her skirt in a whirl as graceful as spun sugar. A third figure emerged, and Cat fine-tuned the focus. Yes, she saw him now, and she would never be able to explain why she knew that this man would be her undoing—his stance perhaps, or the way he seemed to know exactly what he'd come for. A lawyer? A marshal? Someone Wrather had sent? The new owner of the ranch?

With the grace of the vetted elite, he moved from the car, not hurrying but keeping his blond head erect and flicking his jacket loose with a careless thumb. As if he knew he were being watched, he came to a stop and abruptly turned in her direction.

Feeling the impact of the stare deep in her center, Cat lowered the glasses. She stepped behind the Jeep—a ridiculous move, for he couldn't possibly see her with the naked eye. He could have been a medieval king surveying his armies, the captain at the wheel of his ship, a half-naked savage high atop a pinnacle with the wind whipping at his trousers, outlining long, powerful thighs.

The wind tossed his tie capriciously over one shoulder. Reaching into a pocket, he drew out his sunglasses to fit them behind his ears. Cat felt the undertow of fear a cowboy knows when he hears the deadly rattler in the darkness. The sun was setting the sky afire now as it dropped lower and lower. The wind was tearing the clouds into rags and hurling them toward the mountains.

"Whoa, girl," Crowe said to his horse as if he had worked everything out in his mind. He tossed his .22 into the Jeep with T. John and clucked to Sal. The horse trotted obediently alongside his own mount.

Cat could no longer postpone the inevitable. Dragging off her hat, she tossed it distractedly into the back of the Jeep.

Her hair was soggy and matted. Shaking it out and combing it with her fingers, she excavated several pins and gripped them with her teeth, battling the wind for the tangles and braiding an untidy swatch to cascade down her back.

"We're right behind you, Crowe," she called, and took a final, disturbed look at the stranger.

Crowe was already trotting toward the house, Sal in tow.

"Okay, Johnny," Cat added with a pretense of optimism that was draining more and more strength out of her. "Head 'em up, drive 'em out. And don't frown so. Everything's going to be all right."

The boy did not reply. Neither did he believe her.

From the first moment she'd put her foot upon Santa Fe soil the night before, Donna Hessing had been seething. Not only had Brad refused to take her hint, the morning had been an even more maddening failure—frustrating hours spent on the phone with secretaries and clerks and receptionists who wouldn't know a decision if it Xeroxed itself on their behinds, all to insure that this very situation with Catherine Holmes did not occur.

Yet here they all were, up to their kneecaps in another newsworthy incident. This latest development would waste no time finding its way into the county statistics to catch a clever reporter's eye. By evening it would probably have earned its own little piece in print. Didn't Catherine Holmes know of the word *anonymity*?

"This is outrageous," she fumed to Brad, and accidentally stepped on Lawrence's foot with the spike heel of her shoe. "The Holmes woman has already said she would leave without a fuss. So what in hell is that brontosaurus in uniform trying to prove?" She inclined her head to the sheriff and his deputy. "Thomas Holmes isn't even in the ground yet, for heaven's sake. There is such a thing as a decent interval."

Wincing, Lawrence prudently stepped back to give Donna more room. "Down, girl. You'll melt your diamonds."

"And what have you done to help, Sir Genius?" Donna pointed an accusing finger at Brad only to find his hands stuffed dourly into his pockets. "McGrath will be a human dart board if Catherine Holmes is taken to jail. Are you listening to me?"

"It's kind of hard not to, sir," Brad retorted, as he dragged his attention from the sight of a Jeep nosing down one of the nearby slopes and disappearing into a gully.

Pulling a face, Donna stalked past them, mumbling under her breath, "Uncivilized bunch of cretins. Coming out here with guns. I have to do everything myself, or else the whole world turns to mud. I should have Catherine Holmes on *my* side."

Goodyear rolled his eyes at Brad, but Brad was scratching his jaw in preoccupation. Donna's complaints were legitimate. Judge Constanza was on a holiday in Taos, and Donna hadn't been able to get the extension of the eviction time limit she'd been counting on. Sheriff Lobos was well within his rights to haul good old C.H. and the children away this very day.

Leaving Donna to bear down upon the sheriff under her own legal steam, Brad commenced upon a tour of the premises. A person could learn a lot about people's characters by their surroundings.

The ranch house itself was no picture-book hacienda. It was a weathered clapboard mess, its sprawling origins lost amid the numerous additions that angled outward in disorganized spokes. It was stark in its neatness, however. Beyond the orderly vegetable garden, laundry was hung upon the tautly stretched clothesline, not draped over the wire but pinned in orderly rows so that the wind billowed the worn sheets like sails and whipped the threadbare towels to sweet-smelling freshness. No clutter marred the grounds.

Brad had to smile at the snow-white cotton boys' briefs and the bikini panties all pinned in a row, different sizes of bras, all threadbare but well mended and with no telltale safety pins.

The outbuildings were as immaculate as the house and the laundry. Water was at a premium here, and the shrubs consisted of the native variety, their beds bordered with stones. Connecting the outbuildings to the main house were more bordered walks, and the grass that had been seduced out of the ground was clipped and trimmed. Evidenced everywhere were repairs, not with fresh, new lumber but with old wood planks that had been carefully salvaged and joined in patches as perfect as a tailor's stitching.

Chalk one up for you, C.H. I take back the long red fingernails.

With a smile he loosened the knot of his tie and unbuttoned the top of his shirt. He drew back his cuff to look at his wristwatch.

The deputy was wandering around, knocking on doors and bellowing, ''Miss Holmes, Miss Holmes? Anyone home?''

The place could have been dead. Brad peered through the open window of an outbuilding. Inside were two chairs that had just been upholstered in a cool, crisp pattern of blue-and-white checks. To one was pinned a tag: ''Mrs. Tate.'' To the other, ''Phillips.'' A loom was in the process of being dismantled.

C.H. had taught the children a livelihood? Maybe the bottle-blond hair should go, too. Pulled into the center of the room was a long crate packed with rolls of fabric. Beside it were hammers and chisels and tools. A sewing machine had been packed. Sitting on the floor was an electric fan rotating back and forth.

Beyond Brad, the sheriff and his deputy were conferring, dark patches of sweat staining their underarms. In exasperation Donna had stalked away and plopped down upon the seat of the limo to fan herself, her wonderful shoes caked with dust and her legs sprawled in unlawyerish disheartenment.

The strains of an engine prompted them all to turn. By the time the Jeep was popping over the last rise, they had all glimpsed it several times—up and down, up and down.

Loping alongside it, they saw now, was a magnificent Indian right off a superb Remington canvas. Around his head was a strip of blood-red cloth, and his shoulder-length locks bannered handsomely in the wind. The Indian had a sense of destiny, Brad thought with fascination. In his hand were the reins of the second horse, riderless, a gun in the saddle holster.

The Jeep came to a screeching halt, and a backwash of dust momentarily swallowed it. Sensing movement behind him, Brad swiveled to see the deputy returning swiftly from one of the outbuildings, dragging a reluctant girl who was battling him every step of the way.

"You!" he was snarling as he prodded her forward with great difficulty. "Get over there and behave yourself."

"Take your filthy, rotten, stinking hands off me!" she screamed, and kicked and swung at the man with crazed, chubby fists. "Leave me alone or I'll claw you to pieces. I'll grind you into hamburger and feed you to my dog. Then I'll kill you, *I'll murder you in cold blood!*"

She was short and stout and dressed bizarrely in overalls that were two sizes too large, and she was totally unimpressed with the deputy's authority—an interesting study in women's lib, to Brad's mind.

But much more interesting was the woman climbing out of the Jeep. With an intuition that rarely missed, Brad knew she was the one he'd come to see. His own preconceptions of what McGrath Johnson's lover would look like, however, were so disparate from what he saw, his jaw dropped like a boy's who has just discovered girls.

"Sweet Judas, honey, don't you do anything by the book?" he muttered under his breath.

She wasn't wearing a hat. The low angle of the sun struck the back of her head, making the volcanic mass of her hair appear to have been captured by a photographer's misty lens. Her face would be quite pretty beneath the soil—finely sculpted and strong, her brow high and clear, and her mouth wide and set into a strong, smooth jaw. Yet everything about her surface appearance obliterated that beauty. The dirty plaid shirt buttoned at the wrists and bloused about her waist seemed deliberately to disguise any softness of breasts or dipping curves. Her hips were obscured by men's worn jeans, and their extra length had been stuffed into the tops of her boots. Over the jeans were scarred, leather-fringed chaps that had undoubtedly seen too many years of service before she'd commandeered them. On her hands were leather work gloves, and she was working her fingers deeper and deeper into them as she surveyed the scene with sharply flickering eyes.

Brad had the numbing sensation of having been made the butt of a prankster's joke. This woman, this Catherine Holmes, was no crazy. She might be a bit untrendy—underscored and in italics—but she was no crazy.

The dog, meanwhile, having been alarmed by the girl's screams, had streaked protectively toward the deputy and grabbed herself a mouthful of uniform trouser cuff, causing the deputy to go through ludicrous contortions in order to prevent his leg from becoming an entrée.

"Get away! Get, you mangy mutt!" he bellowed, as he tried to rid himself of the canine and hold on to the girl at the same time.

Lady's teeth found the delicacy they sought. Roaring with pain, the man released the girl and fumbled for his revolver.

The driver of the Jeep, a frail redheaded scarecrow of a boy, gave a shrill scream and tumbled out to race for the dog. Flinging his arms about the pet's neck, he placed himself between man and beast and hunkered low, shivering and cowering as he offered himself.

The scene was distasteful in the extreme, and Brad, moving swiftly forward, meant to end it even if he got himself arrested in the process.

"Deputy!" Catherine Holmes's voice carried with the stinging authority of a whip.

Holding his punctured leg, the deputy had no choice but to acknowledge the sharp accost. So did everyone else, for the moment was hers to command.

Brad had never seen anything like her, though he doubted that she had an inkling of the rare nobility she displayed. Even her unkemptness could not disguise it. He was near enough now to see flashes of fire in her magnificent purple irises, and the flush upon her neck. From everywhere, he sensed children appearing, drifting out of the house and from behind the shed to watch with startled eyes. Several small black boys and one of the most beautiful blond girls he'd ever seen came to stand on the outskirts of the small gathering.

Catherine Holmes was sending messages to them with her stunning violet eyes. In unison, they all turned to look at him.

His impulse was, foolishly, to smile, though he couldn't have said why. But the deputy was giving the girl a shake and threatening her with juvenile court if she didn't show some respect.

"Let her go, deputy," Catherine Holmes ordered as her posture became one of crystalline strength. "Now." With a sweeping disdain, she placed all the new arrivals into one camp.

Brad hadn't expected to be cast as part of a SWAT team. So much for Good Samaritanism, he told himself disgustedly, feeling as if he'd just had his hands slapped. Wrather Johnson had hit the nail on the head, all right; Catherine Holmes was different, even fascinating, but she had the most vile sense of indiscrimination he'd ever known. Let her get herself out of this mess.

The utter fragility of the moment in which they existed moved Catherine deeply. The air between them rippled with sexuality, and Catherine wanted to turn and step away, but she was rooted to the spot.

With ever-widening eyes that were riveted in shock upon the tall blond stranger, Babe was scribbling furiously upon the slate of her romantic's mind. The deputy had lost interest in her now. She had clumsily regained her balance only to see Cat confronting what had to be, without a doubt, the most gorgeous hunk of the entire human species.

Catherine's eyes collided with his openly assessing gaze, and she was aware of the increased beating of her heart and a crazy stab of excitement. She searched the man's eyes for a clue as to what would happen, and she saw a stirring there.

The man was making no effort to hide the fact that he found her very attractive indeed. There was no doubt in his mind that before too long she would be under his protection, for suddenly, surprising himself by its intensity, he was hungry for a woman—this woman!

Catherine wished for one wild, mad fraction of a second that they were alone. Her anxiety caused her to move, and the moment was gone. He lifted his eyes to her disheveled hair. Her eyes flickered to his neck, then away. He, too, let his gaze wander downward to her straining breasts.

Ugh! Prose as purple as an eggplant! Cat wasn't looking at the man that way at all, but in the spitting, back-arched way a cat would defend her kittens against a hunting dog that was sniffing too close.

And the man—as he stopped dead in his tracks, grinding his teeth in a scowling, calculating way, appeared for all the world like Robin Hood in twentieth-century garb who'd decided on the spot that the Sheriff of Nottingham was a much better bet than Maid Marian, and to hell with her and hers.

Babe wanted to shriek at them both that they weren't playing their roles.

Cat was speaking to the sheriff in a tone that was little short of insulting. They had locked horns before over T. John and were old opponents. "Well, I see you got your orders, Sheriff Lobos. You'll forgive me if I don't invite you in." Then, more kindly to the wilting older woman: "Hello, Elenie. It's always good to see you. Did you try the recipe?"

The small woman hopped forward and grasped Cat's hands with effusive patting and shaking. "It was delicious. I used the plain gelatin just like you said, and the girls absolutely *loved* it." Her face abruptly fell. "Oh, my dear, I want you to know I wish I had no part in this, no part at all. I was horrified when I heard, but I am responsible to my superiors, Catherine, dear. We can't allow the children to be turned out into the streets now, can we? Oh, this is dreadful, simply dreadful."

"Yes," Cat said with a tense dignity, and gave the woman's hands a bland pat before releasing them. "Isn't it?"

"Oh, dear," the woman wailed as the sheriff rolled toward them. "Oh dear, oh dear, oh dear."

"I don't want to have to do this, Miss Catherine," Lobos said with gruff authority as he hitched at the belt circling his wide girth. "I know you got a good thing going out here, but the law is the law."

"Heaven forbid that we should break the law." Cat glanced disdainfully at the parked county car, her fingers trailing absently upon Lady's head, for the dog had trotted over to hunker loyally at her feet.

On the opposite side of the Jeep, Crowe was still mounted, looking like Sitting Bull planning the Battle of the Little Bighorn. Pressing her lips into a thin line, Cat walked over to speak to him.

The sheriff's small eyes receded farther into their pockets of flesh as he reached for a cigar and stripped the cellophane from it. He tossed the paper heedlessly to the ground, bit off the end and spat into the red dirt.

Cat turned back in time to see Tucker picking up the cellophane and Lobos sending a pale cloud of smoke to join the rest of the ozone. The sheriff pointed to Crowe with the glowing end of his cigar.

"Who's the buck, Miss Holmes?" he said.

Hostile seconds spun out. Cat glanced cryptically at the strange blond man of the limousine clique. A line slashed between her curving coal-black brows.

"He works for me," she told him.

"Been here a long time, has he?" Lobos persisted.

"What's the problem?"

"No problem. What did you say his name was?"

"I didn't. It's Crowe."

"Crowe *what*?"

"Crow *bait*," the deputy supplied with a raucous bark before he became the target of Cat's scathing glare and became instantly sober, adding sheepishly, "Just jokin'."

"His name is John Crowe," Cat snapped succinctly.

The sheriff swaggered to his car and reached inside for the transmitter. After speaking, he waited for a reply, spoke again and replaced it. There was no sound at all now except the snuffle of the horses and the wind striking the eaves of the buildings, plus the occasional spit of static from the radio.

"Well, ma'am," Lobos announced theatrically, "it looks like you've got yourself a bit more trouble."

The wind caught Cat's hair and flung it in all directions. She unconsciously lifted one gloved hand to hold it down. "Say what you came to say, sheriff."

"It seems your buck there walked right off the mental ward up at Santa Fe. Did you know you were harboring a dangerous man here, Miss Holmes?"

A stir occurred within the group from the limousine. Cat saw the man conferring with his people and the woman turning to look at the sheriff. The man's agitation was a low, gritty rumble, and the woman kept shaking her head.

"Crowe's no more dangerous than I am," Cat boldly declared, though nervousness was tinting her earlobes now and staining her cheeks.

A leer spread across the sheriff's shiny face. "Then perhaps I'd better make sure if he's the right John Crowe. You there, Crowe, get off the horse, easy and slow. Just walk on over here to the car. I don't want any trouble, now."

The hackles of Lady's neck rose, and she came to her feet and growled a warning. Cat exchanged a look with the proud, sullen figure seated on the horse. It seemed as though he had lived this scene a hundred times before.

Suddenly his nostrils flared, and he drew his lips back from his teeth. With a look at Cat that was one of an animal who knows it's trapped but who intends to make one last stand, he hurled Sal's reins to the ground. Wheeling his mount hard about, causing the horse to rear with a fearful whinny, he gave a bloodcurdling whoop. In a billowing cloud of dust, he charged through the gate and across the ragged slope of the clearing, thundering across the desert toward the foothills.

The moment seethed with confusion. Barking furiously, Lady chased after the Indian. Sal skittered, and T. John scrambled after her. The sheriff rolled to his car.

"After him, after him!" the deputy bellowed.

As long as she lived, Babe guessed she would never forget the man from the limousine striding across the yard toward Cat, as if, in this one moment of earth's great history, the two of them had been sucked into the eye of a hurricane and the furor outside ceased to exist. With her masks stripped brutally away, Cat peered up at him with pale, parted lips. He pulled off the sunglasses as he stared hard at her, the skin stretching tautly over the bones of his face. Neither of them moved, nor did they speak. They seemed to mutely accept the circumstance, much as two drivers are powerless to stop, knowing all the while their cars are on a deadly collision course.

He moved his arm in a gesture of protection, and before she could collect her wits, Cat took an eager step toward him, her expression as beautiful, as luminous and trusting as a girl's when she runs to meet her lover.

Suddenly, the magic was gone. Cat was once again a mother, feral in her determination to protect her own. She darted for Sal where T. John stood holding the reins.

At first it seemed her intention was to scramble up into the saddle and dash madly after Crowe. Instead, she rose limberly on her toes and dragged the .22 out of the scabbard. Turning to the sheriff, she cradled the weapon in the crook of her arm.

Her voice rang out. "Don't try to stop him, Sheriff Lobos!"

A new danger came with the settling of the dust. No one moved except the sheriff, and he conferred across the distance with his deputy, then held out his meaty hands as he wheezed, "Now, now, missy. Don't you go gettin' yourself in hot water."

"I'm already in it, but I'm not going to let you drag Crowe down, too. The man's done nothing wrong, and you know it. This is an invasion of privacy."

"The hospital—"

"He could take that to court and win."

Ugliness twisted the sheriff's face as she shot down his arguments. "Put down the gun, Miss Holmes."

"I'm going after Crowe."

"You're not goin' anywhere." He reached behind him for a pair of handcuffs. "Behave yourself, and come along before Constanza makes it worse for you. I've got a paper right here in my pocket—"

"You think I care about a paper?" In a blaze of righteousness, Cat flung her head high. "If Crowe gets hurt because of this, you'll answer to the law yourself, officer!"

Sheriff Lobos had never had a woman of Cat's stature defy his authority. In a state of shock he watched her dart toward the Jeep, Lady racing madly at her heels.

The dark-suited stranger reacted with lightning reflexes, sprinting for the Jeep and issuing orders as he ran. "Work this out with the sheriff," he shouted to his staff, moving sideways like a boxer. "Put in a call to Gary up at the state's attorney's, Larry. Donna, fly to Taos if you have to, but *find* Constanza, whatever it takes!"

"Brad..." The woman was hurrying after him, astonishment taking precedence over grace.

"Are you crazy?" the other man yelled.

"And deal with the social worker about the children," Brad added, one hand cupped beside his mouth.

"Brad!" The blonde came to a stop, totally stymied. "What're you *doing*?"

Brad had broken into a dead run, and as Crowe disappeared beyond the horizon, Brad reached the Jeep. Babe watched his assistants move toward the sheriff, who was rushing for his car. The deputy was skulking around the barn like a coyote. Whooping and yelling, Scooter and Tucker and Steamboat raced to climb the fence for a better view, but Diana was as pale as a sheet and was shrinking against the side of the upholstering shed, wringing her hands fitfully at her breast.

In the midst of the bedlam Babe smiled a wise, knowing smile. She wasn't in the least bit worried. Everything would be all right now. The hero had arrived, and Cat was as crazy as could be if she thought she could escape this wonderful, glorious man. Why, he was even better than Patrick Swayze!

Chapter Four

Not once did Cat consider, as she torched her bridges and sent her whole life shooting up in flames, that the .22 was empty. Was she out of her ever-lovin' mind? she chastised herself.

She knew only that Crowe, for once, was being predictable. Crowe would go to the hunting cabin up in the mountains. After darkness fell, he would gather what he needed of the supplies stored there, and he would disappear. Then it would be only a matter of time. He would wander around the country for a while, picking up odd jobs here and there, but eventually he would be arrested on some minor charge of vagrancy or disturbing the peace. By the time the snowball stopped rolling, he would be behind barred windows and doors again, this time for many, many years.

Unless she did something. Other than that vague "something," however, Cat had no idea what she would do as she raced for the Jeep, the fringe on her chaps whipping and her heart pounding, a needle taking stitches in her side.

Grabbing the steering wheel, she slammed a booted foot to the running board, preparing to toss the .22 into the back and haul herself into the seat. An arm shot across the opening. A hand closed over her own gloved one where it clutched the wheel.

She gaped in shock. A hand like that could have belonged to a high-steel man or an oil-field rigger, but it didn't. She snapped up her head to confront the sharp, steel-gray stare of Mr. Establishment himself.

She swallowed. The binoculars had told only half the story. What this man didn't know about infighting didn't exist. Instincts of self-preservation stormed her heart. "Who *are* you?" she demanded, and strained unsuccessfully to break his grip.

"God," he said in a terse, Eastern accent.

Cat envisioned herself laying him flat with her fist, but she caught a breath instead. "*He* sent you. Wrather sent you."

He neither confirmed nor disagreed. He glanced over her head at the sheriff and the deputy sneaking toward them in a roundabout way. Urgency sandpapered his words. "I'd think about what I was doing if I were you."

But with his Fifth Avenue suit and Establishment finesse oozing from every pore of his body, he wasn't her. Even his shoes intimidated her, and the smartness of the Rolex banding his wrist...and his flawless body...his tough, tanned neck...wheaty, golden hair, thinning a tad at the temples but perfectly suitable to him.

Of course Wrather had sent him. He was exactly the kind of man Wrather *would* send—a GQ-gorgeous, ruthless strong-arm.

"You can do one of two things," she blurted grittily as she jerked free. "You can stand there and let me shoot you, or you can get out of my way. One way or another, I'm leaving here. And you can tell Wrather I said no."

As she spoke, she swung the barrel of the .22 sideways until it pressed meaningfully across the center of his pants zipper. His instantaneous perception—of her fierce scowl, the gun pointed at his groin and her indomitable determination—made him smile, not outwardly but deep inside.

She was outflanked, Cat thought, and not by the uniformed men who had come for her. She glanced desperately over her shoulder. "Please," she wailed.

He stepped out of her way. Trembling, she thrust the .22 into the space between the seats. The sheriff was talking on his radio. Far away, Crowe was lost in a cloud of dust as he thundered across the mesa. Damn Crowe for putting her into this position!

Scrambling beneath the wheel, Cat reached for the key, but the man had placed one hand on the back of her seat and the other on the windshield. He leaned toward her.

"If you leave here, Miss Holmes," he warned grittily, "these men will come after you."

"And you won't?"

She twisted the key in the ignition. The engine coughed, sputtered and died. She tried again. The same thing happened. She jiggled the key with a frenzy and pumped the accelerator.

"Not now, you dinosaur," she pleaded softly, and caught sight of the deputy less than a hundred feet away, breaking into a run.

The Jeep roared to life. Cat's foot slammed the clutch to the floor, and she ground the gearshift into low.

"Don't be a fool," he was saying. "It's only contempt of court. If you run now, it'll be resisting arrest. And you try something with *that* thing—'' he indicated the .22 lying beside her ''—it'll be assault with a deadly weapon.''

But adrenaline had flooded Cat's veins now. She popped the clutch, and the Jeep torpedoed from the site, dust roiling out in its wake and the blur of a dark suit winking in the side of her vision. Astounded, she saw he had vaulted into the back of the Jeep with an agility that defied description. In her rearview mirror the deputy was running, then staggered as a great cloud of dust engulfed him.

The speedometer shot instantly to thirty. Only now did the man's words begin to sink in. *Resisting arrest!*

But it was too late to turn back. The desert was unraveling on both sides, and the terrain felt like that of the moon. Cat's knuckles were aching beneath the gloves, and she wished, in those seconds, that she really were on the moon. The faster she went, the less her bottom stayed connected to the seat.

The ranch was completely out of sight. The man yelled something at her, but she couldn't hear.

She shoved the accelerator more desperately, hurling him backward to sprawl over boxes and tarpaulin-covered cans. A terrible oath reached her ears. One of the cans bounced out the back and was quickly left behind. Through the debris, he fought his way forward, hurling things right and left until he reached her seat and, with raspy gasps tearing from his lungs, locked his arm about her neck.

Oh, no. Cat struck blindly at his head and missed. Her hair was whipping back into his face, and he was battling it to locate her ear.

Cupping it, he snarled, ''Stop this machine, woman!''

''No one asked you to come!'' she shrieked, and tried to shake free.

"If you don't stop this thing, darlin'—" he tightened the hammerlock, his breath searing her cheek "—I'm gonna rearrange your pretty little spine."

He underscored his warning with a jerk. He was perfectly capable of doing it, Cat knew, and though he didn't seem the type, who knew what a stranger would do?

"You do," she shrilled with a panic that was impossible to disguise, "and I'll roll this thing!"

The Jeep had its own opinions about that. It struck a hole and nearly threw them both out, and whether he believed her or simply wearied of the outlandishness of her behavior, he let her go. With the swing of one limber leg over the seat, he managed to get his footing and climb the rest of the way across and slide down into the seat.

Considering that most men in a similar situation would have been lying on the ground with multiple contusions and abrasions, his grace was well-nigh obscene as he lifted his hand in a facetious salute, then realized a lens of his sunglasses was shattered. Snatching them from his face, he tossed them over his shoulder.

His grin had the effect of a flashbulb popping in her face. "Hi," he said, his eyes crinkling deliciously at their corners. "How're you doin'?"

For many years Cat had considered herself an expert in the mendacity of the human smile. Every disaster she'd ever experienced had been disguised with a smile. If that premise were true, *his* smile, all one thousand watts of its high-voltage candlepower, promised a most gruesome death indeed. Now he would probably grab hold of her hair and, smiling, lop off her head.

Her guess wasn't far from the mark. Without warning, he made a quick grab for the wheel, and, hardly seeing it coming, she reflexively caught him in the pit of the stomach with her elbow.

"Damn it!" he thundered.

Indiana Jones couldn't have kept the Jeep under control after that. As the world spun crazily and Cat lost her grip on the wheel, the mindless machine plowed down into the next ravine and bulldozed its way up the opposite embankment. The wheels screamed. The transmission sounded as if it were shearing every nut and bolt out by its roots. How they remained inside at all was a miracle.

She never really understood how he managed to get on top of her, he was just there somehow—covering her, smothering her, pressing her back against the seat and hammering at her leg with a fist until her foot slipped off the accelerator and the engine began, blessedly, to unwind. They came to a coughing, sputtering, undignified stop, and the engine died with an unappetizing *spghat*.

Dust drifted down silently. With its settling came the waves of aftershock: the awareness of pulsing breaths, thudding heartbeats.

Cat blinked against the stiffness of his white collar and wondered if there were a chance in the world that she could save face with a heart attack. So hopelessly tangled were their arms and legs, she hardly knew where her body stopped and his began. One of her arms clung to the gearshift, one to the back of a seat. The lower part of his torso was fitted with unyielding intimacy between her legs, and her right heel lay appallingly in the center of his back.

He slowly lifted his head to look around them, then he braced his weight onto his hands and waited until she looked up.

"There was a minute or two, there," he said, grinning, "when I thought we might live through it."

Laughter wouldn't have been entirely inappropriate. Or hysterics. Cat felt much more capable of the latter than the former, and she was certain of it when, to her utter horror, she realized he was enjoying himself.

Sweet Aunt Gussy! Her eyes widened, then narrowed. What did one do in such a circumstance? Pretend that she didn't know that he was pressed against her in a way that was little short of immoral?

"If you say 'What's a nice girl like you—'" she shoved at his chest "—you're a dead man."

He pulled the grin to one side in an attempt to appear properly chastened, but didn't shift his position or move off her.

"Actually, I was thinking of referring you to a friend of mine who does promotion for the Indy 500," he said. "With any luck you might get a few endorsements out of it. Maybe even a television commercial. You know how it works—they bring out the camera crews and take pictures of you shooting your gun, and you stand beside the Jeep, swaggering a little, looking tough and telling about your shampoo...."

Cat thought she could have strangled him with her bare hands. "Do you know you nearly got us killed, you macho...*Casanova*!" she railed, and made another attempt to disengage her pelvis from his. "Can't you find a woman the regular way?"

Brad Zacharias had never been the kind of man to make up lies about why he was, at thirty-seven, still a bachelor. But neither did he broadcast the truth—that he was simply too selfish to become involved in a string of liaisons that would go nowhere. As a youth, hidden behind glasses and a stack of textbooks that had gotten him pegged as an egghead, he'd grown accustomed to living with his own company. When he discovered that girls found him adorable because of that very shyness, he went off the deep end and nearly suffered sexual burnout at seventeen. After that, he became their best friend. Once he was discharged from the army and in a position to play the field in a grand way, however, his name had already become synonymous with Joseph Lowell's. He was much too vulnerable to gossip to take such stupid risks.

Besides, affairs were not only time-consuming and nerve-racking, they were costly. He'd seen too many promising careers go down the tubes because of sex, and frankly, he'd never met a woman who was worth it.

As the years of his bachelorhood drifted by, though, he'd noted a strange phenomenon...all the really fine women he knew ended up married to his best friends. It was a disturbing situation. Then a second phenomenon occurred... those same hostesses, the wives of his best friends, started making invitations of a different nature—purring, late-night telephone calls and deliciously murmured propositions in public places, stolen, subtle caresses in not-so-subtle ways, a hand beneath the table, a risqué wink in an elevator.

Rarely did he take them up on any of the offers, but he'd gotten spoiled, he guessed, for as he gazed down at Catherine Holmes behind her veil of hair and saw nothing but contempt blazing in her luscious violet eyes, he was shocked.

And consummately offended. *Contempt?* For *him*—woman's best friend?

Somewhere inside, a painted clown reared back, hands braced on his sides, roaring with laughter. *Finally getting your comeuppance, eh, Zacharias? Before you even have a chance to turn on the old charm?*

She attempted to thrust her hands between them. Failing at that, she lashed him with a series of scornful, may-you-burn-forever looks.

In a voice ten degrees below freezing, she said, "Wrather will have your job for this."

Surprised, for Wrather Johnson wasn't the name he expected her to drop, Brad scowled. "For the record, Miss Holmes, I'm not on the payroll of Wrather Johnson."

The curl of her lips called him a bald-faced liar, even though they did remind him of sweet sherry. "Everyone is on the payroll of Wrather Johnson."

"Really? Does that include you?"

"You bastard."

"Tsk, tsk, tsk. Don't be bitter."

Was this man for real? Not for a moment did Cat believe he wasn't working for Wrather, and that he should be in her life at all, interfering and knowing about her when she knew nothing about him, was intolerable.

She struck the side of his shoulder with a fist—a stupid, ineffectual violent gesture that was like touching flint to tinder. A slow smile curved his lips and made her suspect he had his own points to prove. She hit his shoulder again, more fervently. She didn't care whether Wrather had sent him or McGrath or Elenie from Social Services. He was Establishment, all boxed up and knotted with a white tie, the kind of person she'd tried for years to trick into accepting her and who rejected her at every turn. In silence she fought him, clawing, kicking, pummeling, wriggling—all for nothing, for the harder she battled, the more cockily he overpowered her. The silence only amplified the strange irony of their struggle.

Presently he gripped her wrists in the manacle of one hand and, laughing softly, pulled them high over her head. His face hovered over her own as, between her thighs, his sexuality became more insistent.

Cat grew shrewdly docile.

"Don't stop now," he teased.

"You're a monster."

"That's unfriendly."

"*You*'re unfriendly."

He winked playfully. "I'm *very* friendly. Unlike some I could mention."

Through slitted eyelids, Cat watched in disbelief as he hesitated, then bent closer. He was, insanely, about to kiss her, and though she despised the reason for it, it had been so long since she'd even touched a man, she was paralyzed by the very thought of it.

He pulled back to frown at her, his lips hovering above her.

"Well," she rashly dared him, "go ahead and do it. What're you waiting for?"

Brad was remembering her affair with McGrath and wondering what her list of demands would be. Hush money from McGrath, most likely. Or some promise of security if and when McGrath became president. Revenge, perhaps, because the Johnson men had made her a casualty.

But she didn't say anything. She was watching him as a person would look at a washed-out bridge, knowing there was nothing to do except turn around and find another way. In his mind he saw a small, wiry-haired girl who bravely laughed whenever she was hurt.

He'd handled things badly. He wished, suddenly, that they could begin again. With a grimace he said more gently, "Who did you really think I was, Catherine Holmes?"

Her reply conveyed no emotion whatsoever. Her eyes had slipped behind some door that had no key. "I have no idea."

"Zacharias. Bradley... Brad Zacharias."

"Well, Bradley Brad Zacharias, either let me up or get to the business you came here for. Unless..." she dipped her words in a bath of acid "—unless this *is* your business."

This was the appropriate moment, Brad guessed, when he should belt her one, right in the mouth. No wonder Constanza had held her in contempt! What a tongue!

"Oh, hell." He swung around to his side of the Jeep and out the side.

The desert they had just crossed, he saw now, was full of stunning contrasts. Yuccas and prickly pears dotted the land, and thorn trees etched evil patterns against the sky. Beyond, raw canyons and straggly ravines pushed at the majesty of the mountains. Darkness would happen quickly out here, he figured. They could have been at the end of the world. The ranch was miles away.

She was scrambling around on her own seat now, busily repairing herself. When he tossed her an offhand look, she had slipped to the ground in a swift flash of arms and legs, and before he could guess what she meant to do, she gripped the stock of the .22 and drew it from between the seats.

Stepping backward, her booted feet spacing themselves so that her chaps showed the insides of her thighs, she lifted the gun into the crook of her arm.

Brad's first impulse was to laugh. "Is that all you know how to do?" He extended his hand in a pleasant, indulgent way. "Look, Catherine, let's be reasonable—"

"*Miss Holmes* to you!" She motioned him briskly from behind the Jeep with the gun barrel. "You had your turn. I'm on top now."

Now he did laugh, and he shrugged his lost-little-boy gesture that was a sure winner. "Okay. I apologize for the skirmish. I mean, I sort of apologize. Heck, is this because I didn't kiss you? That can be corrected very—"

"Stay right where you are."

Sighing and beginning to wish he'd never heard of Catherine Holmes or McGrath Johnson or DevCorp and knowing that if he'd turned in his resignation to Lowell as he should have done he could be in a simple little office this very minute, working at a simple task without looking like a fool, Brad let the seconds fizzle hotly between them.

"Well, well," he presently drawled, curling his mouth caustically down at the sides, "whatever happened to the code of the West?"

"Out from behind the Jeep, please, Mr. Zacharias."

Brad gnawed his lip for a moment. "You know—" he shifted his weight and gestured expansively "—I've lived in New York for years and have never once been mugged."

Her look gave him second-degree burns.

"Spent all that money on the burglar alarm and never got to use it." He reached up to undo his tie and left it draped about his neck. "Don't get nervous, now." He flashed his old killer smile. "This thing is strangling me."

"Be quiet." Ignoring him, she consulted her wristwatch and the sky and their proximity to the mountains.

She didn't do very much for a guy's ego, Brad glumly decided, and considered taking the gun away from her. Pretty dangerous business for a city boy—sheriffs, Jeeps, guns.

"Then I come down here to this godforsaken place," he added sullenly, "and get held at gunpoint. Figure that one out."

"Would you please stop talking so I can think?" She didn't look at him when she spoke.

"You don't mind if I breathe, do you?"

"Shut up."

Despite his better judgment, Brad laughed, and she flushed so prettily and so sumptuously that a door opened inside him that had been closed for a long time. He wanted, illogically, to protect her, but from what? Or from whom? Wrather? McGrath? Himself?

"It's getting dark," she was saying with enchanting seriousness. "I don't have all night to catch up with Crowe. What I would really like for you to do, Mr. Zacharias, is deliver a message to Wrather for me."

Did anyone ever tell you, my darling, that if you'd stop fighting the world for a few minutes, you could have it in the palm of your hand? You could have me in the palm of your hand. You might anyway, God help me.

Clearing his throat with a nervousness that wasn't his style, Brad said, "I told you, Miss Holmes, I don't work for Wrather Johnson."

But she was earnestly working out the message. "First of all, I'd like you to explain that I'm really hacked off about the way McGrath has handled this whole land thing. It was totally unnecessary. If he'd simply told me ahead of time that he was going to sell the place, I could have done something. But right when Tom had to go to the hospital? I'm only one human being." She looked him honestly in the eye. "Tomorrow I must bury my father. Do you know what I've been doing all day? Trying to round up a few head of no-account…" Instantly nervous, she smoothed back her hair. "I'm sure you're not interested in all that."

But he was immeasurably interested, and Brad wondered if he should explain that Wrather had already confided in him about her affair with McGrath. *Bad idea, Zacharias. The worst you've ever had.*

"I think it's safe to say, Miss Holmes—" he smiled mildly "—that Wrather knows you're unhappy. In fact, I'd be surprised if the whole of New Mexico hasn't come to that conclusion by now."

She promptly snapped into focus. "You mean because I filed a lawsuit? What else was I to do? And look, while you're at it—" she moistened her lips more placatingly "—would you tell Wrather that I called. I didn't forget, I really did call."

Confusion pricked at the back of Brad's neck like a tattoo needle. Forget what?

"And please try to explain it nicely," she added, looking him up and down as if to ascertain if he were trustworthy, "the way I'm telling it. Don't throw in a lot of personal opinions and make things worse than they are."

Quickly, Brad bluffed, "So, that was *you* who tried to call."

She angled him a suspicious look. "You know about that?"

"Shouldn't I?" He fastened his interest upon the maddening little pulse at the hollow of her throat. *Please don't lie to me, Catherine. Please don't disillusion me with a lie.*

She had begun to walk toward the Jeep, obviously intending to leave. "I admit it was…childish, hanging up like that."

"Yes, it was." Brad wanted badly to know what had happened between Wrather and her before that phone call.

"I was having—" she made a self-deprecating sound with her teeth "—what you might call a bad night."

With a discipline that caused Brad pain just to watch, she wearily lifted her foot to swing into the Jeep. "Is there anything you want me to tell McGrath when I see him?" he asked quickly, stalling.

"I have a lawyer." She started to throw the .22 into the back and thought better of it. She glanced over her shoulder. "Why should I want to tell McGrath anything?"

It wasn't at all the scenario Brad had planned from his office in New York City. Damn it, why hadn't he been better prepared? Why hadn't he known more?

"Catherine—" he took several genuinely awkward steps toward her "—I realize this is a bad time in your life. I know your heart's been chopped up in little pieces, but do you think causing this trouble for McGrath is going to make the pain any easier to bear? I'm sure he regrets very much the inconvenience he's caused, and if you'd try not to let your own regret—"

"Regret?" As she swung toward him, the .22 coming with her, the question was a burr in her throat. "You think McGrath feels *regret*?"

"Of course he does. Any man would."

She stood shaking her head as if his density amazed her. "I've known McGrath for a long time. He throws that word around and doesn't know the meaning." She gave a fair imitation of McGrath's superprofessional diction. "'I regret I can't help you, Catherine. I regret things are pressing me. I regret you came to me at this time.'" She squinted sharply. "You wouldn't understand. Forget it."

Brad was at an utter loss as to what to say. Across the distance that separated them—miles, years, lifetimes—he wanted to touch her mind. The silence went on too long and, though he sought one, he could find no bridge. Presently, sincerity being the only way, he said simply, "Try me."

She was gazing out at the encroaching darkness. Pressing the center of her lip with a fingertip, she smiled a brief, unhappy little smile, lowered her hand and looked at her feet as if touched by his lack of eloquence.

"I don't see how people live with their priorities, that's all. You know, I've gotten down on my knees and begged. I've offered my soul for pennies. No charity, I've told them, the children will work for anything they get. A fair day's work in exchange for shoes, for clothes—for a few of those things other children have—so they won't always be on the outside of life, looking in."

Her artless fervor was a thing of incredible beauty when she turned toward him. "What does it take with you people who sit behind the desks? There's no shortage of money. It's all going into building bombs and missiles and making millions of dollars on Wall Street so someone can steal it.

Meanwhile, here I am with a mute girl who needs psychiatric care that I can't give her. I've got a scarred-up little junkie who wants to go home to his mother but who's afraid because someone on the police force tried to rape him. I've got an Indian who's run off to hide in the woods because someone committed him to a mental institution and gave him shock treatments for having no social graces. Now he can't get a job because he has a record of mental illness. And I have no place to take them, Mr. Zacharias, where they can heal. You speak to me of *regret*? If you want to know the meaning of that word, you have to look into the eyes of my children.''

Shaken to his roots, Brad's breath was trapped somewhere inside him. She hadn't said the right words at all. Maybe it had to do with the extremes he found himself in— the out-of-scale desert that suited her so well with its mountain-ringed horizon, its roses and ochers and greens and tree-covered folds. Maybe it was her fire and courage against such odds. How many women would dare go up against men like McGrath and Wrather Johnson?

Something monumental was happening inside him, not in his brain but in his heart of hearts. His past seemed to be meeting his future, and he understood now why he'd never found the right woman. He'd been looking at fancy Washington parties, on ballroom floors and in highbrow New York offices. He should have looked on a rambling ranch out in the desert of New Mexico.

The knowledge went through him with such force it took his breath away. He wanted to prolong the moment, to make her smile, to make her see the folly of offering her love to a man like McGrath, to make her see…that it would be much, much smarter to offer *him* such love.

With a belatedly mischievous grin, he lifted his hands slowly toward the sky.

She blinked at him and turned away, then spun back in surprise. "Put your hands down," she mumbled, and shook her head. "Don't do that."

He didn't move.

"Please, you're making me feel like a . . . a—"

"Jerk?"

Her reply was to look at the sky, which was a stunning palette of purple and black and orange.

Brad laughed because she made him feel as if twenty years had suddenly dropped off his age. "But darlin'," he drawled sensually, adoring her, "every good shoot-'em-up I ever saw had a hands-in-the-air scene." He took a deliberate step toward her, capturing her astonished eyes and refusing to let them go.

Caught off guard, Cat wondered when she'd lost control of the situation. She might be holding the gun, but who was stalking whom now? Just what kind of a man was this Bradley Zacharias?

"Don't be ridiculous," she huffed, and, without lowering the barrel, began clumsily inching backward for every step he took forward. "This isn't a shoot-out."

"Then you wouldn't mind getting rid of that thing, would you, darlin'?"

With one lingering look, he stripped the clothes right off her. Cat's cheeks stung as if he'd thrown pepper in her face.

"Now, you wait a minute," she rashly declared. "I don't want to shoot you, Mr. Zacharias."

To some nonexistent person in the sky, he said, laughing, "Ah, that's a relief."

He was playing a game, the wretch! And it had nothing at all to do with the .22!

Jutting her chin stubbornly, she narrowed her eyes. He was still Wrather's man. He was still the enemy. "But I will," she lied. "Shoot you, that is."

Without warning, his laughter surrounded her—deep, gut-rich music that made her know she would miss it when it stopped. Cat ground her teeth. A person had to be on guard every single minute, didn't she? Right when you thought you had your life all worked out—no risks, no surprises—then along came a man whose laughter and smile could make you like every other woman on earth and had you wondering if there weren't someone out there for you. You could almost imagine that he was the one, with his laugh and his drawl and teasing, steel-gray eyes.

He turned down one corner of his mouth in a sensual, seductive way. "It was a joke, Catherine," he explained huskily, as if they'd been lovers for a hundred years. "Give me the gun now, and behave yourself."

The sun had fallen behind the mountains. Being in the darkness with Bradley Zacharias was about as dangerous as a situation could get, she guessed.

"You wouldn't shoot an unarmed man, would you?" he was taunting.

"How do I know that you're unarmed?" she hurled back in his face, thrashing in her mind for her next move.

"You want me to undress and prove it?"

Before she meant for it to, Cat's own laughter rippled merrily out through the dusk, and she immediately stopped, snapping her mouth shut. "Why don't you just do that, Mr. Zacharias," she challenged with a triumphant gleam in her eyes, for she knew she had him now. "Why don't you just undress and prove it right here before heaven and me and all those little green men in outer space."

She knew she had called his bluff now. *Sorry, Zacharias. Better luck next time.*

His eyes, in the shadows, were little more than gray slits framed with gold. He puckered his mouth and tapped the toe of his expensive shoe upon the hard, packed earth. Then he straightened his shoulders and, chuckling, let out his breath. When he was certain that he had her undivided attention, he smiled a strange, calculating smile and began drawing off the coat of his suit.

Cat felt her face growing stiff. Surely the imbecile wasn't serious!

He shrugged out of the coat and dropped it languidly to the ground as his grin flashed whitely in the shadows. "Never let it be said, sweetheart, that I'm not a reasonable man."

Chapter Five

It was, Cat supposed, the way that wars began—a flippant dare to the wrong person, a tiny battle of wits that got out of hand. Brad Zacharias's suit coat was a pool of spilled worsted upon the ground, ten times worse than any glove slapped across the jaws.

From the center of her dilemma Cat glared at it. Moisture was collecting on her palms. How did she get out of it? A Freudian retort? Coquettishness? Huff him off with a coy, lilting laugh?

There was very little lilt left in her at the moment, and she doubted that Brad Zacharias possessed a single drop.

"Forfeit the game, my love," he drawled, chuckling, "or make your move."

Cat would have strangled before conceding the victory. Drawing in her breath, she smiled and drew strands from her cheek. "Shock tactics are wasted on me, I'm afraid."

"Boy, no one gets the goods on you, do they, Catherine Holmes?"

"Actually, I've always hated being called 'Catherine.'" This, with a ploy of exaggerated patience.

His right eyebrow was an amused question mark. "And you always get what you want?"

"If I did—" rich crimson stained Cat's cheeks "—we wouldn't be having this conversation now, would we?"

"That depends."

With an expression ranging from that of a lawless gypsy to a cocky Wall Street gambler, he blandly began unbuttoning his shirt. *One, two, three.* With the slip of each small button, Cat's nerves popped like rubber bands. A rivulet of liquid fire trickled into her veins. He was dead serious!

Prolonging the stripping of his tie until his grin had destroyed her bluff, he dragged it from beneath the stiff collar. By the time the tie had joined the coat on the ground— purest Oriental silk, it went without saying!—Cat could hardly breathe. Darkness wasn't coming nearly quickly enough.

Without a word he removed his gold cuff links and slipped them into his pocket. Cat expected him to laugh, to ask if he'd gone far enough, but he merely took off his shirt and squinted at all the soil he'd picked up, before adding it to the collection. Then he hooked his thumbs beneath his belt, spread his legs like a pirate bent on plundering a captive ship—ravished maidens and keelhauled sailors, the whole bit—and waited.

Your move, Catherine.

I'm not going to play your stupid, little boy's game.

Sorry, darlin', you already are.

With a haughtiness Cat prayed was a match for any of the women he knew, she boldly swept the line from his shoes up the trousers to the tan-fleshed ribs and his chest where crisp, coppery hair was lightly curled. She viewed corded muscles and sinews with disdain as they stretched from the precision of his wrists, up his arms to the broad span of his shoulders.

You're merely showing off that great bod, she telegraphed when she reached the twinkle of his eyes. *I've outlasted you. Admit it.*

He chuckled softly. *You think so?*

Cat snapped her brows together and lifted the barrel of the .22.

"Easy, easy," he crooned. "I'm working as fast as I can, my love."

She stamped her foot like a spoiled child. "Mr. Zacharias, I have to tell you I find this highly offensive."

He seemed not the slightest concerned. "What d'you want for nothing, sweetheart? My manhood?"

"Oh!"

Before she could turn away, he unbuckled the belt and whisked it through the loops to drop it upon the ground. It was insanity! Both of them knew he wouldn't take off his pants, yet his fingers gripped the zipper. To Cat's horror, he didn't slide it slowly as a stripper would tantalize his audience, giving her a chance to recant, but made quick work of it—skimpy black briefs, a suntan mark low on his hips, a discreet swell, intriguingly muscled thighs.

Cat's tongue was glued to the roof of her mouth, and her feet had taken root in the ground. Off came the pants. And when he hooked a finger beneath his briefs so that black curls winked flirtatiously over the band, some wise and wonderful phantom finally stepped into her body and gasped, "All right, all right!"

"You mean..." His triumph was a deep rumble in his chest. "You mean I win?"

"I believe you're not armed, yes."

"Well, I *knew* that, darling, but did I win?"

"Damn you! Yes, yes, you win! A thousand times, you win!" Cat flung her hand toward a heaven that had to be howling with glee. "Whatever you want! Mercy!"

"Don't be overgenerous, sweet Catherine," he murmured as he stooped blandly for his pants. "I'm not *that* nice."

Slumped upon herself, Cat kept her head bent. "There is something seriously wrong with the English language," she choked, "when you can use the word nice in any possible connotation with yourself."

He was not only a bad winner, he rubbed it in. Gloating was in the jingle of his coins and in the cockiness with which he scooped up his shirt and shrugged into it. He left it open so that its tails flapped about his wonderful thighs, and he tossed the jacket into the back of the Jeep as if it were nothing but a rag.

He reached for the gun that she had, in her chagrin, let swing to the ground.

"I think I'll carry that, sweetie," he said happily. "If you shoot off your foot, you'll probably make *Time* magazine. Then I'd have to forfeit my citizenship and move to Saudi Arabia. I'd probably catch some disfiguring disease. Do you want that on your conscience?"

"Take it." Cat was more than glad to get rid of the hideous thing. "It's not loaded, anyway."

His pause was that of a stone falling into a deep, deep well. With an indulgence that made Cat question everything she had learned since she was born, his face assumed a boyish respect.

"You went through all that business with Sheriff Lobos with an *unloaded* .22?"

A malice-trimmed smile twitched at her mouth. "He didn't ask me if it was loaded."

His regard of her intensified. "And me?"

"You didn't ask me, either."

For a moment he savored the irony of that, accepted it manfully and walked over to prop the gun against the Jeep. Returning, he stood above her, his smile different now—more honest, one that went straight for the jugular. No one alive could have hidden from that smile, Cat thought, flinching as if she'd been stung.

The silence spooled out between them awkwardly. His smile gradually disintegrated. The slow, lingering solemnity that took its place was even more disconcerting. He drew in his breath, and his nostrils flared.

"C.H.," he said softly.

"What?"

"What, *what*?"

Cat was struggling to keep things in perspective, but he was much too close. His sexuality charged the very air around them, and she didn't think he had the slightest idea of how brutal it was.

"Catherine, I didn't come here solely at Wrather Johnson's request." He seemed to see through her skin, into the marrow of her bones. "I work for a man named Joseph Lowell. Lowell..." Hesitating, he rubbed a palm over his hair. "Joseph Lowell, and others, have made a considerable investment in order that McGrath will be the next president of this country, Catherine. Theirs is probably one of the most important investments of this decade. It's my job and the job of my staff to see that nothing happens to jeopardize those plans. *You*, sweet lady, were the one thing we didn't count on."

Cat's feet took a step backward as if they were no longer taking orders from her brain. "I have an unfortunate habit of being that, I'm afraid. Ask anyone."

"Here you are, one woman in this great big state, and in the last few weeks you've managed to undo what it's taken us a very long time to establish. You've got people upset, you've got the press printing ugly things about McGrath. You've got his father running around stopping airplanes. You've put my whole career on the chopping block. My future looks very dark indeed because of you, Catherine Holmes."

Laughter crept up from behind, and Cat's lips curved. She pulled a face. "Would you *please* call me Cat?"

"Cat?" he repeated idly, squinting, then shaking his head. "I don't think so. A kitten, maybe. Kitten Holmes. That's you." He chuckled at his own joke. "I'll put you in my pocket, Kitten Holmes."

If his behavior toward her had been personal before, now it was organic, predatory. He was no longer smiling as he watched the rise and fall of her bosom and the way her hands kept tugging nervously at her gloves. And he looked lower, much lower, as if he were imagining what the insides of her thighs would feel like.

"I, uh—" Cat lifted her chin in a pretense of formality "—I think you should finish getting dressed now, Mr. Zacharias."

He sighed, as if deeply disappointed. "First things first? Wrather Johnson did authorize me to make you another offer, Catherine. On behalf of the family."

The chilliness of the evening suddenly drifted past Cat's flesh and reached her bones. It turned her to granite. She felt like a statue. "What offer?"

"Of another place to live. He'll set you and the children up—"

"Forget it."

"But it would be a partial solution. It would get you off the hook with Constanza. I've sent my people clear to the state's attorney general, but it's doubtful that he'll get involved in something of this nature. You could be in real trouble here.''

''I'll go to jail. It's a matter of principle.''

''Don't be stupid. You won't go to jail, but it could wind up costing you a lot of money.''

So still did she remain, with her gloved fingers covering her mouth, Brad thought she was reconsidering. Was it possible that she didn't know what she did to people? That she made it impossible for them to ignore her? In a full room, *she* would be the one who stood out, and the less attention she called to herself, the more she would draw: ''presence,'' the movie people called it.

Constanza had Brad's sympathies. Even Brad didn't know what to do, and he, God help him, liked her.

Without a word, she turned and walked away, not as one broken but as one who has learned to find another way. Instinctively he followed, aching to draw her into his arms and shake some sense into her.

He caught the edge of her sleeve. As gently as a butterfly would have rested upon the top of her wrist, he turned her. Surprisingly she didn't resist, and he lifted his fingers to her face, intending to press away the tiny frown and smooth the weariness from the sides of her mouth, but he didn't have the courage. She was the one opening *him* up with her tactless looks, stripping away the superfluous images he'd learned to project over the years, searching to see if a real Brad Zacharias was beneath all the complicated Establishment grillwork.

He had no idea what she saw, only that, for him, seeing wasn't enough. Not nearly enough.

''What else will you do?'' he asked softly. ''Where will you go if you leave here?''

She shook her head and offered no complaints, no tantrums, no self-pity. "I don't know."

"You can't just *not* know."

Her eyes were a hundred years old. "It's all right, Mr. Zacharias. You have your job, I have mine. I didn't ask you to come here, you know, and I didn't ask for your sympathy, though I do appreciate it. I'm going to get into the Jeep now, and I'm going to drive into the mountains as far as I can. When I can't go any farther, I'll get out and walk because if I don't, Crowe's going to get himself killed. I'll bring him back, and then I'll bury my father. It was never my intention to cause trouble for McGrath, only to provide a place for the children, and Wrather *did* promise Tom. The children and I will leave, yes, and we'll make it somehow. But I won't withdraw my lawsuit. It's not right—what McGrath has done."

If he'd had the sense of a rubber duck, Brad would have turned on his heel and hiked back to the ranch. Catherine Holmes obviously still loved McGrath, to feel so strongly. He doubted that anyone could get inside her as much as McGrath had done, the blackguard, and frankly, why should they want to? She might have her own style and she might be unique, but she had a chip on her shoulder the size of a Mack truck. What she would do to a man's ego wasn't to be imagined, and what she would do to a *lonely* man . . .

The sky was deeply purple and black now. The moon was thin in the sky, pale and milky among the first white scattering of stars. The breeze off the mountains sounded like distant rain.

Throwing to the winds all the caution that thirty-seven years had taught him, Brad stepped to her back before she reached the Jeep. He closed his arms about her in a slow, suspended motion that was so careful, she could easily have stepped away.

Yet she stood quite docilely in his embrace, catching a tiny little breath as he fit himself to her back. Her voice was the color of the night: "What are you doing in my life, Mr. Zacharias?"

Brad shook his head with more honesty than he wanted to show and considered drawing her hair aside and kissing her nape. "I don't know. I've been asking myself that ever since I got here. I don't like not knowing."

She was so devoid of coquetry that her self-possession appeared stronger than it really was.

"But I have to do this, Catherine," he said, and turned her slowly around to face him. "You know that, don't you?"

She stood quite still between his hands. "I know you're here," she said simply, "in this place, but . . ."

Cat was not oblivious to the mistake she was making when she let Brad lift her arms one at a time and place them about his neck. All her intuitions told her that he was very selective about whom he held.

And neither did she take it lightly. But her whole life seemed to pass before her eyes as he bent his knees to align himself with her before molding the front of his body to hers.

As he straightened, her feet all but left the ground. "I'm in what place?" he whispered as the heat of his breath upon her temple did terrible things to her equilibrium. "Here, in your head? Are you thinking what I'm thinking?"

He closed his teeth upon the lobe of her ear, and the hard ridge of him strained against her belly. Cat received the impact deep in her woman's center only to have it ripple with a retroactive ache that attacked her senses and tightened her nipples with a delicious, drugging pain. Her legs began to tremble, her hands to shake.

Don't do this, Cat. This is madness. Didn't Wrather teach you about this kind of man? She held herself as taut as rapier steel.

"No," she lied breathlessly as her head dropped back and her hair tumbled over his arms. "Not in my head."

"Then where?" he demanded as his body followed to bend over hers. His lips found her throat. "Here?"

Cat knew her tiny moan pleased him, and her power to do that, to affect him, went to her head like too much wine. "No," she groaned stupidly as his lips trailed lower, over her shoulder to her collarbone.

"Here?" His voice was knotted with urgency as he nibbled the buttons of her shirt.

Cat could not speak. Memory was battering at the fortress of her woman's soul. She shook her head. His breath seeped through the frail shirt, the skimpy cotton of her bra. Somewhere deep inside she was alive in a way she hadn't been since she was a girl alone with her dreams. She wanted to scream to the stars twinkling above them: *I have never felt so cheated in all my life as at this moment, because I cannot let this happen.*

Quickly, before he could push her over a line, she pulled herself up by his shoulders.

"You don't understand," she gasped, and stepped away. Yet, before he could move, she returned just as swiftly to rise on her toes and press her mouth to his.

"I guess I don't," he mumbled, and crushed her in his arms, slanting his lips hard upon hers, gathering intensity, demanding, insisting, his tongue parting her teeth and searching for answers to incredible questions that had not yet been asked by either of them.

Only the failure of Cat's past rattling about her feet like rusty chains brought her back down to earth. What they were doing was too dangerous in far too many ways. *He* was too dangerous! Though the taste of him caused a storm in her blood and the nuances of being wanted after so many years of rejection were healing, she stepped back and covered her mouth in dismay.

"I have to go," she said on a quivering breath. "The ranch is about four miles that way." She lifted her hand and let it drop weakly in the general direction of the ranch. "If you keep the North Star in front of you, you'll reach it before too long."

Wishing she had never been reminded of what it was like—all that terrifying, driving need—Cat turned and stumbled in the darkness to the Jeep. As she was climbing in, his hand prevented her yet again, except this time it was possessive. It took her by the shoulder and propelled her to the passenger's side, and when she was there, he picked her up and deposited her inside.

He placed a kiss upon the ends of her flying hair. "Whenever I take a girl to a party," he said gruffly, "I always take her home. And if you don't mind, my darling—" his flinty eyes meaningfully probed hers "—I'll do the driving this time."

At sixteen, Cat had learned the truth. Sex wasn't love. Love wasn't sex. Love didn't come in pill form, neither was it to be found in a stranger's bed. Real, enduring love had very little to do with a bed at all.

She had also learned, after hunger for that love had fixed her affection futilely upon Wrather Johnson, that love and men weren't necessarily synonymous. How amazed she'd been at the wealth of love in the shy, reaching arms of a child. She could exist quite nicely without a man, she discovered. The key was persistence, to tackle tough jobs by degrees. Chip away at them. Break them down. Never give up. Everything yielded—eventually.

But to look across the Jeep and watch Brad Zacharias as he drove, a man's man who had catapulted into her life one troubled afternoon and made her question all that she'd learned at such cost, was shattering.

All the girlish vanity she hadn't gotten a chance to indulge came rushing back. She wished that she looked better, that she was pretty or that she could at least break even with the women he must know; but it had been a long time since she'd liked her body and herself that much.

Longing hurled her into a fantasy of him—not as he was now, wearing his Dior shirt and trousers and wonderful Cordovan shoes and having the look of the city to him—but of him beneath the angry western sky, stripped to his waist, competing with nature and winning, his back burned red and his jeans unbuttoned at the waist, the muscles of his arms sweat-stained and capable of harnessing power she could not conceive of. She was bringing him water. They did not touch, but looked at each other as he tipped the dipper and streams spilled to his heaving chest—not a casual imagery, more like that of a woman caring for an old and comfortable lover or a wife for her husband.

Wrapped in the cloak of darkness, Cat made furtive adjustments to her clothes. She smoothed and tucked in her shirt. She hid behind a shoulder and scrubbed grime from her wrists and a cuff. Casually, making sure he did not notice, she buffed the tops of her boots on the legs of her Levi's. Inclining her head so as to shelter herself behind her curtain of hair, she hastily wiped her face on a sleeve and tried to remember if her brows were plucked or if dark circles were under her eyes. She would have made an arrangement with the devil himself for a lipstick!

Driving was a constant process of stopping and starting and grinding reversals. Brad mastered the rough terrain of the foothills with an ease that exhausted her. He was amazingly quick, his coordination flawless.

Up this high, ponderosa pines blanketed the farthermost sections of Running Wolf Ranch—lovely, hazardous slopes, the backyard of the gods. The greenery seemed to grow out of the rocks, crowding along the ravines, which resented the intrusion of the vehicle. Against the sky, the mountains were insistent black fists raised in defiance.

Crowe would be having a much easier time of it on horseback. She had been to the cabin only once, and that, too, had been on horseback—with Tom one blistering Sunday afternoon shortly after they had left Wrather's garage apartment in Santa Fe. They'd ridden up to get an overall picture of what the ranch consisted of.

"The cabin was built long before McGrath bought the place," Wrather had explained to them before. "It's falling down, but don't worry about fixing it. Someday I might do some hunting—maybe, maybe not. Just leave it alone and concentrate on the ranch house and getting well."

Wrather had never come hunting. She'd never seen him again or spoken to him. She'd joked to Tom as they pondered the scragginess of the herd wandering around in the desert, "Now I know where the ranch got its name. Any self-respecting Wolf really would tuck tail and run. A sad affair, Tom, very sad."

Tom had laughed. "Around here we call that character building."

Tom had always loved Crowe like the son he had never had. During his illness, they spent long hours lazing in the sun, Crowe listening tirelessly as Tom rehearsed his sad life, for Crowe never placed blame. She was glad Tom didn't know about the Indian's recklessness that had not only sent his own life spinning out of control but had forced hers to take yet another unplanned detour.

A buttress of mountain suddenly erupted just in front of them. The Jeep came to a violent, screaming stop. Thrown forward, Cat felt the blow across her middle from Brad's outflung arm. The breath left her in a tiny *whoof*.

"Oh, my," she gasped, clutching his arm in stunned surprise, then laughing when, a second later, drunk with relief, she realized they could have been smeared upon the rocks.

"Damn!" Brad let out his breath.

The engine had died. He twisted toward her, pushing back her hair and feeling her arms and legs to make sure she still had them. "Are you all right?"

Was it the easy, familiar way he touched her that made her suddenly so weary of being on the fringes of life? She threw off his hand and blurted pettily, "You mean besides having lost my father and having no place to live and facing the possibility of going to jail, do not pass go, do not collect two hundred dollars? And risking death by stone crushing? Sure, Zacharias, other than that, I'm perfectly all right. You bet. Yeah. Fine. Perfect."

Slumping, he chided her with the edges of his mouth. "Catherine, darling," he intoned, "you're a lesson to us all."

Cat thought it would have given her great pleasure to black both his beautiful eyes. "Zacharias, would you do the world a favor and shut up?"

"You're all right." He sighed resignedly. "No doubts about it whatsoever."

Cat mumbled under her breath that he was a scoundrel and a barnacle. "You might as well leave the engine off," she said petulantly, and tumbled to the ground.

"We're here?"

"As close as we can get. It's up there...I think."

"But you're not sure."

"I was only here once. Give me a break."

Brad shut off the lights and pocketed the key. "In the daylight, naturally."

"Naturally."

"Great."

He, too, swung out of the Jeep and took his suit coat from the back, slinging it over his shoulder as Cat pulled on her gloves. The air was much cooler here, and he buttoned his shirt, to the relief of Cat's libido. In the distance, the sound of rushing water blended with the soughing of wind in the trees. Dew was pungent with the smell of pine.

"It's a hellish walk from here," she said, and squinted through the darkness, praying that her memory would not fail.

"I hadn't really planned on going in that direction, myself."

Cat scrambled up a steep slab of rock, accidentally sending a spray of small stones showering down upon him—jewels cast aside by a careless deity.

Stepping out of their tinkling path, he stared a moment at the sizable heap about his feet, than at her with a touch of malice. He signaled a T with his hands. "Time out, lady."

Laughing, Cat shrugged with proper innocence. "This is tough territory, city boy. Maybe you should wait down there."

"Not on your life." Taking a handhold, he started pulling himself up the slope.

"I hadn't expected it would come to that, myself," she cheerfully retorted to the top of his crew cut.

With a few well-timed moves, he reached the top. His breath was coming quickly as he tossed his jacket up, then followed it to tower over her.

"I don't know if I should walk so close to you, Kitten Holmes," he growled threateningly. "What with that blood-letting rapier wit of yours, they might never find my body."

"Why, Mr. Zacharias—" she coyly fluttered her lashes "—I do declare, I think I detect a hint of fear in those words. I'll slow the pace on your behalf. Do try not to lag behind."

He nibbled the inside of his jaw. "Give me a little time, darlin'. I'm still learning the rules of this game."

Cat had to physically repel the powerful attraction he had for her. Wheeling hard on her heel, she started up the next, more rugged slope. "That's the difference between us," she tossed over her shoulder. "You play games and I don't."

Scrambling around in the darkness over strange, treacherous territory wasn't high on Brad's list of priorities. He relished even less having Catherine Holmes's delectable little rear moving less than a hand's reach in front of him as she hiked up the side of the mountain. He couldn't remember the last time he had wanted to touch a woman with so little provocation—to simply hold her, aside from all the connotations of desire.

For the first time he was having to cope with a woman who did *not* come to him but was forcing him to go to her. Her game was an unconscious one, which was her immense appeal. Fantasies were blurring crazily in his mind and had been since the very beginning; not the quick, earthy sexual machinations that he had consoled his mind with year after monkish year—all those swimming images of naked women who spread themselves before him and did every imaginable thing his heart could desire—but something closer to reality. He could see himself undressing her, and the act itself was as exciting as sex. He could feel the eroticism of silk that revealed only the most tempting glimpses of flesh, the arch of her foot, the sensual slope of her underarm and the smooth space between her breasts.

Her heel was just above his head, and he reached up and caught it, giving it a playful jerk that drew a yelp of protest.

"I think you play the game, all right, Catherine," he said to her boot. "The question is, do you ever win?"

"Well, maybe you know all about winning."

She climbed out on the plateau and began tromping through the pine trees where the footing beneath them was soft and cushiony with earth and a carpet of needles. Her voice carried back. "You and Wrather Johnson obviously discussed me. Didn't he tell you about my colorful past? All my bad habits?"

Panting, Brad stopped to lean upon a half-rotted tree. The telling would never get any easier. Why not do it now and have done with it? Put it behind them.

"He told me about your...involvement, Catherine."

To Cat, his words were like a bandit jumping out of the darkness and grabbing her about the head and holding a knife to her throat. The only thing that spared her total disgrace was that he couldn't see the anguish on her face when she stumbled over her feet and came to a stop.

Wrather had told? He had made her look like the loser she was? Cat wanted to crawl beneath one of the rocks. She wanted to hide so she would never have to look into those merciless gray eyes. And she'd been worried about smudges on her face and dirt on her boots?

His footsteps crunched softly as he walked close behind her, sending a chill up her spine and making her shudder with humiliation.

"Now, before you go and make something out of that," he told her, "I didn't ask to know, Cath, and I didn't discuss it with him. He just told me. That's all."

If she could have made her feet work, she would have run away. She could sense his sympathy wanting to touch her in some sort of consolation, and she balled her hands into fists and squeezed until her nails scored her palms. *Keep away from me. Leave me alone. Don't look at me.*

"That's a part of my life that I don't talk about," she said in a dark, wooden voice that didn't resemble hers.

"I can understand that."

"Can you, now?" She laughed an ugly, hideous sound.

Brad cursed himself. Of course he'd had to tell her, but his timing couldn't have been worse. She was right. It was none of his affair, yet he knew, deep in his heart, that he had to find out if it was truly over between McGrath and her, because if it were true, and even if it weren't . . .

He placed his hands awkwardly upon her quivering shoulders. "Catherine . . ." His voice broke.

Jerking away, for she couldn't bear to feel the pity in his touch, Cat hugged herself. How pleased the gods must be. For one brief, sparkling moment she had thought part of her might be salvaged. But her past had waylaid her. Again.

"I don't need understanding, Brad Zacharias," she said with a razor blade in her tone. "I know exactly what I was. I was a dumb, stupid girl from nowhere, and he was grand and had money and lived the life of a movie star. I had a child's crush on him that got out of hand, and, like a fool, I wasted half my life. It's over now. You don't have to be afraid that I'm going to go blabbing to some gossipmonger. Do you think I *want* the whole world to know how stupid I was?"

Brad had a painful perception of how hazardous life was. He'd been going along, doing pretty well, and now he was in the position where a single word from her, a tone, could knock the breath out of him. He hadn't intended this to happen. He didn't want it to happen!

"Did I say that, Catherine? You are the most *un*stupid person I know."

She still refused to face him. "Why did you really come down here to New Mexico? I can take the truth."

"I came to take the pressure off McGrath's political career. That's my job." Brad took a step toward her, and she finally turned, moving back, her hand extended in warning.

"That's all I came for," he added softly.

In the stillness, water was gurgling. The wind was tucking itself into the boughs of the trees. A coyote howled his lonesome plaint, and Brad wondered if the Indian, Crowe, was somewhere out there in the blackness, watching this painful scene.

Presently she cleared her throat and recovered her poise a bit. "I'm going to tell you something, Mr. Zacharias, but I don't really know why. I've never told this to another living soul, not even to Tom."

"You don't owe me any explanations, Cath. You don't owe anyone."

"But you want to know, don't you?"

"Yes."

"Why?"

He smiled unhappily. "I don't think you want to know *that*."

A sad amusement softened her face momentarily, but with the return of her memories it quickly faded. She touched her fingers briefly to her lips, as if remembering their kiss. She inclined her head the slightest amount.

"We never made love," she said softly.

The words took a moment to sink into the bedrock of Brad's understanding. Wrather had been mistaken? Or had he been misinformed? Nearer to the truth, perhaps, was that he *assumed* McGrath and Cat had had an affair. Wrather had readily admitted that he and McGrath never discussed it.

A wave of eagerness overrode his relief and filled his head with spinning dreams. With a sudden lightness, he started to go to her, but she had turned and started walking again.

Just like that? Just like that. With a casualness that was one of the most difficult poses he'd ever been called upon to strike, Brad caught up with her and swung into step. Presently she looked across at him, a faint, grim smile tipping up the corners of her mouth. How perfectly she fit into this wild black night with her hair and her strong, lithe body and her mysterious challenges that made him want her more earnestly with every passing minute.

"I suppose you win all the time, Zacharias?"

Brad hadn't the faintest idea what she was talking about. He frowned.

"Those games you play," she explained.

"Oh, those." He chuckled. "I win. Absolutely."

She had set a quick pace. Brad was so absorbed in watching the way she moved, he hardly noticed where they were. He stopped and looked around.

"And when I want something very, very badly," he added to the clearing they had stepped into, not caring if she heard or not, "I have been known to cheat."

"The cabin," she said.

"Where?"

She pointed. "There."

Chapter Six

The terrain unfolded quite suddenly into an open space bordered on its fringes by whispering pines. Large enough, Brad speculated as he followed Cat, that a helicopter could have landed.

In its grassy center sat a primitive log shanty with a crudely laid chimney. Along one side stretched a bench with a stack of firewood at one end. A circle of stones enclosed the place where an open fire had burned—rather recently, it seemed to him. Beyond it, the plateau spilled over the cliffs into the darkness.

"Is that the flow of the River Styx I hear?" he mused in a cryptic aside as he walked across the clearing and peered over the edge.

She had fit her hands into her back pockets and was rotating, studying the trees in the opposite direction. "I'd be careful if I were you, Zacharias." Her words were absently spoken. "The Furies are waiting to get you."

Delighted, Brad reached into his pocket. "Catch," he said when she turned, and flipped a penny. "Can't have you caught on the wrong side of the river with no money to get home, can we?"

She missed catching it by a mile, and the penny disappeared into the grass. Laughing, she removed her gloves and stuffed them into a back pocket. She stooped to search through the sprigs without success.

Brad hungrily watched the flex of her waist, the way it flared invitingly into her hips. How strange it was that at this moment she seemed to have been a part of his life forever. When he looked at her, he felt surrounded by... home.

"You seem to know right where I'm going to go," she quipped.

"I just wanted some company. Forget that penny. Here's another."

"No!" She looked up from her hands and knees and added with more wistfulness, "I want this one."

"Why?" he asked, which meant that when this was over, it wouldn't be the end of them.

She finally found the penny and pounced upon it, laughing as she sat back on her knees and waved it in triumph, but she seemed to read the unspoken question in his eyes, and her smile slowly faded. Embarrassed, abruptly shy, she rose to move deeper into the clearing and turned in a circle, her insistent sensuality silhouetted against the sky.

"Crowe?" she called, and waited for a reply, watching, scanning.

Startled, an owl flapped away, making a pewter stain of the moon for a second before disappearing in a wide, breathtaking arabesque over the treetops. All living things seemed to have vanished. There was just the wind in the pines and the whispered secrets of the water in the distance.

Placing her hands beside her mouth, she called louder. "Crowe, it's safe to come out. This is Brad Zacharias. He's not with the police. Come on out, please. It's very late."

Brad could imagine the Indian standing motionless in the shadows where the trees were thick, his hand muzzling the horse.

"I know you think they came for you, Crowe—" she was speaking to all directions as she rotated "—but they didn't. If anyone's in trouble, it's me." She tapped her own shoulder, then shivered from the cold. "You know Constanza and me." Her words dwindled with the dismal reminder. "You know me."

Brad placed his suit coat about her shoulders, and she shivered as his hands remained upon her arms—not squeezing, not patting, but at peace with themselves. A deep and terrible longing crept out of hiding inside him. His heart felt bruised with wanting.

"I don't think he's here, Catherine."

"Oh, he's here." She continued to study the shadows. "Crowe just doesn't trust people easily."

"Who does?"

The moon had edged the night with silver paint. Where they stood, the mountain was pearled and misty gray, but above them where the woods were thick, the shadows tangled so densely that seeing anything was impossible. So long did they remain fixed in the tableau, waiting, that the owl returned to perch in the top of a half-dead tree and hooted his low, chanting approval.

Their mutual heat presently reached through the jacket, from her to him, from him to her. Presently she handed the jacket back to him.

"Let's go inside," she said with a gesture at the cabin. "He'll come when he's ready."

With a small smile, she strode toward it with a business-like *swish, swish, swish* of her chaps. She disappeared inside, and Brad, wondering glumly if he were destined to follow her the rest of his life, ducked his head and walked through the door.

"Wait there," she commanded softly from the dark interior. "I remember a shelf. There might be a candle."

Reaching into his pocket, Brad located the lighter he kept with his change. He held the flame high so the shreds of light danced eagerly into the corners, and his eyes widened with disbelief.

"What in the name of..."

The word *cabin* hardly did the place justice. Expecting rough, moldering boards and sour dirt, he saw what was more like a hedonist's daydream—a glittering, eccentric fancy lifted straight from the pages of *A Thousand and One Nights* and transported, live and in color, to the Jemez Mountains by chartered flying carpet.

Though the "cabin" was windowless and crudely walled, its rude floor was covered with luscious fur throws. Before the primitive fireplace were great piles of inviting tasseled pillows—velvet and nubby raw silk and shimmering satin. Along one wall were low mounds of decadently plush furniture and against the opposite, drapings of tapestries and an evilly luxurious chaise and a velvet footstool.

The "kitchen" had no modern conveniences, but there was a compact area for cooking with a portable stove. Near it was a rich supply of liquor and a rack of glittering stemmed glassware. Hung from the ceiling were various lamps with wicks in need of trimming. And beyond a partition was the seduction of a bed—pagan indulgence of silk sheets and a quilted comforter left in sensual disorder by its last occupant.

More correctly, its last *occupants*, for the room harbored unmistakable secrets of women, from the sultry garter belt and wispy stockings draped carelessly across the back of a chair to whiskey glasses, still with lipstick stains on them, scattered over a small tabletop. Long, slender cigarettes were crushed in the ashtrays, and the residue of marijuana.

Brad saw himself being played for a fool, but he wasn't sure by whom. Catherine? Wrather? McGrath? Just what was going on? There was something insidious and sinful about the whole place, and his original impression about the helicopter wasn't far off the mark, it seemed. People flew in, did their thing, then left. What people? What things? Why?

"Why, we're just full of little surprises, aren't we?" he said with heavy sarcasm, and let the chips of suspicion fall where they would.

Cat was stunned. When she'd last been inside the cabin, the place had been four gutted walls and had recently been used for cleaning fish. But she was even more stunned by Brad's insinuation that she knew about any of this. How *dare* he? How *could* he think that the sweet French perfume in the close night air might belong to her?

And other smells not nearly so sweet, smells that were, dangerously, a murky part of her past.

"Whoever was here," he was saying as he moved about the room, "obviously left in a hurry."

With whiplike determination, Cat moved to the small table beside the bed where the trappings of someone's hasty fix lay—the needle, the spoon. She looked up to see suspicions drawn on his face that were even more ugly than those drifting through the room like a poisonous gas.

"Your friend Crowe?" he accused as a sudden breeze snuffed out the lighter.

"No," she said angrily.

"Who, then?" He flicked the lighter repeatedly without success.

Cat slumped from the force of his speculation. He had crept up on her from behind and had cut through the walls of her hard heart with a blowtorch—an ordinary man who was on a job he hadn't particularly wanted, who made her laugh and remember what happiness was like. Now he was exposing the core of her so that she could look right into herself and remember the terrible mistakes she had made with her life.

Through her teeth she said, "Maybe it's your good friend McGrath, Zacharias. Stands to reason, doesn't it, since he owns the ranch? Maybe good old McGrath has been dealing a little sauce on the side, hmm? Maybe that's been paying your salary. Or maybe he just kept this as a party place for his important friends. I'm surprised you're not one of them. It's perfect, isn't it? And if anything happens, he can always blame Crowe."

Cat snapped her mouth shut. She had said too much. From far away the noise of the stream seemed to grow louder until it was a torrent bursting through floodgates and sweeping her beneath the surface where bubbles roared past her face. She was drowning in her own past.

"Or me." She turned woodenly as the truth dawned. "So *that*'s why McGrath sold..." Spinning around, her lips pale as a wraith's as her heart broke, she placed the truth between them, dragged it out into the open like a corpse. Her whisper was that of a child unfairly punished. "He would blame *me*."

With a small, strangling sound, before Brad could stop her, she rushed through the room, pulling open the doors of the cupboard, lifting the pillows before the fireplace, ripping at the sheets, throwing back the mattress with the energy of a crazy woman.

"What're you doing?" he demanded, and grabbed her wrist.

Cat looked down at his hand wrapped around her wrist and wanted to smash him. She could have trusted him, damn him! She could have truly cared. One more minute of his sweetness, and she would have been pouring out her life at his feet like a burnt offering.

"Looking!" she cried. "Leave me alone!"

"Looking for what?"

"The stash, the evidence!"

"Damn it, Catherine!"

Brad had never meant for the situation to become so nasty. He hadn't even meant to imply that she knew or had anything to do with it. He attempted to catch her into his arms, but she twisted free of him, seeming obsessed with ridding her life of the cabin and everything in it.

"Wait!" He stumbled in the darkness and crashed into a chair. "Damn! Would you wait just a dad-gummed minute? I don't think you ought to touch any of this. If none of these prints are yours, and the police were to ever..."

In her delirium, Cat collided headlong with him, and Brad's arms closed about her like a vise. In the shadows he saw the sense of betrayal large and desperate in her eyes.

"*If* none of them are mine!" she cried furiously, doubling her fists. "*If* none... You really think that I've been up here? You think—"

"Don't put words in my mouth, Catherine," he ground out.

Cat abruptly found herself lifted off the floor with a strength that defied her to resist. Her legs dangled limply against the strong, anchored power of his, and her head snapped back painfully.

"I didn't say that, and I didn't mean it," he said.

"You thought it, Zacharias." The words were ripped hoarsely from her throat, though they weren't the ones she wanted to say at all. "You thought it, and you know—"

"Listen to me—" he tried to hold her head still so she would be forced to look at him "—I'm not accusing you, Catherine. I'm trying to protect you."

"Oh, well..." she sneered. "You mean you've decided to stop protecting McGrath and start protecting me, now?" Hands braced on his shoulders, she stared at him with ruthless honesty.

Brad slumped in dismay. "Cath—"

She wriggled futilely in his arms. "There is an old proverb, Brad Zacharias, about how a house divided against itself cannot stand. In your trade, I think they call it a conflict of interest."

Like the blade of a medieval sword their conflict whirred in the air then thrust, into the ground between them—terms delivered, boundaries laid out and to be crossed at one's peril, man versus woman, love versus sex. Brad wasn't proud of the anticipation that curved his lips and narrowed his eyes to slits as he looked between them to where the curves of her breasts were flattened to his chest and the secret hollows of her that should have been satiny with feminine sweetness slipped farther and farther beyond his reach. She was wrong about him, dead wrong. He'd been wanting to love her, not destroy her, and now she had superimposed upon that desire something repulsive.

"Damn you," she flung in his face.

"Then if I'm damned, my darling," he said with lustful relish, "I might as well be damned for aught as for naught."

She had pushed him too far. Had she not been so vulnerable to him as a man, she might have been able to stop him with a look, but he knew—he had known since that first kiss—how on-the-edge she was, and he was ready to prove it now, bending over her in a ravenous search for her lips, her hair in his face, the heat of his desire reaching through all the layers of clothing and past mistakes.

Cat saw herself naked and needful before this man, feverishly guiding his lips to places she hardly knew herself.

"No!" she groaned and struck blindly at him.

But his kiss was smothering her cry, and he was clasping her head in his hands and silencing her tongue with his. One of her hands was crushed against his chest, and when she tried with feeble, whimpering blows to fend him off, he swept her up in his arms and half walked, half stumbled with her to the bed.

They fell upon it together. Cat ended up beneath him, straddled, his hips pressing hard against her belly. "You can't do this!" she choked.

Laughter was buried in his chest. "Can't I?" He tore a button free on her shirt. "We might as well even the score, eh, Catherine? Shall I get the gun? Point it at you this time and see what happens?"

Cat had always thought, with a twinge of secret vanity, that her one, true woman's beauty were her breasts, with their full Botticelli roundness and firm, pink nipples, their tendency to sloop without drooping and their pale, creamy tops that were feminine even when the rest of her was as virile as a man. But no one had ever looked at them against her will before.

His thumb flicked lightly, and the bra clasp slipped free, spilling the curves that were even more pale and more luminous in the darkness. Both their breaths roughened, and she saw dark desire in his eyes.

Without his touch, without any provocation at all, her nipples tightened, pouting at him. She could have drawn his head to them. She thought she would break if she didn't. She relished the feel of his hands upon her, and she could have learned all the symmetries of him and touched him in a way she had never touched a man before.

But she looked where he looked, and she saw only white portions of herself against a marring tan that was several shades darker. She hadn't been allowed the luxury of tanning evenly. She slaved in the sun, not played. And she slaved because she was so stupid—like now, painting herself into a corner.

She couldn't keep the rasp out of her voice: "Are you satisfied now?"

His sound was that of an animal when it has run too far. With a shake of his head he groped for her hands and, lifting them to his lips, kissed their palms and placed them upon his eyes.

"He was a fool," he said thickly. "How could he not have loved you? God help me, I would've loved you."

Neither of them spoke as he slowly stretched out alongside her and gathered her into his arms, holding her for long tender moments with her breasts hidden against his shirt, stroking her hair, skimming the contours of her back and her waist, sighing.

"I'm sorry," he said at length.

Cat didn't know what to say. She couldn't remember a man ever apologizing to her before. She sighed softly against his pocket. "I'm not easy, Zacharias. I'm sorry I'm not easy."

He chuckled ruefully. "Catherine, sweetheart, tell me something I don't know."

Cat found an odd contentment in letting her fingertips simply ride the rise and fall of his ribs when he breathed. When things were calm, he was actually a very nice man. That niceness was his talent, though—a net he could throw over her at will, holding her immobile.

Contentment gave way to foolishness, and she felt as if she were in a sensual vise where nothing in the universe existed but his muscles playing beneath his shirt and the insistent hunger for her that made him taut against her side. A hazard, that male hunger, and highly unreliable. Men wanted anything with breasts and hips and a mouth.

"Are you hungry?" she drowsily asked, her cheek resting upon his heart and absorbing its steady beat.

He laughed soundlessly. "That depends, love. Hungry for what?"

"Don't be obscene." She appalled herself by giggling.

"It's *my* hunger, I can do with it what I will."

"You're an evil man. There's food here if Crowe hasn't beat us to it."

"Ah, yes . . . Crowe."

Releasing her, Brad took a secret pleasure in watching her repair her clothes. He loved everything about her now, even things he did not know. Once more he found himself ambling in her wake, watching all her moves, his only satisfaction that of knowing she could accuse McGrath as quickly as she could love him.

"Are you following me, Mr. Zacharias?" she said as she stooped to peer into a small cupboard beneath the wine-glass rack.

"Absolutely."

"Voilà. Look what I found."

She produced only two cans, both without labels. Crowe could very well have been there already; the cupboard was bare. Brad wondered if he were watching them even now. He twisted to find the doorway empty, then propped his foot on one of the footstools and braced an arm on his knee.

"I love surprises," he said.

"I don't."

"Come on. Where's your sense of adventure, Catherine?"

"I've had enough adventure for one day, thank you very much." She straightened only to crack the shelf of glasses with her head. "Ouch!"

"Poor Catherine," he crooned, and didn't lift a hand to help her. "I think this might be a good place to say that I'm very easy to cook for. My mother, God bless her, is an awful cook. Do you know till this day I like burned toast?"

"Why, you're just a prize catch, aren't you, Zacharias," she purred as she riffled a plastic container and found a can opener, which he immediately took to open the cans. They proved to be, fortunately, Boston baked beans.

"You'll make someone a wonderful husband when you grow up," she said, her search for a plate finding none that weren't dirty. Grabbing two spoons, she poked one into each can. "Dinner is served."

"And since you're taking such an avid interest in all this, I might as well inform you that I'm completely housebroken, I know how to do laundry, and I'm very handy at fixing toasters—to burn the bread in—and repairing vacuum cleaners and that sort of thing."

She screwed up her face in a comical squint. "Why are you telling me all this?"

His grin flashed. "Just in case you're ever in need of that kind of information."

Laughing, Cat shook her head and delved into one of the cans for a bite. Once indulged, her hunger overcame her, and she lifted the can from his hand and rapidly wolfed down half its contents.

He was watching her as raptly as a doting parent hovering over a difficult child. She paused long enough to cast an eye on his baked beans. "Are you going to eat those, Mr. Zacharias—"

"Why do you keep calling me Mr. Zacharias?"

He had stepped directly before her and braced his foot upon the lowest shelf. Cat could hardly have called his blatant display of masculinity immodest after what they'd been through, but heat nonetheless rose in her throat as she gaped at it.

She took a quick bite of beans for fortification and talked around her mouthful. "Because it's your name."

"My name is Brad. Spoken gently, of course. Say it." His eyes were making searching forays into her own as he leaned closer. "Say Brad, Catherine."

"Mr. Zach—"

"Gently."

Wanting to smile but not daring to now, not when he was looking at her as a mountain lion would allow a poor rabbit a few more moments of life before having lunch, Cat looked everywhere but at his braced leg and grimaced, shaping her lips soundlessly about the name.

Leaning even nearer, he murmured, "Not that gently, darling."

She flattened herself to the wall at her back and clutched the can of beans to her bosom. Moving closer, he pressed every part of his body against her except his right hand, which held his own can, and his left, which he braced beside her head.

"Say my name, Catherine," he urged huskily.

"Well, I might if you weren't crushing the breath out of my body," she squeaked.

The dazzling, heart-stopping flash of his smile, the catch of his breath, the burn of his eyes, the swelling insistence of masculine dimensions—Cat was aware of them all.

She wet her lips nervously. "Brad," she whispered softly.

His breath was seductive upon her cheeks as he smiled down at her. "Again."

She smiled shyly. "Brad. Brad, Brad, Brad. Now, will you let me go?"

He didn't. "You know that something important is happening here, don't you, Catherine?"

Her voice grew so brittle, it sounded as if it would shatter like ice. "I know that something is happening, but I can't...I don't—"

Without relinquishing her eyes, he removed the can from her hands and set it, along with his own, aside. His lips lowered, searching hesitantly for hers, and Cat watched them gradually fill her vision until there was nothing but him: the slightly askew nose, the whisper of his breath, his smell, his clean, short hair.

"It's important that you know I don't go around doing this kind of thing," he said. "Do you believe that?"

Cat was someone else, a stranger from a dream. "I've made too many mistakes in my life, Brad."

"I've made my share."

His mouth brushed over her cheeks, her eyelashes, his fingers finding the nape of her neck beneath her hair. When his lips had traveled everywhere, measuring the slope of her jaw and the plane of her nose, the shape of her ear and the width of her brow, they found a dewy corner of her mouth and nibbled lightly, making sure she understood he was asking for the kiss, not taking it.

She didn't struggle when he fastened his mouth to hers and tasted and explored until her mouth seemed more his than hers. When the kiss became more urgent and he was burying his fingers into her hips and lifting her up, she slipped her arms around his neck.

She whispered, "Brad, I want to tell you something."

He was tasting her everywhere—her shoulders and her chin, her throat and her ears. "What, sweetheart?"

"A long time ago..."

"Yes?"

Cat could hardly speak for the sensations he was causing. She pushed feebly at his shoulders. "After I got straight..."

"Yes."

"I was...I was so scared of having caught something, you know? Some of my friends were on the needle. They were kids, like I was, and we were all in bad trouble. I took a lot of tests after that. One reason was I thought—" she dropped her head to his shoulder, sighing "—I thought that *he* might want me more if he knew I hadn't caught some awful disease or something."

He stopped battling her for the tails of her shirt and sought her eyes. "You don't have to tell me this."

"Yes, I do. I was lucky, Brad, but I promised myself then and there that I wasn't going to ever risk my life like that again. And go through that horror? D'you know what I'm trying to tell you?"

His mouth reached for her lips, then drew back. He looked into a distant past, then back to her as he comprehended.

"Do you think you're the only one who considers that?" He watched her measuring him for wisdom. "Hey, I like women. I've always liked women. Okay, okay." He grinned. "What I'm trying to say is that when I was young, as compared to you when you were young, I *really* liked 'em. A few times I was certain that I was in love." He shrugged more seriously. "But eventually I realized it was their good humor or their legs or the way they danced that I was in love with. For my own reasons, Catherine, I don't sleep around, either. They're not even noble reasons; quite materialistic, actually, and I'm a little embarrassed to say that. The bottom line is, I'm the safest man on this planet, but I would never make a woman worry about her life. It so happens that I like my life, too. And about what happened on that bed over there, I could never hurt a woman. But you know that, don't you?"

Deep in her most frightened, primitive heart, Cat knew a lot more. He was stealing her heart right from under her nose. She was half in love with him already. She wished she had the strength to deny the forces that were hurling them into some star-crossed collision course, but she couldn't. There was McGrath. What about Wrather? What could possibly come of this? It was hopeless—the two of them. His job was to take care of the very man she hated. He represented a whole way of life she hated. It was a soap opera, an impossibly bad novel.

"I think we'd better eat," she mumbled, and very gently put him from her. "Crowe's around here somewhere. It's just a matter of time."

After a long, thoughtful pause he stepped back to let her pass. "Yes, it's just a matter of time. Let's build a fire outside. I don't like this place. It has the smell of evil about it."

They waited for Crowe outside. Taking blankets and beans and the scattered pieces of their emotions, they built a fire higher up, beside the stream where it slewed down the mountainside to collect in a shallow pool before dropping into the gorge. While Cat gathered wood, Brad got his lighter working again and coaxed the kindling to catch.

Crowe, Cat knew, would spot the fire. The mountain was cold now. The wind whistled through the desolate slopes, and the trees gossiped among themselves about the two crazy people who could have been comfortable inside the cabin but who elected to brave the chill all because of a silly feeling.

As the fire caught and smelled of pine, the stars seemed as large as asters above them. Cat let herself flow into the limitless night. Her need for sleep drifted in upon her like fog. After they ate the scanty fare, Brad arranged the blankets and invited her into the haven of his arm to wait.

"He won't be much longer now, I'm sure," she said sleepily.

"While we wait, I'll tell you my life story," he said. "Where do you want me to begin?"

She laughed. "Tell me everything, beginning with the last two hours."

"Witch. Close your eyes."

"They are closed."

"Once upon a time..." he said.

With his arm cradling her and his thumb moving back and forth in a caress of her cheek, he told her about growing up in Seattle in an ordinary middle-class family. He was the only son among four girls, and when he'd gotten the position with Joseph Lowell, he was full of idealism and the certain knowledge that he would make a difference in the world. He told her about seeing his dog get hit by a truck when he was nine and how he had held her in his arms while the vet put her to sleep. He told about how he had cried, and his sisters had made a special box and worn nice dresses when they buried her. Cat told him about her mother's divorces and her stepfathers and about the time she had hidden in a closet in Lincoln, Nebraska, and plotted how she would go to the police station and beg them for bus fare so she could go home to her father. But her stepfather had found her and made her sit at the table, and every time a tear slid down her cheeks he would say, "Did anyone ever tell you that you're too emotional?"

"Tell me, Brad, when did you realize that you would spend the rest of your life just being a plain old mortal man?" she asked, holding herself close to his warmth.

He rested his chin upon the crown of her head. "I've suspected it for some time now. I just didn't know where to place the blame until quite recently."

"And now you know?"

"Absolutely."

Stirring, Cat raised herself on her elbow and gazed at him from beneath drooping lids. Gone were all the *GQ* specifics she'd seen before. Now he was merely a slightly rumpled man with a five o'clock shadow who was tired and a bit hungry. He was on the same level of human survival as she was herself, and she wondered why she'd ever found him threatening.

"Then tell me whose fault it is," she demanded brightly, and scooted nearer the fire. "I'll break their kneecaps and won't charge you a thing."

With a grip of her ankle, he pulled her back to his side. He placed her fist upon her own knee. "Have at it, Mafia mistress."

She pretended to swing a punch at him. "That's not nice, Zacharias."

"Don't haggle over details. I'm trying to share a deep personal experience with you, woman."

Grinning, she touched her forehead. "I've got four stars stamped right here for 'good listener.'"

He rose up to make a thorough inspection of her forehead and kissed it in four places. Then he drew her down until her cheeks rested upon his chest.

"I've been trying to quit Joseph Lowell for years," he said. "It didn't seem right to me, having power over people's lives like that and letting others believe things that I knew in my heart weren't true. That's what it's about, you know. The 'prevail' of power. But the struggle never stops, because power has to accumulate more power, protect the power it already has, hoard it. That's what's so sad. Power prevails until it becomes powerless, and the struggle goes on, eating its tail.''

The silence had its own voice. He was, Cat knew, only just now facing something that she had faced at sixteen—his own helpless mortality. There was something in his wistful sigh that made her love him a little—that plea for her understanding that a man wasn't a knight on a white charger who could work miracles and create Camelot, but just a man.

"People live with what they're given, Brad. I hate too much, you worry too much. Neither of us can change a thing.''

"We're a matched set, then.''

"No. I've copped out, Brad. Now I just fight back. But you're working within the system, and if anything ever gets done, it's by men like you who don't want the power for power's sake.''

Without warning, he sat up and took her by the shoulders and looked at her until Cat felt as if she'd been opened up by a surgeon's knife. "You understand, don't you?''

She wanted to hold him but didn't dare. "I understand that life is gray. I hate the grays, but that doesn't change the way it is.''

He caught her close to his chest, his voice rough with earnestness. "I'd like to turn my back on everything and just let it go down with the ship—McGrath and his father and Lowell. But too much is invested in me. I've staked my honor on McGrath, and now I have to give him the best I've got. It didn't matter before I met you—well, it mattered, but not in the same way. Now it matters like hell, and I realize I don't have one bit of control over my life. All this time I've been priding myself...''

Releasing her so abruptly that she fell back, he swiveled around and let his head drop between his bent knees. "Christ, I don't know what I've prided myself in."

It wasn't a thing a man told a woman. Men didn't want their weaknesses to show for fear it would mar their strengths. Brad Zacharias was baring his soul.

Kneeling, she timidly placed her hand upon his back, and when he leaned back against her, she wrapped her arms about his middle. "Weaknesses make a man human, Brad, and human beings are the toughest, most admirable things in existence. I admire you very much for that honesty."

The fire fizzed and sizzled, and the symphony of the night drew very close. Without looking at her, he said, "Are you going to tell me about it?"

Cat knew exactly what he was asking. The hunger of her own kiss had given him that right, and though she admired him for his honesty, she didn't think she could surrender her own.

Shifting abruptly so that her back was to his back, Cat bent over her knees and picked at the fringe of her chaps. "Why do you want to know?" she mumbled. "Why can't you let it rest?"

"I don't think you want to know the answer to that question. Yet."

A pine knot popped. Turning, he circled her waist and snuggled until she fit between his legs. The sensation of being surrounded resurrected other feelings in Cat, and she nervously moistened her lips.

"He told me that when I graduated from college we would do something special," she admitted. "I knew what he meant. Like a little fool, I'd done nothing for four years but tell him how much I loved him. It was my own fault—all of it. I didn't know then that men liked the chase of it more than they liked the prize."

A strip of leather fringe came loose in her hands, and she worried it between her fingers. "Anyway, I killed myself for four years, making myself into something that would fit into his world, and..." She laughed bitterly. "Can you believe it? I was actually faithful to the man? I didn't go out, I didn't date, I just kept building that castle in the air. Oh boy, did I build!"

Even the fire burned lower, waiting. She went on, "When I was ready to graduate, I bought the most gorgeous evening gown you can imagine. I hunted for weeks, finding the perfect lingerie. I went on the Pill, I shut my eyes to all the guilt, all the signs I should have seen." She shook her head.

A long silence ensued, broken only by Brad's eventual prompt. "Go on, Cath."

Cat was trembling now. Not once had she shared with a living soul what she was about to say. That she should be telling it now was something she didn't understand. She tossed the bit of leather into the fire, wishing it could be her memories of Wrather Johnson.

"He called and put a message on the phone that something had come up and that he'd get back to me." She bit her lips until she tasted blood. "I waited, and I waited, and he—"

"Catherine—"

"He knew I was waiting." She dropped her head to her bent knees. "That's what hurt more than anything. He knew."

His sigh seemed, to Cat, to scrape her flesh like a blade. He pulled her so close that she was part of his breaths. "I'm sorry. I shouldn't have pressed you. Don't cry."

Lifting her head, she drew in her breath with a ragged, audible sound. "I wish I could cry, Brad. I would give everything if I could wash it out of my head the way some people do." In a voice as cold as the stones of the mountain, she said, "And don't be sorry for me. My hate keeps me alive. It makes me keep fighting. I'll never forget, not as long as I live, how I felt that night. I don't want to forget. I learned the heart of man that day—"

"No."

Not wanting to hear a commentary about herself—what could he tell her that she hadn't told herself a thousand times over?—Cat covered her ears and attempted to move away, but he caught her hands and drew them to her sides. His thighs were strong and insistent against her back. His knees strained aggressively along the outsides of her own. And he felt taut and needful against her.

"Brad..."

She struggled to escape, and his fingers closed about her shoulders and bit deeply. Striking him off, she scrambled from between his legs and twisted to see gaunt lines framing his mouth. He was hurting as much for her as she was hurting for herself, and for the first time ever, she didn't want to fling her outrage at the world and scream, "It serves you right!"

"Oh, no," she whispered, and knelt until she could touch the line between his brows, the grief alongside his mouth. "Don't feel bad for me. I'm all right. Please don't hurt for me."

Coming up on his knees, he captured her face in his hands. "I've had it so easy, don't you see? All my life, what I've wanted, I've taken. When something needed doing, call Brad Zacharias, the old Miracle Worker."

She shook her head. "Don't say this to me, Brad. I can't take it, not now."

"Is there a right time to tell you?" He was tracing the arch of her eyebrow with a fingertip, and his breath sounded as if he'd run forever to reach her. "To tell you that I want to fall in love with you until it burns me up? That I've looked for you in women all my life? That you're the most wonderful thing I've ever seen?''

"But I'm not. I've done terrible things. Please..." She covered her head with her arms. "Please don't say nice things to me. I'm not used to it. They melt me to pieces, and then I can't..."

"Then let me melt you to pieces," he mumbled thickly, and, by a process that Cat wasn't quite sure of, drew her hands to her sides. Turning her, he pulled her down upon the blankets beside the fire. "Let me heal you, Cath. Let me heal myself in you."

The fire was reflected in his eyes like shards of gold. As he took her hand and lowered it, closing her fingers about the aching part of himself, she watched the lines at his eyes tighten with a look akin to pain.

She was afraid to know how much he wanted her. She drew back her hand. Her hair swirled between them. "I wouldn't be any good," she mumbled.

But he wasn't listening. He was groping for her mouth with his, and the sounds he made prompted her own whimpers and her own shifting and turning and clinging. He was drawing himself upon her so that his weight and his hardness were undeniable.

"I would disappoint you," she whimpered into his kisses that were blurring together.

"Hush, Catherine," he said, finding the zipper of her jeans. "Be quiet and let me fall in love with you."

If she believed him, Cat told herself as his hands seemed to be everywhere, everything would fall apart. Life had taught her that too well. That she desired him back had nothing whatsoever to do with it.

But his touch was drugging her as surely as the chemicals she used to swallow so many years before. She was floating, she was moving in a dream as he removed her jeans and chaps and pulled her shirt free of its buttons. Hardly knowing where one kiss ended and the next began, she slipped her hands beneath his shirt and thought she would surely burn to a cinder for such madness.

Brad had no such doubts. He pressed his lips to her ear and said silly, breathless things as he battled her for the wisp of her panties. In the first moment of panic when she knew it would truly happen, Cat pressed her knees tightly in denial.

"Brad," she said in protest. "Brad, just a minute . . . Brad, I want to tell you something. Brad—"

"Shh, shh." He persisted until his knee had pried hers apart, and then with his fingers he slipped past that one boundary Cat had sworn would never be crossed. "I've been looking for you for too long, sweetheart."

Cat's cry was a little girl's cry as he learned the way she was fashioned. He was making a brief negotiation with an item from his wallet and placing himself where his fingers had been, and in one last shuddering effort to protect herself from calamitous failure, she tried to slip from beneath him one more time.

But he coiled his hands into her hair and filled her with a quick, piercing thrill that would make everything different forever—fears, recriminations, past and future. Then there was only him, moving and kissing her and adoring her until he couldn't talk anymore and, much sooner than he wanted, driving to that ultimate end where he was, as women from the beginning have always known, vulnerable to her.

Later, the taking of him to her breast was as natural to Cat as a mother reaching for her newborn child. She lovingly moved her hand over the crispy stubble of his hair and kissed his brows and his eyes. So much was missing, not because she'd had no sexual climax, nothing like that, yet she was satisfied; he had seen the worst of her and none of the best, but had still desired her.

Yet she wasn't going to hurt them both by pretending that anything could come of this night. It was out of time, out of place. They both knew where they had come from and where they must go. For now, though, in the quiet peace of the fire and the mountain, she could almost believe.

Chapter Seven

Crouched invisibly beneath the boughs of a pine, Crowe was keeping watch. He'd known when he rode away that Cat would follow; it was the presence of the stranger that frightened him. He'd been inside the cabin when the man and Cat climbed the slope, and he'd filled a sack with all the food he could carry.

What frightened him even more was that she'd lain beside the man and let him love her in the way that men love women. He felt like a man seeing his wife be unfaithful, and his hands were bruised where he'd slammed them against a stone. Yet, in an eerie, unsettling way, he was glad.

He was tired now. The last night at the ranch he hadn't gone to bed at all but had grieved for his dear friend, Thomas Holmes. He'd waited for Cat that night—walking outside and stripping off his shirt to lie upon the cool stone flange of the cistern.

He wanted to see her before he left. Moving any nearer, however, was dangerous. The man did not sleep but merely rested beside the fire, holding Cat in the curve of his side as she slept.

With surefooted, silent steps, Crowe moved from the safety of the tree, drawing closer until his presence was felt. Cat stirred uneasily in her sleep, and, murmuring something unintelligible, the man bent his head and kissed her brow.

From his vantage, Crowe could distinguish the rough, tired features of the man. He smiled and adjusted his arm about Cat's shoulders and, with a deep, contented sigh, lowered his face into her hair and drew in a long, wondering breath.

On impulse, for it was contrary to all that life had taught him, Crowe stepped into the open and waited silently for something, he didn't know what. As if Crowe had called a name, the man gradually turned, and across the moonlit space they looked—two men who didn't know each other except that they had both fixed their affections upon the same object: Catherine Holmes.

They did not speak, they did not signal. It was simply the relinquishment of a certain protective caretaking from one hand to another. As if he understood and accepted his new task, the man inclined his head. Satisfied in some strange and ancient way, Crowe turned on his heel and disappeared into the darkness.

In Cat's dream she was roused by the sound of a storm gathering far in the distance. Once begun, it seemed to come quickly, and the thunder was a drumroll that crescendoed with ever-growing power, louder and louder until, in the dream, she was thrashing her arms and flailing to swim up to the surface of a river that had closed over her head. A soothing voice whispered, "It's okay," and she sank once more into the warm, swirling current that carried her deeper, deeper to the lost Atlantis.

Cloak? Thunder?

"Babe?" Cat gasped, and snapped instantly awake, sitting up with a jerk, clutching the blanket and blinking at the darkness and hearing the reassuring crackle of the fire.

Seconds passed before she remembered where she was and what she and Brad Zacharias had done. Brad was getting to his feet.

"It's all right, Cath." His voice, gritty with weariness, was reassuring. "We're in the mountains, remember?"

Far away, the Jeep's engine revved, and the roar of it echoed up through the ravines. In horror, Cat scrambled to her feet, forgetting that she was naked beneath the blanket and grabbing it none-too-gracefully about her.

"It's the Jeep!" she cried.

Brad was searching for his shirt and pulling it on, tucking it into his trousers and looking for his shoes. He smiled grimly. "Good thinking."

"But who—"

"Crowe, I expect. He came to say goodbye while you were asleep."

With her eyes wide as plates, Cat swirled the blanket around her. "Why didn't you wake me?"

Their eyes clashed briefly as he studied the gleam of her naked arms above the cloth, and her sleepy disarray, her ludicrous attempts at modesty as if nothing had happened.

He shrugged, grinning boyishly. "It wasn't that kind of goodbye."

Crowe had seen them? Cat shuddered. He had seen Brad lifting her up to meet him? Her own hands clutching him in that eternal pagan offering? Oh, God!

"And you gave him the keys to the Jeep?" She cringed.

Reaching into his pocket, he tossed the keys to clatter upon the stone at her bare feet. His teeth flashed whitely in a grimace. "He obviously didn't need them. A very resourceful man, your Crowe."

While part of her mind wasn't inclined to argue, for she could all too easily imagine Crowe moving about in the darkness like the ghost of some ancient tribal warrior, Cat couldn't believe that she and Brad were now at the extreme boundary of the ranch and on foot. She met his warm regard and noted that it was growing more warm by the moment.

"Put out the fire while I get dressed, Brad," she murmured wryly, and gathered her clothes into a tiny heap, not daring to imagine what she must look like or how she was going to get dressed without exposing herself even more.

"That, madam, may be something of an impossibility."

Beneath the blanket, Cat wriggled into her jeans—no mean feat and one that required the balance of an acrobat. She fumbled with her bra and shirt.

"If it'll make things easier," he said around smothered laughter, lowering himself to a stone beside her, shoes in hand, "why don't you just ask me to turn my head?"

"Turn your head, you wretch."

"Do you think I'm crazy?"

Affording him only the briefest glare now that she was dressed, Cat dropped the blanket and wobbled on first one foot, then the other as she dragged on her boots and mumbled to herself.

"When I get my hands on Crowe, I'm going to wring his Apache neck." Rising, she buckled on the chaps and wriggled into their leather contours with an innocent provocativeness that set Brad's teeth grinding. "I can't believe he did this after I stuck my neck out ten miles."

By the time she was dressed, the Jeep was long gone, naturally. Taking a few steps toward the darkness, Cat puckered her mouth into a pensive circle and turned to find Brad watching her from his shoelaces.

She lifted a helpless shoulder. "Now they'll get him for car theft."

He finished tying a knot. "Not if you don't report it stolen."

"Then they can say I helped him escape."

"From what? He hasn't been charged with anything."

The moon had spilled its silver paint over the angles of his face. She'd been right, Cat thought. He had a way of putting himself high above a situation and not letting the details cloud his judgment.

Without the slightest intention of doing so, she lowered her fingers to the stubble of his crew cut and drew their tips over the bristling ends. He reached up to trap her hands, and she gave him an Indian burn. He howled, and she dodged his outswung arm, laughing.

"I've wanted to do that ever since I first saw you." She giggled.

But he had turned and snaked one purposeful hand to grab her ankle. Slowly he reeled her in to him inch by inch, until she was standing in the wedge of his legs and could have hugged his head to her waist and given him a dozen Indian burns.

Yet she closed her arms about him and stood gently stroking his brow. "Why do you believe in Crowe now when you didn't before?"

His answer came without hesitation. He was cradling the backs of her legs. "Because you believe in him."

"You know what he'll do now? He won't even use the Jeep. He'll leave it somewhere so we'll find it, and that'll make him all the more easy to catch."

"You like to worry."

"I do get carried away sometimes, don't I?"

"Thank God." He laughed.

Looking out at the peaceful blackness, Cat was struck by the hugeness of space and their own smallness upon the earth. Brad had bent his head, and his breath had found the front of her jeans and was seeping deeper and deeper beneath the denim until its heat was burning her.

She started to laugh, but her breath caught in her throat.

"Since he's gone," he was muttering, as his own breathing quickened and an alarm system switched on inside Cat, "I guess there's no need to hurry, is there?"

A red light was flashing in Cat's brain, but so delicious were the sensations he was causing, she wished she could drown in them. This was no leisurely and casual caress of a woman he'd just made love to, but a flagrant new conquest from a different quarter altogether.

"Brad," she whispered, trembling as he moved his hands more knowingly over her hips and between her legs, "Brad, this isn't . . . Brad, please, we have to go. We have to—"

"We should have done this before," he murmured, and reached up for her zipper.

She pushed him away. "Crowe might . . ."

But he was discovering her shape through the soft, old jeans. "Crowe is gone, and we're still here."

He persisted in seeking that one, inevitable spot that would slip through her defenses, and Cat, drawing in her breath, knowing a dozen things to say that would stop him cold, could say none of them. He had bewitched her, and her eyes were closing and her head was dropping back in surrender, for she didn't want him ever to stop, not for a thousand years, as he touched the exact spot and, rising as she gasped, caught her in his arms.

The world stopped turning. Cat closed her hands into the front of his shirt and tried to breathe. He didn't stop once it was over, but made it happen all over again.

"No!" she managed to choke at last, and stumbled, half blind, to droop against a friendly tree in the darkness so he could not see her face.

"Stay away from me, Zacharias," she warned, heaving and holding out her hand in protest.

Chuckling, he walked over to lean against the same tree and looked enormously pleased with himself. "It's not a crime to be human, Catherine. A very smart lady once told me that human beings are the most admirable things in existence."

"It's a lot more than that, you lecherous opportunist, and you know it."

"'Lecherous opportunist'? You can do better than that, can't you?" He proceeded to extinguish the fire. "So, now what do you want to do?" he asked over his shoulder. "Climb on your trusty steed and ride back to the ranch?"

"I want to guillotine you first," she said flatly, sliding down to rest and get her bearings. "That wasn't fair."

He laughed. "I'm not sure I can find a guillotine up here."

"A big rock will do, thank you."

"Aw, Catherine." Returning, he stooped beside her and lifted the curtains of her hair. "I don't think you've ever heard of the proverb 'What's good for the gander is good for the goose.'"

Cat peered out to glare at him. "I don't want to talk about it."

"What did it feel like?"

She refused to smile. "What did *you* feel like?"

"Great."

"Then use your imagination."

He chuckled. "I can see you don't like to talk after sex."

Why was everything he said and did so perfect? "What you see, you renegade, is worry. How are we going to get home now?"

"Easy. Take my jacket and let's go. I have a feeling that Crowe left us his horse."

He slapped her on her most sumptuous fanny and strode vigorously to the outcrop of trees they had fought their way through so laboriously during the climb up.

"Wait!" she yelped, scrambling to her feet.

"Get a move on, lazybones."

His shoulders were forcing the branches aside as she clambered after him. Cat threw a final, desperate look at the cabin. Should she do something about the evidence lying around inside? Would it protect Crowe if she destroyed it?

Brad was beyond her with a dexterity she couldn't match at two o'clock in the morning. Going down, blessedly, was easier than coming up. Now it was a matter of lunging into Brad's back or balancing on his shoulders to keep from plunging down the side of the mountain. He was wasting no time, and branches switched them soundly for intruding into their domain.

Once at the bottom, however, they were confronted with logistics. There stood Crowe's horse, her reins tied to a tree with just enough slack that she could nibble the tidbits of green grass at her feet.

With a skeptical cock of his head, Brad scratched his jaw. "Let's see now..."

Thinking about the miles they would have to ride the beast double, Cat smirked and said, "I'm sure you know just everything about horses, Brad."

"Of course I do," he wryly replied, being the racer of horses, not the rider. "I saw *Black Beauty* twelve times."

"That's it?" Cat threw back her head in a laugh. "Brother, this should be good."

"As you're so fond of saying, I'm a city boy."

"Talk about taking the boy out of the city... Well, who gets up first, you or me?"

"I do, obviously." Brad chuckled grimly and untied the reins to lead the horse to a large stepping stone. "Stand out of the way, Catherine. I'm going to use my best Clint Eastwood for this."

Cat tucked a tired smile into his jacket which lay about her shoulders. "I can hardly wait."

His attempt to mount bareback wasn't too bad for a city boy, but the horse, accustomed to Crowe's flawless expertise, kept prancing out of the way.

"Actually," he said with graceful humility, "I think I would be less at risk if you mounted first, Catherine."

She made a face. "First we make a pact on the pain of death that we will never disclose this to a living soul."

Grinning, he made a stirrup of his hands, accepted her boot and heaved her onto the mount's back. "Now," he said, "scoot forward, darling, and hold the reins. And for pity's sake, turn your head."

Laughing, because she was growing more addicted to him by the minute, Cat obeyed. "Boy, am I chalking up blackmail ammunition against you, Brad Zacharias."

"Don't get too smart for your britches, madam." He groaned as he pulled himself up. "God, this looks easy when Burt Lancaster does it."

"Butch Cassidy you're not."

"At least I'm not one of The Three Stooges."

Cat was overcome with giggles. "The night is still young. Never mind me—" she tried to stop laughing "—I get this way late at night. Dementia something-or-other."

After a number of what Cat suspected were extremely ungraceful moves on both their parts, they settled themselves upon the poor horse. Brad reached around her for the reins.

"You can relax now," he murmured into her hair. "The master has taken control."

Just how literally she should take that information, Cat didn't want to consider, but the horse was dutifully picking her way down the incline and out onto the more level ground of the desert. Cat sighed with the most contentment she'd known in months.

"You seem to be a movie buff," she said peacefully into his shoulder. "Did you see *The Electric Horseman*?"

"You're not comparing me to Robert Redford, are you?"

"No, the horse."

He laughed. "Yes, I saw it."

But Cat's eyelids were much too heavy and the smell of him much too wonderful, his strength far too seductive. Deep inside her she was still warm and tender from having been loved, and the world was far away, hardly touching them at all.

"What's your point?" he asked.

"I can't remember," she whispered as she gradually melted against him in her dream.

She would have sworn he placed his face into her hair and said, "I love you, Catherine Holmes."

But that was another dream. "I love you, too," she said, for it was all right to say such things in dreams. No one had told her so, but she knew it was true. Babe Polansky would have heartily agreed.

"You're gonna wake her up."

"*I* ain't gonna wake 'er up."

"Be quiet, then."

"*You*'re the one gonna wake 'er up. *I* ain't gonna wake 'er up."

"Would you shut your face and get her shirt for the laundry?"

"If I do, she'll wake up. She'll be mad."

"The pants, too. Be careful. You dropped a sock."

"I don't wanna do this. Look at what you done. Now she's wakin' up."

"Oh, brother."

"Are you gonna get it!"

Two sheepish, beaming smiles burned through the tops of Cat's eyelids, and Scooter's sweet, nonstop voice said in a booming stage whisper, "Hi, Cat. Me and Tuck just come to get th' dirty laundry. Everybody's still sleepin'. Hey, Cat, there's a man downstairs in th' kitchen makin' phone calls like crazy."

"Ohh." Cat swore her head was a cantaloupe that had stayed out in the sun too long. She pried open one eye and was instantly blinded by gritty light streaming through the window whose curtains had already been stripped and packed. The room was foreign in its naked state, and she hated the sight of the boxes stacked around the walls. The only furniture was the bed she was lying on.

"Scooter?" she groaned, and tried to blink the rust from her eyes. "Tucker? Gad!" She dropped back to the pillow in exhaustion. "What time is it?"

"The man from the big car, Cat," Scooter reported with a grin and nine-year-old gregariousness, "he asked if we was hungry and then started makin' pancakes. Just like that. When he asked what kind of syrup I wanted I said Miz Butterworth, but we didn't have no Miz Butterworth so I had t' take maple out of th' Easy Flo spout."

Wincing, Cat scrubbed her cheeks with her palms. Every morning without fail she woke at four-thirty and while the house slept she prepared for the day. If she awakened an hour later, the kids were already leagues ahead of her, and the whole day was out of kilter.

With Tucker and Scooter bending over her, shaking their heads like two surgeons consulting about a hopeless case, she tried to slip into the familiar, practiced ritual: call funeral home, round up cattle, find rented house—cheap rented house. No, find Crowe first, talk to lawyer about the trouble she was in with Sheriff Lobos, about Judge Constanza, too. No, ask Bradley Zacharias about that.... Bradley, Brad...

Oh, God, he was here! Cat's eyes snapped open with a panic, remembering everything. Mercy, mercy!

"See—" Scooter was hissing triumphantly to Tucker at the back of her head "—I told ya she'd be mad. Tuck's the one that woke you up, Cat. I didn't do nothin'."

"Go away," she wailed. "What did I ever do to you?"

"We have to do laundry, Cat," Tucker gravely explained.

"Do you know how much sleep I've had the last three days?"

"Everything's boxed up. Nobody's got no clothes."

Scooter plopped himself upon the mattress at Cat's feet and happily repeated himself. "There's a man downstairs, Cat."

She knew, she knew! "Of course there's a man downstairs." She dragged the pillow over her head.

"Who?"

"Bradley Zacharias," she mumbled.

"Oh." Scooter pondered the name, as if it explained everything.

Sitting up, Cat tucked the sheet beneath her arms. "He slept here," she said.

"We know."

"Then go away."

Giggling, they headed for the door.

"Wait!"

They stopped, posing for her in their hand-me-down jeans with the cuffs rolled up six inches and the socks drooping about the tops of their tennis shoes. Their shirts were bleach-splotched and stretched out of shape. Ordinarily it wouldn't have mattered, but with Brad downstairs, she was strangely embarrassed.

"Is that the best you've got?" she questioned.

"Everything but our funeral clothes is packed," Tucker patiently explained.

She heaved a thunderous sigh and waved them on. "Okay, okay. Just . . . do the best you can."

Tucker gave her one of his famous shrugs that meant anything anyone wanted it to except that he would follow his own intentions, which is exactly what he always did. "We're gonna miss Tom, aren't we, Cat?"

A quick muscle of regret pulled in Cat's neck. In all her trouble, she'd almost forgotten how the children adored her father. Swirling the sheet about her bare legs, she walked over to hug them.

"It's good to know he doesn't hurt anymore, though," she whispered, as she stroked the curly heads and placed kisses upon each.

"Yeah," they mumbled as they held her tightly. "We know."

"It would be selfish of us to want him back, just so he could be sick."

"Yeah."

As the boys trudged obediently downstairs, Cat hesitated, feeling guilty about the surge of anticipation that flooded her, knowing that Brad was downstairs. She would bury her father today, yet all she could really think was that she was alive, and that for the first time in years she was glad she was alive.

Hurrying, she moved about the room, snatching clean clothes from the boxes that were stacked against the wall. She rushed down the hall to the shower and prayed no one else would waken before she was through. Once she was showered and shampooed, she rubbed a circle in the steam of the mirror and wanted to die. Her hair had been whipped into a black tornado.

She slumped. Please, not today.

Searching through one of the boxes for conditioner, she found only scrubbing cleansers and disinfectant. She raked at the tangles with a comb, but finally muttered a curse and twisted the entire mess into a doughnut on top of her head and sped back to her room to dress.

Not until that moment did she realize just how far Brad Zacharias had brought her with his intimacies and his smiles. As she stared at herself in the paisley skirt and blouse that had before been perfectly suitable, she saw how she must appear to others: a neat, ordinary, homespun Western woman; a sparrow, a little brown mouse.

And the wretched irony was that before Brad came, she'd been relatively satisfied with that—at least resigned. Now she felt as if she were in the last stages of some terrible terminal condition like bubonic plague.

"Look in the mirror, Cat Holmes," she said with ruthless cruelty and traced over all her worst flaws. "See what a fool looks like."

No man in his right mind would jeopardize even part of what Brad had for the kinds of trouble she represented. And the trouble that she *was*. What did she think? That Brad would marry her, for pity's sake? That he would move to New Mexico and take up ranching? Or would take her to

New York, along with a whole household he wasn't responsible for?

"Grow up, Cat." She leaned against the door for a moment until she felt she had accepted the truth. Then she moved out into the hall as she did every day of her life.

"All right, rise and shine, you misfits of society," she called in her tired, droning drill-sergeant voice as she walked down the hall knocking on doors. "Feet on the floor. Breakfast in fifteen minutes."

Babe poked a chubby face outside a door. "Oh, no. I was right in the middle of a chapter."

"Finish it later, sweetie," Cat said, and spied the familiar yellow pad spread open on Babe's tousled bed.

Heaving, Babe turned to her room, but then swiveled back to sniff the air like a bloodhound on the trail of a juicy rabbit. She homed in on Cat and, brows lifted in surprise, stood on tiptoe to test the back of Cat's ear. "What *is* that smell?"

Cat scowled fiercely and tried to wave the girl away. "What smell? There's no smell."

"Giorgio?" Babe exchanged a wise and knowing look with Diana, who had also appeared in the doorway looking like a startled blond angel. "It's Cat," Babe informed her. "She finally made it home last night. Oh, by the way, Cat, *that man* is downstairs."

Cat prayed to the saints for patience. "I know, dear."

"Tsk, tsk, tsk." Babe strutted back into her room as Diana flashed a broad smile and followed her. "Giorgio?" Babe muttered blithely to herself. "I think I'll just finish the first chapter today, Diana."

Cat thought she could have strung Babe up by the thumbs with the straps of her own tote bag. As the girls were ducking back inside, Bingo, the lanky twelve-year-old from across the hall, stepped out of his own room completely dressed because he'd slept in his clothes again.

"Oh, gi-irls..." he crooned, catching Babe's attention with the piece of yellow paper he waved over his head.

The page had obviously been retrieved from a wastebasket, having been wadded and smoothed a number of times. "Hey, Cat, I want you to hear this." Bingo paused in a dramatic aside before beginning to read, "Another day of high romance on the ranch, folks."

Horrified, Babe lunged at the boy, and Bingo scampered out of reach, laughing and waving the paper high above her head. Then he read, "He swept her into his manly arms and brought his lips down hard upon hers. 'Oh, darling,' she moaned as her heart beat wildly within the full globes of her breasts. 'All my life I have waited for you. I have never loved before and will never love again.'" He grinned. "Full globes of her breasts. Oh-ho!"

Other doors had opened by now, and a chorus of titters rippled down the hall. Flaming a vicious scarlet, Babe shook the walls with her thunderous gallop after the culprit.

"Give me that, you pukeoid!" she shrieked as Bingo skittered adroitly toward the stairs and down them, pausing halfway as he continued to read, "His kisses were burning brands upon her love-bruised lips."

"I'll kill you, Bingo Means!" raged Babe.

"Oh, do stop threatening to kill everyone, Babe," ordered Cat, her voice weary as she marched down the stairs to the prankster and held out her hands. "Give me that, Bingo, right this instant."

"Aww, Cat."

"I'm not joking. You had no right to go into Babe's things."

Babe was in tears. "It wasn't even revised yet, you jerk-off!"

"I expect you to apologize to Babe, Bingo," Cat said. "With sincerity."

Duly chastened, Bingo sheepishly handed over the confiscated paper and got his first good look at Cat, his expression running the gamut of surprise. "Jeez, you wearin' lipstick, Cat?"

There was not the slightest resemblance to anything pleasant in the look Cat gave the boy. "Go wash your face, Bingo."

"I did already. What's that I smell?"

"Pancakes," T. John supplied, hating scenes.

"Giorgio," Babe unhelpfully confirmed.

"Wash your face again, Bingo!" Cat commanded, and felt the onslaught of a ghastly mood.

"Oh, fudge."

"Then, come to breakfast," she told them all glumly, wishing she had time to race back to her room and scrub the skin off her face and climb into the reassuring squalor of her jeans and chaps. "We have company."

Chapter Eight

The floral pattern of the linoleum in the ranch-house kitchen had faded, and the red roses were rusty, their green leaves bleeding through with black and brown. The old-fashioned square windowpanes were yellowed with a permanent film that showed now that their curtains had been packed away. In places the floor groaned from old age, and the beams complained. The enamel on the refrigerator had worn thin, and the sink was chipped.

Yet the walls of the old room staked out a territory that kept the savage jungle outside and everyone safe inside. Its warmth invited laughter. Dominating it was a great table Tom had constructed for the children by joining together three outdoor picnic tables and painting them a homey, reassuring cream.

By the time Babe and the other children had loped down the stairs and burst through the door, Bon Jovi was playing on the portable radio, and Steamboat and Tucker had laid out the paper plates they'd been using since packing for the move began.

Babe Polansky stopped dead in her tracks. Brad Zacharias was standing at their cookstove, serenely turning pancakes on the griddle.

He hardly resembled the man who'd climbed out of the limousine the day before. He was staggeringly sexy, having confiscated a pair of Crowe's old jeans and an army fatigue T-shirt with the sleeves ripped out and slashed halfway to the waist. A hole had worn through a front pocket of the jeans revealing a bit of blond-haired thigh. The toes of the scuffed boots tended to turn up at the tips.

Babe wished immediately for her notepad. Only this morning she had written her revision of chapter one. *With a feeling of sensuality,* she had penned, *Catherine fit her mouth to his and quivered with response to the taut male muscles beneath her hands.*

"Oh, Catherine," he murmured. "I love the taste of you."

Suddenly Catherine was hungry to know the heat and textures of his kiss, to feel the delicious velvet roughness of his tongue sliding over hers. Her body jerked. Her arms clung. Their knees were widespread now, their stomachs and breasts molded flat together.

"You're so beautiful," he breathed. "Nothing can keep us apart."

He gently twisted her nipples between thumb and forefingers, sending currents downward to meet the fire between her legs. His hands flattened her milky white orbs with their tips pinched against the edges of his hands.

"Say you want me," he groaned, probing her ear with the warm, wet point of his tongue. "For always."

"I am yours," she cried, and arched against him.

Now Babe moved in a daze through the kitchen and poured herself a glass of water. Over the rim of the glass, she furtively watched Cat and Brad Zacharias.

Cat hardly glanced in the man's direction when she entered, but smiled briefly and turned down the volume of the radio. She seemed to take an inordinate interest in Steamboat's uncombed hair and Diana's bitten nails.

How could she not look at the man? Babe wanted to screech at Cat. He was the most hunky thing she'd seen on two legs!

And Brad's glance at Cat was just as infuriating. His smile held a hint of mischievousness for a fraction of a second, but the suggestive telepathy was missing. No telltale blushes or murmured private jokes.

Babe didn't think she could choke down a single bite. Taking her chair, she sat picking her napkin to pieces as T. John lingered above the stove, his hands stuffed into his pockets, too shy to introduce himself.

"You're T. John, aren't you?" Brad inquired, as he looked up and wiped his hands on the towel that was tucked into his waistband like a quarterback's. He extended his hand. "Brad Zacharias. A pleasure, John. Did everything work out with the social services lady last night?"

T. John's grin was eager to trust. "She ain't gonna put us in foster homes or nothin'. Said we could stay one more night out here till somethin' was worked out with Cat. Ms. Sepulvada's okay, I guess."

Brad tracked the boy's hesitant look at Cat and chuckled. "Something'll work out, John. I'm sure of it. How d'you like your pancakes?"

Cat was calmly helping the boys take their seats. Yet when Scooter turned suddenly and buried his small face into her waist, sobbing horribly that he couldn't bear to leave his home and go somewhere he didn't know and have to eat with people who didn't have good table manners and grow up to be a hooligan, she unraveled. She dropped to her knees beside the boy's chair and rocked him back and forth in her arms.

Brad Zacharias, Babe saw, laid down his spatula.

"It's all right," Cat crooned, and sleeked back his hair from his face, "everything's going to be all right, Scooter. You'll see. You have the most beautiful table manners in all the world, and nothing could mess them up."

The silence that stretched out was like the inside of a shell, traveling around and around and around through the big room and echoing the same unspoken fear of leaving that they all had. Babe was caught up in it herself.

"Listen to me," Cat said, her words including them all, "whatever happens, you will be grown-up and take it like champions. Even if I'm not there for a little while, Scooter, you'll be a man."

"But I'm not a man," he howled at the top of his lungs. "I'm just a scared little black boy. I don't want to be no champion. I don't know how."

Smiling even as her eyes grew more deeply purple with compassion, Cat went through the ritual of kissing and petting and explaining how he would never be alone because he had himself and about how life wasn't about being great, it was about being good.

From deep in her woman's heart, Babe watched Brad Zacharias watching Cat. At first she thought he intended to turn the small, golden cakes on the griddle and was wiping his hands on the cloth at his waist. But he wasn't wiping his hands, he was wiping his mouth on the back of his wrist and swiping at his eyes. He had the haunted look of a man who was watching something die.

Babe knew that what she had been writing was drivel. She had been watching two people fall in love, yes, not with

gushing purple prose, but with a quiet, stately dignity all
their own. She knew now what it must have been like between them in that first desperate moment—their voices,
their touches, the sighs of garments being removed, his
gravity as he lay on top of her, his mouth open upon her
breast, her pale cheek, his back and the scratches upon his
shoulders, the chafing, the flashing seam where their bod-
ies joined and the wondering discovery of pleasure and pain
and heartache.

In a moment so fleeting it almost didn't exist, Babe saw
Cat look over the boy's weeping head to seek Brad. A
thousand voices were in her search, and he seemed to hear
them all with an exquisite helplessness.

Releasing Scooter, Cat moved to the window. She leaned
her head upon the glass, sun-splashed in her skirt and
blouse, her nape pinkened charmingly as she stood totally
alone.

"Hey, Steamboat," Brad said, as he quickly took up
Cat's slack and started around the table with a great stack
of pancakes. "How many, storm trooper?"

"Can I have extra syrup?" the boy bargained, oblivious
to the deeper emotional currents swirling thickly about him.
"Cat don't let me, says it'll make my teeth rot out."

"Well," Brad drawled with good-humored horror, "I
ain't gonna give it to you, either. You think I want t'die?"

"Cat wouldn't kill you, Mr. Zacharias," Tucker soberly
remonstrated.

Brad's smile reached back to his own boyhood, and he
bowed with appropriate acquiescence. "I stand corrected. I
didn't mean die...literally."

"Tucker's an affliction," Babe observed sympatheti-
cally. "God made 'im that way. We're used to it."

"And Babe takes a rather Machiavellian view of life, Mr. Zacharias," Cat added without turning around. "One learns to be careful."

"I wonder where she gets it," Brad murmured, also without looking up.

When breakfast was done and T. John shuffled out to see to chores that he and Crowe usually tended together, Tucker trotted faithfully off to do the laundry while Steamboat and Bingo and Scooter trudged out to the upholstery shop to finish crating supplies.

Babe grabbed Diana's hand in a tizzy. "Come on," she hissed, and whisked the surprised girl from the room and up the stairs as queries blazed mutely on Diana's face. "There's a place I know," she insisted. "We can watch everything that's going on."

As they reached the landing, Diana pulled back on Babe's hand and waved her finger back and forth in refusal. Exasperated, Babe stamped her foot.

"It's not eavesdroping, Diana. It's art, damn it. And art has to imitate life. How am I supposed to know about life if I don't ever see it? Now, don't get mental on me, girl. Come on."

Cat swiftly found herself alone with Brad and a sink filled depressingly to the brim with dirty glasses and sticky cutlery and bent paper plates. She moved about the room for a moment, touching things, picking them up and putting them down, not knowing the answer because she hadn't understood the question.

"Well," she said eventually to the sink, her hands braced on her sides when the silence became unbearable, "you remember the old one about how into every life some rain must fall."

Brad was also moving about too casually, cleaning the batter from the stove. "Look at it this way," he said to the grates, "every cloud has a silver lining."

Cat smiled. She picked out the plates and stuffed them into a garbage sack and sorted the utensils. "What about 'Everyone has to learn sometime,'" she said with a growing fervor.

He chuckled. "I like the one about life being a bowl of cherries, myself."

"Or 'A little bit of sugar makes the medicine go down.'" Cat thought her laughter sounded as if it had been run through a food processor.

"'You never appreciate the water till the well runs dry.'"

Sighing, she held the syrup bottle beneath hot, running water and wiped it dry. "Then there's the one, 'Laugh and the whole world laughs with you, cry and you cry...'"

The sound of running water filled the huge vacuum of their dilemma. Staring at the clear, steaming ribbon, Cat thought she was falling victim to hypnosis. Ever since that first moment when she'd awakened, she had been kidding herself, hadn't she? No, long before that—when she'd stood on the hillside and watched the steaming pennons of dust that had brought Brad into her life like a hurricane.

Now it was too late. She had fixed her love upon this man, and no matter how blasé she tried to sound, when he left, a great hole would appear in her life that nothing could fill. How had she been so stupid as to let that happen?

She looked up. He was standing at the opposite end of the table, his big, wonderful hands braced on the back of a chair, a boot resting upon the rung, the jeans conforming softly to his frame and reminding her of how hard and knowledgeable he was. He was a good, kind man, who fit easily into the old kitchen with his scruffy cowpoke's clothes. He'd never asked to be put in the position he found himself in.

Swiftly—for she must hide the bits and pieces that were left of herself—Cat spun around and noisily threw open the doors of the cupboard to find liquid detergent packed in a neat little box along with the soap tray and Windex and Comet. Hardly knowing what she did, she drizzled the rich golden liquid into the water.

"I always knew you were flexible, Mr. Zacharias," she heard her voice say with almost flawless poise, as a mountain of bubbly rubies and pearls and diamonds exploded beneath the stream. "But the culinary arts? I'm impressed."

She didn't dare turn off the water for fear he would hear her heart crashing. *Say something, Brad. Anything!*

She didn't hear him moving any longer, but she could feel him staring into her back. Don't turn around, she told herself.

As surely as a needle turns to its magnetic pole, however, she slowly pivoted to find him, not stripping away the layers of her masks but chipping his way through the crust of his own. He looked so purely unhappy that not touching him was unthinkable.

She took a step without meaning to, her hand extended, her lips parted with unspoken words. He, too, moved toward her, but her distress was so acute, Cat saw again the worlds between them and stopped. She felt her head moving back and forth in protest.

"It's not dark now, my darling," he said softly as he moved toward her with a gypsy's easy grace. "The stars have all gone in. There's nowhere to hide."

"Brad, I don't know how..." She took a step backward. "The day's going to be horrible."

"You don't have to make promises to me, Brad. Please don't put us through that."

"We're not going to have a moment to ourselves." His footsteps were whispery soft.

"Brad, I've thought it all through, and I know what you're going to say."

"In two days I have to fly back to New York."

"What happened last night . . . was wonderful, but—"

"I've been on the phone arranging for people to come finish—"

"I want you to know I'll never forget—"

"The funeral will take up most of the afternoon, but after that—"

"I couldn't bear it if you thought—"

The collision of two worlds. The knowledge that nothing else existed. The inferno. The torment. The hopelessness. Though Cat didn't know quite how it happened, she was in his arms again. Everything in heaven and earth was wrong, but he was kissing her everywhere, smothering her, devouring her, holding her head between his hands as sounds of misery rumbled in his throat. Both of them knew, as they clung so fiercely, that it would never be enough.

"I love you," he groaned between her inflamed flurry to kiss all of his face at once, and his hand and his shoulders and his wrists.

"I know, I know," she breathed.

"I couldn't sleep for thinking about you and wanting it all over again."

Lifting her off the floor, he turned in a circle and buried his face into her neck. He let her slide the length of him and sleeked his hands over the curves of her hips and her back. He captured her eyes, the wonderful glittering violet of them.

He shook his head. "What do we do?"

Her answers were as nonexistent as his. She couldn't get close enough. She wanted to stay in his arms where she would be safe and nothing could ever hurt her again. But that was a child's way, and she hadn't been a child in a long, long time.

So she rose on her toes and tried to accept and find a detour around her heart. "I love you, Brad," she whispered fiercely. "I don't know how, I don't know why. But always know that."

Releasing her, Brad led her by the hand to a more private niche of the kitchen between the wall and the pantry. Leaning there, he drew her into the spread of his legs. If he studied her for a hundred years, he didn't think he would find her the same twice. She seemed constantly on the verge of a mood that would change his life.

He traced the long line of her throat and the curl of her ear, the heavy froth of her hair. "You are without a doubt the most difficult person I ever met, Catherine Holmes."

She held his face between her palms, smiling. "I don't expect anything, Brad."

"Well, I expect everything, damn it. This isn't going to be easy, you know. If one of my people had done what I've done—taking advantage of a woman with her back to the wall, putting her interests before a man who's laid his good money down for their loyalty... I'm not sure I even believe in McGrath Johnson anymore, Catherine. Everything I've spent the last years working for seems to be in a shambles."

Cat wasn't sure she knew what he was saying. "Brad, in the last few hours I've made more mistakes than I could pile on this table." She narrowed her eyes. "And I know what you're thinking."

"Do you, now?" The gray of his eyes twinkled.

"You're an honorable man. Of course I do."

"What do honorable men do when they find themselves in straits?"

Cat swallowed. He wasn't playing fair, making her state it in twenty-five words or less. Maybe she had concocted his feelings.

Hesitating, she said the words reluctantly. "They jeopardize things. I can't let you jeopardize anything because of last night."

The amusement faded from his face. "Is that what you think is at jeopardy here? 'Anything'?"

"All right! The future did cross my mind, but only for a few minutes. Then I woke up and smelled the coffee, Brad. It wouldn't work, not in a thousand, million years."

"But if it *would* work in a thousand, million years, would you want me?"

He was looking at her with such desire, Cat was embarrassed to the roots of her hair. She tried to smile, but nothing about her face would work. He picked up one of her fingers and began to nibble on it.

Cat clutched it to her bosom. Was this a proposal of marriage? Was that what she was hoping for? She couldn't think about that, and that wasn't his meaning. She looked distractedly around them and saw the floor an inch deep in water and more gallons spilling over the countertop.

"Great Scott!" she wailed, and hurried, slipping and sliding, to turn off the wretched tap.

The next moments were chaotic—mopping, wringing, sopping, cleaning, drying, cooling off. When it was done, and they stood in the midst of an extra washing-machine load of wet towels, they were left with the cruel realities of what loving was all about.

"I'm all right," she made herself say when he started toward her. She held out a restraining hand. "I'm okay. Really."

His eyes said flatly that he hated her smile. "Well, I'm not, by God."

Cat wanted, suddenly, to be alone. The burden of such a decision was crushing her, creating more problems than it solved. She wiped her hands on the one remaining dry towel while, from outside, the sound of a car's approach reached them.

"They've come for you," she said dully, calling attention to the things that would always be coming between them. "You have an appointment with McGrath, remember? My advice is to lie, Brad. Hey, tell a really good one. Tell him I'm okay."

He muttered an oath so foul, Cat wasn't sure she heard correctly. He strode irately across the still-wet floor, saying how he would go to his hotel and change clothes, then attend a press conference with McGrath and his staff that Lawrence had arranged for. Then they would pick up Travis Tanner at the airport. By then it would be time for Tom Holmes's funeral. And then...

From the kitchen door, he turned to point his finger. "And then we'll talk. You're not as cool as you pretend to be."

She wasn't cool at all; she was without hope. Beyond the window, she could see Donna Hessing's beautiful face as she moved briskly down the rock-bordered walk. The woman was Grace Kelly, Deborah Kerr and Dina Merrill rolled into one. She simply couldn't face the woman standing in the middle of two dozen sopping-wet towels with her paisley skirt glued to her legs!

"I have to get ready for the funeral, Brad," she said.

"I'll sit with you and the children at the service."

"I don't think McGrath or your staff would view that too well."

"You think I give a flying fig about that?"

"Yes." Cat closed her eyes.

The front door did not shut gently when he left.

Upstairs, Babe had hurried to the place in her closet where the floor was broken and a person could place his eye to the gaping crack and look down into the kitchen. She had often used this device to time her comings and goings so as to lessen her time spent at the sink washing dishes.

After removing the boxes she kept piled upon it and arranging herself and Diana in the small enclosure, she hunkered down and motioned for Diana to learn the business of becoming a voyeur—an absolute necessity for any kind of success in the literary arts.

"They're down there somewhere," she said after a moment of looking without finding them. "They have to be." She peered up at Diana in confusion. "They didn't go outside, did they?"

Diana shook her head no.

"Well, I'll be tied in a bow, if that don't beat all." The kitchen, as far as Babe could tell, was deserted. Not a sound anywhere. Except... except that water was running out of the sink and flooding the place!

"Good grief!" she shrieked, and grabbed the mute girl by the hand and went tearing down the stairs only to look in the door to find Brad and Cat mopping up the water and wringing out the towels.

"Maybe it's just as well," she said with an Emily Brontian fortitude, as she drew the girl out of sight so they wouldn't be pressed into service. "After watching the two of them at breakfast, I don't think they know what romance is all about, anyway. I want you to know, Diana, that this is totally pitsville for my career. It's really quite sad, quite sad, indeed."

* * *

"Okay, Larry?"

"Like hell, boss."

Working together for so long had caused a verbal short-hand to develop between Brad and Lawrence Goodyear. They were in Brad's hotel room in Los Alamos and had twenty minutes in which to finish dressing and meet Cat at the funeral home. Showered, shaved, wearing a different suit with a fresh shirt whose collar was starched to the consistency of cardboard, he adjusted the knot of the new silk tie Donna had bought at his request. He had just sent out for a steak because the press conference had lasted too long and McGrath had wanted to be reassured afterward that everything was going smoothly with Catherine Holmes. All morning long he'd been lying through his teeth, reassuring McGrath that everything was perfectly fine, until now he was so deeply entrenched in deceptions that every word was colored with four different meanings.

Lawrence Goodyear was poring over copies of the *Santa Fe New Mexican*, the *Albuquerque Tribune*, the *Taos News*, and the *Los Alamos Monitor*, where he'd gotten McGrath front-page coverage in all. In the background of the same press photo were Brad and himself. Tucked inside on page three of the *New Mexican* was an inconsequential update on the lawsuit filed by Catherine Holmes. "According to sources," said the reporter, "both parties will reach a mutual agreement soon." On page six was a two-line announcement of Thomas Holmes's funeral service.

With the drapes drawn and the television turned on without the sound, depression was thick in the room. Brad braced his shoe upon the edge of the coffee table and was about to buff it when the telephone buzzed.

Lawrence answered it, then extended it to Brad. Brad mouthed, "Who is it?"

The media man shrugged in ignorance.

"Brad Zacharias," said Brad, fitting the receiver beneath his jaw.

"Hello, Brad? Wrather Johnson."

One wrong move, Brad told himself as the strength drained out of his shoulder, and he wouldn't have to worry about resigning. He motioned to Lawrence for the carton of milk on the table.

"Where are you, sir?" he asked, and pried the container open, drinking from the paper spout.

"Home. Just flew in. I thought I would pay my last respects to Tom. How is everything going with the problem we discussed?"

Wiping his lips on the back of his hand, Brad wondered why he was putting himself through this. "I've seen Miss Holmes," he said mildly. "There was a bit of confusion at first, but I think she should be moved out sometime today."

"So she's agreed to drop the lawsuit against McGrath?"

"We've been discussing it, sir." *Actually, I'm in love with the woman, and if it's all the same to you, butt out.*

"Well, I'm sure you're doing your best, son. I trust you implicitly, you know that."

Brad hated himself. "Yes, sir."

"She is going to let us find another place to take the children, though?"

"Ahh, actually, she's quite adamant on that score, sir."

"You mean she's turning it down?"

"In a nutshell, yes. As you say, she's quite proud." *And wonderful, and you were wrong about her. She didn't have a flaming affair with your son!*

"No one in their right mind turns down an offer like that."

"Well, she did, sir." Brad smiled and finished off the milk.

"Well, I'm not too surprised," Wrather said with one of his sighs. "I've got one more tack I might take with the girl. If the press gets hold of this, you know, we could still look pretty stupid."

"Oh, I don't know—Channel Three's running the tape of McGrath visiting the state home for wayward children tonight, and tomorrow we have the Catholic foundling home. Larry's working on one of the Protestant schools, and we'll probably have a tape of that by tomorrow. He'll sprout wings by the day after."

Wrather's silvery laughter drifted smoothly over the wire. "Joseph was right. He told me we could count on you, Brad."

"Yes, sir, you can count on me," Brad said, and folded dejectedly into his chair as Wrather jabbered a few parting amenities about looking forward to seeing him at the service. "Same to you, sir."

"Boy!" Larry said with a whistle when Brad replaced the receiver in its cradle. "Want a real drink, boss?"

Brad squinted at the man. "What's the screwup on getting footage of the Indian school? I want McGrath's shining face out there before dark, Larry, I don't care what he tells you. And get time on tomorrow's noon news. What's the latest on Constanza?"

The media man pulled a face. "He's being a stickler, as we expected. But Donna's working on him, which means he'll come around sooner or later. He'll drop the contempt thing as long as C.H. is off the premises today. Don't worry about it."

Don't worry? Slumping so low on his spine that he was nearly prone on the low-slung sofa, Brad let out his breath in a long, whistling sigh. "I hate this job," he said.

"I saw it, Miss Holmes. It was here."

"Are you sure?"

"Quite sure."

"Would you check again, please? There has to be a mistake. It simply isn't possible."

Grace Bouvier, the middle-aged secretary of Biggs & Watley Funeral Home, was perfect for her job. Cat found everything about the woman to be reassuring in the way a friendly face at the dentist's office is. Even Grace's linen suit with its matching frilly blouse was that of someone's grandmother.

Today Cat needed a grandmother. The paper was open on a corner of the desk. Brad's face looked back at her from behind McGrath's right shoulder.

Somewhere in the huge building an organ was playing "Jesu, Joy of Man's Desiring." Rising, Grace walked in rhythm to its sedate beat to a filing cabinet in the corner. "Please," she invited Cat with a gracious wave, "sit down."

Dressed in her black crepe de Chine dress—even though it was skillfully sewn and a superb fit, it was still homemade—Cat was hovering at the office window, watching the children who waited for her in the neighbor's borrowed van in the parking lot across the street.

She lifted her wrist to her nose where she could smell traces of Brad on her like perfume. She half expected to see him down there, his suit jacket open, his hand moving over the slim side of his vest, looking expectantly up at the window as if he had known all along she would be there watching him.

"Miss Holmes? Miss Holmes!"

Starting, Cat spun around to find Grace Bouvier flipping through a file folder.

"I have it right . . . ah, yes," she was saying. "I knew I wasn't mistaken." She extended the papers as living proof. "See? Everything is already paid for. Exactly as I told you."

In disbelief, Cat took the file and swiftly scanned the financial forms she'd signed several days before. Attached was a check, not her own that was to be drawn upon the money Tom had saved for this day, but a check she'd never seen before. Lifting it out, she saw it was signed by Wrather Johnson. Grace was beaming with triumph.

Confusion was in the drop of Cat's jaw. Wrather thought he could buy her forgiveness by making this gesture? With shaking hands, she lifted the check and turned it over, as if it possessed some magical ability to explain itself.

Without pausing to wonder what the woman would think, she ripped the thing in half, then tore it into smaller and even smaller pieces like a shredder destroying evidence.

"Oh!" Grace exclaimed as she reached to catch the falling scraps.

"It's all right, Ms. Bouvier," Cat said grimly as she tossed the confetti into the wastebasket and found her own checkbook. Standing up, she began to write. "The funeral home will get paid."

"I wasn't thinking of that. Dear me, what—"

Signing her name on Tom's own check with a flourish, Cat ripped it out of the book.

"I think this will do," she said briskly, and snatched the signed form from the file and shoved everything beneath the stapler on the desk. With a snap of her hand, she hit the device with a resounding *whop* and returned the papers neatly to the file folder.

"Case closed," she said, and smiled.

But Grace had been lifting out a larger envelope that had been beneath the forms. "What's this?" she was musing, puzzled. "It must've come when I was out yesterday." Over and over she turned the envelope, then shrugged. "It's for you, Miss Holmes."

With dull surprise, Cat blinked at the Air-Lane Express pack. Opening it, she found a business envelope with the date and the handwritten message: Personal, Ms. Catherine Holmes.

A small line of perspiration beaded across the top of her lip as she lifted the letter opener from the desk. Slitting the envelope, she warily drew out another check—this one drawn on a different bank, made out to her personally, signed by Wrather Johnson.

The amount was ten thousand dollars. In the space labeled ''For'' were penned the cryptic words Interest due.

Chapter Nine

At one o'clock in the afternoon the sun was wheeling high over Los Alamos, and the air was heavy with heat. Four blocks from the cemetery the illusion of coolness on the golf green was lost as players sweated out their eighteen holes. As the mercury climbed, mirages radiated up from the streets and from the highway two blocks away where the world moved past at fifty-five miles an hour, unconcerned that one man's simple life was over.

Biggs & Watley had erected a tasteful canopy over the grave site, dark green canvas trimmed with black. An artificial turf had been spread around the bier to disguise the reality of death.

Flowers were few, as few people had known the deceased. Most of the garlands were from the neighbors who had taken an interest in the improvements being made at Running Wolf Ranch and stopped by upon occasion to make friends. A pleasant floral spray had arrived from

Wrather, a plant from McGrath, nothing from Cat's mother, whom Cat had not seen in over a decade.

Cat sat with the children in one of the special chairs provided for the family. Her legs were crossed so that layered folds of her dress fell in graceful wings about her feet. Those who watched found the vital, motionless intensity into which she seemed to have composed herself to be mesmerizing—reminiscent of matriarchs of another age who believed it to be in bad taste to grieve in public. None of the spectators could take their eyes off her.

She had made a small, unelaborate veil and arranged her hair in a French twist. Her jewelry consisted of tiny gold earrings Tom had given her when she first came to live with him. Other than that, she was simplicity itself.

"'I am the resurrection, and the life...'" the minister said mellifluously as he gazed out over the small group. "We are gathered on this occasion out of love and respect for Thomas Holmes...."

High above the cemetery, on the embankment of the highway, a lone figure sat hunched beneath the shadows of the overpass. To the accompaniment of swishing cars and his own somber reflections, Crowe smoked and watched the funeral of his good friend.

He was uncomfortable being in town—there was too much risk of being picked up by the authorities—but he'd wanted to pay his last respects, and he didn't dare venture close enough to speak to Cat.

Brushing at a bothersome fly, he ground out the cigarette. He would wait as long as he had to. There were things he must tell her, perhaps even tell the man who had spent the night at the ranch, her lover. He hoped Cat would leave peaceably now and stop fighting McGrath, for there was trouble coming that he felt but didn't understand.

Maybe he was borrowing it. Maybe he really was crazy, as people kept telling him. Only two people in the world had ever believed in him; one was about to be put into the ground, and the other was watching it happen while, from a discreet distance, her lover stood in quiet dignity.

In the rear row of chairs between Lawrence Goodyear and Travis Tanner, Donna Hessing sat patting her foot upon the grass. The three of them had just come from KWVT, where a videotape was being edited for the evening news.

Donna hadn't wanted to attend the funeral. When Brad had insisted, she'd gone directly to a fashion mall and purchased a black Evan Picone suit and a large-brimmed black hat, plus summer gloves and a new pair of panty hose. Her shoes weren't new, but in Los Alamos, New Mexico, who cared?

Lifting a gloved hand to shield her mouth, she whispered to Travis who sat on her left. "Take a look at that." At Donna's nudge he angled a look across the cemetery where a long, dark limousine was arriving late, its approach whisper smooth along the street that wove through the grounds.

The car had also attracted Lawrence Goodyear's attention, and the three of them watched it swerve onto the edge of clipped turf to park. The windows were heavily smoked. None of the doors opened, no one got out. It simply sat, purring like a big black cat dozing in the hot sun and watching a bird before making up its mind either to attack or to go back to sleep.

"Keep frosty," Travis said to Donna, for he had been Brad's PR man long enough to expect the worst from every situation. "It's probably no one."

Donna drew her mouth into a regal pout. "It's Mc-Grath."

"Nah."

"Lay your money down."

Travis's pleasantly ugly squint that was part proposition and part disenchantment was a spur in Donna's side. If he'd showed the slightest bit of obsession, she would have dropped him flat, but the thought of anyone being able to resist her was intolerable. Which was part of her great attraction to Brad.

"Wait till Lowell gets wind of what's going on down here," she murmured. "He'll have another stroke."

Travis scowled. "What d'you mean 'going on'?"

Donna smiled with saccharine sweetness and whispered, "Travis, you miss everything. Put two and two together and try to see two inches past your wonderful nose."

She directed his attention with a tip of her own wonderful nose, and Travis found Brad standing a few yards from Catherine Holmes, grim and solemn in his dark suit. His arms were folded over his chest as he tried to listen to the service. His eyes flicked repeatedly to the woman.

"You're crazy," Travis said.

"You didn't see them together this morning. Something *very* interesting is going on."

Travis narrowed his eyes. "Brad's too smart for that."

Donna drolly rolled her eyes at the ceiling of the canopy. If she had a thousand dollars to throw away, she would bet Travis that a certain little item she had placed in Brad's wallet was no longer there, but she could never let Travis know she'd been that dumb.

"You're so out of it, Travis," she purred.

"Let us repeat together the Lord's Prayer," the minister said.

Donna didn't close her eyes. She angled them to Brad, who was angling his to Catherine Holmes who stood as solemn and as still as a queen. Donna wasn't mistaken about

Brad. Zacharias the Great was losing his heart. *More power to you, Catherine Holmes. Make him suffer bloody hell.*

As is the marvelous way of children, their grief, once the service was over, was short-lived. Before they moved from beneath the canopy, their minds were already absorbed with refreshingly healthy matters of self-interest.

"Cat, can I go to the van now? Scooter'll get the front seat if I don't."

"I gotta go to the bathroom, Cat."

"When do we eat?"

"Yeah, I'm hungry."

"Would you make Bingo leave me alone?"

A discreet distance away, the cemetery crew waited for everyone to leave so they could do what they were getting paid for. Cat had done her grieving for Tom long before this day. Surrounded by the needs of her children, she had little choice but to be drawn along in the flow.

Stepping into the sun, she searched for Brad. He was on the opposite side of the canopy, part of a small clique as he conversed with Donna Hessing and two men, one of whom she didn't recognize, and another woman who held a small tape recorder. A reporter, Cat surmised as the children dropped her hands and hurried to the borrowed van.

"Catherine?"

At the sound of her name, Cat froze. She did not turn, nor did she have to; if she'd been blindfolded and dropped into the middle of China in a blinding hurricane she would have known that silvery voice.

"Turn around, darling."

Cat didn't want to obey. A dozen scenarios from the past returned to her, telling her not to. Yet, she slowly turned. The layers of crepe swirled softly about her legs, and the veil, having been drawn aside, fluttered about her face.

He was wearing brown linen slacks and a cream-colored blazer, the perfect attire for a hot summer day. His shoes were so perfect, she imagined herself making a sandwich of them and taking a bite. When he stepped forward and lifted her veil, folding it back over her face like a groom preparing to kiss his bride, her breath came in a harsh, tattered sound.

"Wrather!"

She watched the processes of his recognition after four years. His interest was nothing new, but this was different as he took her apart piece by piece—making his list, chalking up her faults and weighing them against her assets.

"Oh, my dear," he said on an ascending note of surprise and approval, "my dear, *dear* girl." He laughed softly and rearranged her veil unnecessarily and lifted her hands to his lips. "Except that you aren't a girl anymore, are you? Where did she go, little one?"

"I think she died, Wrather," Cat said icily, trembling inside.

Again he laughed, almost without making a sound, as if it were something just between the two of them. "Ahh, not entirely."

His gaze lowered to her throat and her sharply rising bosom. The look of possession was on his face, Cat thought, and she was struck with how unappealing she found it now.

Yet, from habit, she started to lower her eyes, then realized where she was and that Brad stood only a small distance away. She had dealt with a man as an equal now, and never again would she lower her eyes to anyone. She lifted her head in a declaration of independence and exposed the fiercely proud length of her throat.

Choosing the worst possible moment, Tucker ran up to tug on her hand. "We gotta take the van home, Cat," he fretted. "Come on. Everybody's waitin'."

More brusque than she meant to be, Cat answered without giving him so much as a glance. "Just wait for me in the van, please, Tuck. I'll be there when I get there."

Wounded, the boy unhappily trudged away, and Cat hated herself more than she hated Wrather. She looked over her shoulder in an attempt to catch Brad's eye and said, "Why did you come here today, Wrather? You didn't give a fig for Tom and you know it."

He was impervious to her spur. "I came here to reason with you, Catherine, to insist that you let McGrath and me relocate you and these children of yours. I was going to say that if you couldn't think of McGrath's career, to think of the children. But now, looking at you, I see that I've made a slight miscalculation."

A tiny chill shook the bones of Cat's spine. "What miscalculation?"

"Look in a mirror sometime, my darling." He waved aside the retort and probed her with ever-deepening scrutinies. "No, what I'm seeing wouldn't be seen by your perversely critical eye. But I see, everyone else sees—" he gestured expansively "—how charming it is, how...enchanting. I'm planning great things for you, Catherine, at this very moment. Why, you're absolutely irresistible."

He wanted her now? Like some jewel to adorn his finger? Some trophy for his wall? The realization crashed down upon Cat like an avalanche from out of nowhere. After all this time, *he* had decided that she met his approval and that he would care about her now.

Yet the man had saved her life, and what did she do with that? "I'm afraid I don't think in terms of greatness anymore, Wrather," she said as kindly as possible, and wished that Brad would stop talking and look up.

With one of his elegant shrugs and a glance around the premises, he murmured that he was sorry. "I think we should talk about the children, my dear. I've been greatly concerned and I've made some plans that I think will please you. We can't visit here in this heat. Please, come sit with me in the car for a minute."

"We can talk right here," she said, and tried again to catch Brad's eye. Now she saw Donna and the men, but no Brad.

To her dismay, Wrather touched her elbow and began drawing her gently from beneath the canopy. So used to obeying him was she, at first she didn't protest. By the time her wits returned, they had walked to the edge of the grass.

Cat drew her arm from his and vigorously shook her head. "I can't go anywhere with you, Wrather."

Her protest only made his smile more tender and indulgent. The old desire was in the burn of his looks now, that anticipation that had been there at the very end when he had kissed her and made her promise to return. Even the heightened color on his cheeks was a strategy, Cat thought.

"You do owe me, Catherine," he reminded her. "I've made a large investment in you, and you do owe me the courtesy of hearing what I have to say."

With shocking boldness, he touched her throat, and a thousand confusing sensations shot through Cat's body. "I'll put diamonds here," he said, and fingered the burning lobe of her ear. "And diamonds here. I will make you my queen, Catherine. God, you're breathtaking."

Once they were out from beneath the protection of the canopy, the sun hammered down out of a cloudless sky. It flashed off the windshields of cars that were leaving. Cat felt herself melting beneath its burn as if she were a wax dummy.

She stared blindly at the gleaming car that stretched beyond her. Her heart seemed ready to burst. "You never did understand, did you?" she whispered. "I didn't want diamonds. I wanted you."

"Of course you did, darling...."

As if by magic, the door of the car opened. With the delicacy of a connoisseur touching rarest porcelain, Wrather took her hand and drew her forward.

"This is Nemo, Catherine," he said. "You remember Nemo, don't you?"

Cat smiled numbly at the phenomenal hulk behind the steering wheel. Nemo had been driving one of Wrather's cars since the Model T, she thought, and she didn't know if the man had a last name or not. At six feet eight inches and two hundred and eighty pounds, Nemo was one of a kind.

"Hi, Nemo."

"Hello, Miss Catherine." He smiled a child's simple, toothy smile. "How're you doin'?"

Shrugging, she searched again for Brad, but Wrather was urging her into the car. She said, "This hasn't been one of my best days, I'm afraid."

"Sorry to hear about Mr. Tom."

"Thank you, Nemo."

Wrather said in a more gruff, paternal voice as he handed her inside, "Catherine, darling, who do you keep looking for?"

Not until that precise instant did Cat perceive the truth of the situation—that Wrather might have indeed come to the funeral with the purpose of persuading her to accept his offer of a new home for the children. But now he wanted her to leave with him, and he had no intention of being refused.

Panicked, she finally located Brad. He perceived everything at a glance except her motives. Is this what you want? he asked her from across the crowd.

Her telegraphed reply was instantaneous. *Please, help me.*

The gulf between them was wide, composed of pieces of information that as yet were only parts of a whole. She saw him stretch out a hand to stop the conversation. Heads turned to look at her.

Brad was suddenly elbowing his way through people, pushing strangers aside as he hurried and dodged and, once clear of them, was striding with urgency across the grounds. Cat pushed at Wrather's hands, but they had the advantage now. She found herself being smothered with words—silky protests and crooning promises as only Wrather could overwhelm her—about how everything was going to be all right, that he only wanted to talk and put things straight, that she owed him that much after all he had done, that Tom would have wanted her to accept help from his old and dear friend.

Door locks snapped into place like stainless-steel tumblers. The open window whispered shut. Ice-cold air poured into the smoked-glass enclosure, and the partition between the front and back whispered discreetly into place. With hardly a stir the car moved off the grass and onto the street, all in a matter of mere seconds.

Too late, Cat twisted around. "What is going on here?" she demanded. "Stop this car. Let me out this minute."

"Catherine, darling, if you would calm down just a minute."

"Don't tell me to calm down! I'm not going anywhere with you! The children..." Leaning forward, Cat rapped sharply on the partition that separated them from Nemo. "Nemo, turn around. Take me back. Stop this car!"

But they were a block away now, and Nemo was frighteningly impervious to her shrieks.

The car nosed around a turn and started up another street. In a frenzy, Cat lunged toward Wrather, not caring that her dress was showing her thighs or that her veil had been pulled askew. One of her shoes had come off.

Her intention was to attack him with her stored-up vengeance but when she turned, she gaped in shock at a stranger. How oddly…unkempt he looked as he sank back upon the fine leather seat—smaller than she remembered, older, not quite on top of things. Had age done that, or was it she who had changed? Or had Brad, in the short time she had known him, changed the way she would look at other men for the rest of her days?

He cupped her elbow, and Cat saw that age had not diminished his physical strength. Enough power was in those hands to crush her, either in anger or desire.

"Why are you doing this?" she asked coldly, and drew her arm out of reach, unable to bear his touch at all.

He pushed a button that sent a bar sliding out into view. With tongs, he put ice in two glasses. He poured liquor out of a small bottle and extended one glass.

"Drink this, Catherine," he said, his silvery voice having grown brittle. "It'll calm you down."

Curling her lip, Catherine took the glass and, wishing she had the courage to hurl its contents in his face, poured the liquor onto the carpet.

Rather than angering him, it amused him. What he could have had for nothing, he was now willing to go to any lengths to get, it seemed.

"You've not only grown up, little Kitten, you've become a tigress." He stared at her straining breasts, her insistent nipples. He moistened his lips and laid his hand upon her knee. "The tigress—ever a fascinating animal; so sensual, so provocative, so bloodthirsty."

They were blocks from the cemetery now. She wished she had never told Brad about Wrather. He would wonder if this weren't what she'd wanted all along. He would think that she'd used him and the funeral and the children to force Wrather to make his move.

She dropped her head in defeat against the glass. "This is so stupid, Wrather. What do you hope to gain?"

"Why, you, of course."

Cat shook her head. "You will always have my gratitude, Wrather—" her voice was that of an old woman "—but I don't love you anymore. Maybe I never did. Maybe I was just growing up."

"How well do you know Brad Zacharias?"

In a fresh wave of frustration, Cat leaned forward to slam against the partition with her fists. "Open this window, Nemo!" she cried, pounding. "Let me out of here. This is wrong! Damn you, damn you...damn...."

The giant behind the wheel, though pained, did not respond.

Wrather repeated more intently, "How well do you know Brad Zacharias, Catherine?"

Hoping that a thousand volts of bitterness showed in her eyes, Cat glared. Then it suddenly came to her that she should tell him the truth. Trembling, for it wasn't in her wildest scenario, she whispered, "I know him...*very* well."

"I see," he said smoothly. "Do you intend to marry him? Has he asked you? Do you see yourself slipping into his world? Don't be naive, Catherine. You are only just now ready to learn what his world is all about. And you know I speak the truth, as I have always done."

Cat felt as though she were bleeding from every pore. Oh, she hated Wrather when he did this!

A silver smile. An adjustment to his impeccable cuff links. "I made a deal with you once," he said. "I'll make another. If Brad Zacharias is what you want, I'll help you, but first you will pay off your obligations to me. I will arrange for the children to be placed in homes, Catherine. Now, before you throw some pathetic, hysterical tantrum, let me assure you that these children will have better treatment than you could ever have given them. Come to me, Catherine. It's time. I will make you into a queen. My queen."

Reaching out, he drew her back into the seat, and though Cat braced her hands against his side, his grip grew tighter and tighter until she was pinned against him so rigidly that her bones would have snapped had she moved a muscle. He moistened his lips and placed his hand upon her breast.

Her blood turned to ice water. "Let me out of this car, Wrather Johnson."

"You once told me that you lay in your bed and dreamed about me. I'm with you now, Catherine. Close your eyes and dream."

Disgracefully, Brad had wanted this funeral to be over since it began. He wanted the day to be over and everyone to be gone so he could take Cat to a private place and come alive again, bring her alive. When Wrather had shown up, he hadn't been particularly surprised. Now his mind leaped desperately toward Cat, but Mary Delaney's voice kept droning on and on and on.

Mary Delaney, a reporter for the *New Mexican*, had attended the Holmes funeral service at Travis's invitation. Nervous—she didn't often see anyone from New York, much less get showered with attention from them—she tried to ask intelligent questions after the service was over.

"Isn't that right, Mr. Zacharias? That the immigration problem cannot be overrated, that Senator Johnson hasn't given it enough weight thus far?"

Brad frowned. He hadn't been surprised when Wrather's car arrived, but he was thrown off guard when the man made such a point of talking to her. He was leaving now, and Cat was walking him to his car.

"I beg your pardon?" he said, looking blankly at the reporter.

The angle of Mary Delaney's nose was accusing him of rudeness, to say nothing of Donna Hessing's, over which she was peering imperiously. Clearly his coworker wished he would get his act together. Damn! This reporter was important to their work.

Cat was hesitating at the door of Wrather's limousine, and desire went through Brad shamelessly as he watched the breeze lift her skirt demurely and tuck it between her legs. He rubbed the back of his neck as the door swept open in front of Cat.

He didn't understand. She turned, her arm flung outward, and he realized that she intended to get into the car. Then he saw that she wasn't getting into it, she was being *pulled* into it! She was trying to push Wrather away, not say goodbye!

In a look that went through him like a blade, she found him.

If he hadn't known before how deeply he'd fallen in love with her, Brad's doubts would have dissolved in the face of her fear. A murderous rage boiled up inside him. In that moment he was capable of incomprehensible violence.

"Will you excuse me?" he blurted, cutting Mary Delaney off in the middle of a sentence and turning so sharply that he struck her on the arm.

"Oh! I . . . I—" she spluttered.

"Brad?" Donna called to his back as he took a step from them.

Brad turned hard on his heel and started across the lawn at a quick trot.

"Hey, Zach!" yelled Lawrence.

Travis muttered, "Wait for me," and started after him.

"That's the rudest thing I ever saw," Mary gasped. "I've heard that everyone's like that in New York."

"You'll have to forgive him, Miss Delaney," Donna soothed as she patted the woman's hands, then started after Lawrence and Travis, meaning to strangle all three of them. She called back to Mary Delaney as she walked, "They've all been under terrible pressure, Ms. Delaney. Wait right there. I'll be back."

"Well, I never..." Mary said as she watched all three of them chase after Brad Zacharias.

Brad could hardly think as he tried to catch up with Wrather's limousine as it swept away from the grass. He was a good runner, but he saw as he chased the car partway down the street that there was no chance of catching up.

Briefly, he considered what would happen to him if he tangled with Wrather over this. His career could suffer fallout forever because Wrather and Lowell were close, but his career didn't matter now. Nothing mattered without Catherine.

The car was halfway down the street. The brake lights winked at him.

"Hey, man, wait up!" Travis wheezed as he ran up. "Where're you going? What's going on?"

Brushing aside his friend, Brad sprinted to the limousine that he and the team had rented. Jerking open the door, he leaned toward the driver, a young man who looked as if he'd lived his whole life for this one moment to come along.

"You want a quick hundred, Jerry?"

The driver worked his hands upon the steering wheel. "You bet."

"Catch that car."

He laughed as his hand reached for the key. "Jerry's the name and chasin's my game. Git in, Mr. Zee."

Lawrence grabbed Brad's sleeve. "What's the matter with you, Brad? That's Wrather Johnson in that car."

"Yeah, and he's about to get himself accused of kidnapping."

"Brad, you're mistaken. And even if you're not, you can't hassle McGrath's daddy. There could be serious repercussions from this. For all of us."

Brad slammed the door shut. He didn't look at any of them, didn't want to see pity in their eyes. *Poor Brad. He's gone off his rocker over a little nobody.*

"Hit it, Jerry!" he growled as he pulled loose the knot of his tie.

"This is suicide!" Lawrence bellowed as he ran alongside the car.

The car left him standing on the turf, staring in disbelief. Leaning toward the windshield, Brad balled his hands into fists.

"Just catch up, Jerry," he said with tight urgency, "and force them to pull over. I'll do the rest."

"Hot damn!"

"And don't wreck the car."

At first Brad was afraid Wrather had gotten too much of a head start. The streets were in an old part of town. To get onto the highway was a process of making several narrow, twisting turns. As Jerry whipped around a corner they saw the big car streaking along a lane. Jerry, having never been involved in a chase in his life, figured that watching all that television had to pay off.

"Got any ideas?" he asked Brad, snatching a glance.

Brad was twisting to see where they were. He pointed. "You see that service station down at the next block?"

"Yeah."

"What d'you want to bet that the traffic light catches them and they turn right? Cut through the gas pumps and head 'em off."

"I got 'em now, man—" Jerry laughed "—right in the sights of my gun."

"Well," Brad dryly observed, "don't get trigger-happy."

Nemo did indeed anticipate getting caught by the red light, and he veered around the others headed toward the intersection. He zoomed up the right-hand lane, horn blaring. With a squeal of tires, Jerry turned left and streaked down the wrong side of the street to skid through the self-service isles of the station just as Nemo was barreling from his lane in an attempt to cut across. With only inches to spare, Nemo hit his brakes and sent the big car into a broadside skid, leaving great rubber stripes beneath the canopy and barely missing a gas pump.

Even before Jerry brought their car to a stop, Brad was tumbling to the ground. Behind them, drivers were blaring their horns.

The poor station attendant ran out the door, screaming, "What in hell do you think you're doing?"

Brad was pulling on Nemo's door before the huge man realized what was happening. When it didn't open, Brad started around the lovely silver finish, kicking it as hard as he could and banging on it with his fists.

"Open this door, you son of a bitch!" he yelled, kicking and slamming.

Nemo gawked at him, and Brad, enraged, picked up a trash can and, lifting it above his head, intended to send it crashing through the windshield. Nemo heaved out of the car, waving Brad back as he lurched toward them.

"Okay, back off," he thundered.

Brad was well aware that he was outdistanced and out-weighed. He was outeverything-ed as he heaved the barrel into the hulk's middle instead and darted around him to the open door. Nemo stumbled slightly from the impact, but reached Brad before he could unlock the back doors.

"Get out, Catherine!" Brad shouted as he found himself lifted completely off the ground by the collar of his suit.

The next thing he knew, he was slammed against the car. As he fell back, a pile driver ploughed into his middle. Sickened by the blow, he felt his head swim. Nemo released him long enough to peer inside at Wrather Johnson for instructions.

A mistake—what Brad lacked in body size, he made up for in wits and reflexes. Some of the boxing skills he'd picked up at Princeton served him in good stead now, and he staggered toward Nemo to land a series of blows to Nemo's kidneys.

With a mighty roar, the giant turned and lunged for Brad. Brad slammed a low right hook to Nemo's midsection, and the blow was good. The bystanders' breaths were as audible as Nemo's.

The man swung blindly with rage, and Brad moved in on him again, leading with his left, jabbing and stepping back, jabbing and stepping back, a classic tactic that Nemo was not skilled at. But Nemo, reeling, fell upon Brad, and the sheer impetus of the fall nearly knocked Brad off his feet. With breaths raspy and straining, they struggled until Nemo lifted Brad free of the ground and slammed him against a gas pump with a gagging fury.

Brad felt things breaking and tearing inside him. Far in the distance, he thought he heard the scream of a siren. With the desperation of a drowning man, he ducked and literally crawled between the giant's mighty legs to reach the car.

The entire thing had consumed no more than a minute, and it took less than another thirty seconds for Brad to hurl himself onto the front seat and confront Wrather Johnson. In that moment as the two men looked at each other—the older at the younger, the younger at the older—the truth struck Brad with more force than any blow Nemo had landed. Wrather had no time to dissemble. Brad saw, in the man's stunned blue eyes, that it had been *he* whom Cat had loved.

With that knowledge came a defeat he wasn't prepared for. All his lovely little dreams cracked like sugar-glass props on a movie stage. In his ears were the sounds of Cat's heartbreak when she talked about her past love. And he knew, too, that Wrather had deliberately lied to him.

"Why?" he choked as Nemo turned and staggered toward him with the bellow of a bull.

Wrather's look was not only one of contempt, it was one of pity. With a fist, Brad struck the control panel a blow and the locks of the back doors flew open.

"Get out, Catherine!" he ordered.

"You're finished, Zacharias," Wrather said.

"You touch her again, Wrather—" Brad's voice was the slash of a sword "—and I'll bring you down. I'll break you. You can't go far enough that I won't break you."

Cat was scrambling out and onto the pavement. From behind, Nemo grabbed Brad by his suit and dragged him out of the car. Again Brad's body was lifted clear off the ground and slammed onto the top of the car.

Cat raced around the limousine and began pummeling Nemo with her fists. "No, no! Nemo, don't."

The attendant dashed out of the building. "Stop this!" he shrilled. "I've called the police."

But Brad saw none of it. He was being strangled by a gorilla. With a roar, Nemo dropped Brad to the ground and hurled him against the front fender with such force that it was dented. He drew back his fist. With a mighty blow, he struck Brad squarely in the face, and blood gushed from Brad's nose to stream over his shirt.

"Aghh!" Brad yelled, and slumped forward.

Cat thought she was dying. She heard a scream and knew it was her own. "You're killing him! Stop it, Nemo! Please, in the name of God, stop!"

In despair, she climbed up Nemo's back and grabbed a handful of his hair and pulled with all her might as she would choke a mad dog. "No, Nemo! Leave him alone. No!"

She didn't think the hulk even heard her, for he gave her a backhanded shove that sent her sprawling against one of the gas pumps.

Picking himself up, Brad knew he would have only one chance. Gone now was the technique he'd learned in boxing. With blood streaming down his face, he doubled up his fist and struck Nemo with every ounce of strength he possessed. As the man stumbled, Brad staggered toward Cat and pulled her to her feet. Working on the same wavelength, Jerry shot his car into the empty stall and threw open the door.

"Get in!" he yelled.

Cat glanced up to see Nemo staggering toward them, his big arms thrashing at everything in his path. Jerry was leaning over the seat and pulling Brad into the car. Cat placed herself between the two men.

"It's all right, Nemo," she blurted, waving him away. "You've hurt him enough. Go back to Wrather, Nemo."

Dazed, Nemo did as she said.

With a screech of rubber, Jerry whisked them from the scene, and Cat turned to see Brad holding his face with blood streaming through his fingers. "It's broken," he moaned, his words muffled. "That prehistoric beast broke my nose."

"Shh," Cat said as her love for Brad swirled about them like a warm, healing stream. She met the questioning look from the young driver and said, "The hospital."

And in that moment her pain—past, present and future—didn't matter. She was holding Brad in her arms as her hair spilled about them.

"I love you!" he whispered fiercely into the hollow of her throat. "Are you all right?"

"Yes." She held him very tightly.

"Tell me, Catherine."

"I love you, too," she said against his stiff, blood-streaked hair.

"Don't ever leave my side again."

"Please, hold me."

"I can't, Cath." Releasing her, Brad slumped onto the seat and squeezed his eyes shut. "I think I broke my hand."

Chapter Ten

In matters of binding up people's hurts, Cat was unsurpassed. She had even advanced to the stage where she could separate the emotion of the moment from her good judgment, which made her one of the all-time perfect friends and supreme confidants, to say nothing of a really great nurse and not-so-bad mother.

But for this one person, this hurt man whom she had just confessed to love, with whom she was falling more in love each moment, Cat was so helpless that she could do nothing except receive his pain into herself and hurt along with him. Now that her confession had been spoken, what happened next? she asked herself. Did it really change anything to love a person so blindly?

Brad had sprawled with the careless negligence only a trusting lover knows, with one knee flung over hers and a total depletion of his facades. Handkerchief in hand, he dabbed at his face and ran his tongue along the inside of his mouth, searching for tiny cuts. Turning to see his reflection in the window, he grimaced, but even that hurt, and he dropped back to the seat with a groan and held his ribs.

All the insecurities of a lifetime collected in the pit of Cat's stomach. If she *really* loved him, she would get out of his life and stay out, wouldn't she?

"Well," she exclaimed too lightly and too inconsequentially, too airily as she leaned to inspect a tiny bleeding cut in his hair. "I guess we just about summed that up, didn't we?"

He didn't understand her tone. As she attempted to see his nose, he held her at arm's length and studied her down the bridge of it. "What's that supposed to mean?"

Cat wished she'd kept her doubts for another day. "I mean that pain has a way of making you say things, Brad. That's all. Move your hand. Goodness, your face is ruined."

"It's been ruined before." His voice cut as sharply as a stropped razor. "What did you mean just now?"

They were drawing to the finish line of some terrible contest, but Cat couldn't fathom what it was, only that she hadn't wanted to run in the first place, and if she won and lost Brad, she would still have lost, but she couldn't have Brad, so she had lost anyway.

Her reply was made of lead. She looked out the window as she gave it. "I only want you to know, Brad, that I realize that you love me now, but I won't hold you to anything once the bleeding stops."

Brad hardly knew what hurt the worst, one of her logical gems or Nemo's meaty fists. Looking up, then down, he attempted to draw her attention from the city outside. He touched her hair with the good hand he had left.

"Catherine, darling—" *lightly, Zacharias, lightly* "—I have just told you what I've never told another woman in my entire life."

At that remark, she came out of hiding from behind her hair and smiled chidingly. "See?" Her lifted brows drove home her point. "The pain has made you delirious already. Can you remember your mother's name?"

She touched a bruise darkening beneath his jaw. "Let me look at that. Don't worry, I'm the original Earth Mother."

Brad grudgingly corrected himself, "Well, if I said that to any other woman, I'm sure I didn't mean it."

Her laughter was more than he could stand. "I mean," he grated, "I might have *thought* I meant it at the time, but now..."

"I'd stop while I was ahead if I were you."

"Damnation, woman, I've laid my life on the line for you! I faced death by dismemberment for you!"

"The pain has definitely gone to your head."

For the first time since she'd known him she actually had the upper hand! Though Cat could have hugged him, she had him stick out his tongue and moisten the edge of a tissue. She got most of the dried blood out of his eyelashes and finished scrubbing his neck.

"I could really get into this Earth Mothering," he said, and enjoyed a really splendid view down the front of her dress.

She followed the path of his stare and narrowed her eyes. "Just as we suspected, Mr. Zacharias. Your brain is disintegrating. I'm afraid we'll have to operate immediately."

"Oh, you found that out, did you?" He tried to laugh.

She leaned back to take an overall view. "It's really quite a mess, isn't it?"

"My brain?"

"Your nose, idiot."

He was fumbling with the knot of his tie. "This is the third break."

"Some of those rash statements to women you *thought* you loved undoubtedly caught up with you."

"They're going to have to give me a pain medication for you."

With quick, sure fingers Cat pushed his hand away and loosened the tie, stripping it off. Reaching between the stiff collar and his Adam's apple, she freed the button, touching him in a dozen ways that Brad found almost worth the beating he'd taken.

He caught her hand with his good one and murmured above the quiet song of the tires, "Enough kidding around. I have to know, Cath. Did you mean what you said?"

For a brief second, Cat's hands stopped fussing. *Don't be naive, Catherine. You are only just now ready to learn what his world is all about.* Confused, for she had opened a door to a corridor that revealed only dozens of other doors behind which would be other doors, she let her lashes drop to her cheeks for a fluttering moment.

Presently she drew in her breath and continued unbuttoning his shirt, pulling it free of his pants with trembling fingers, which Brad seemed to find irresistibly endearing. "Did *you*," she asked, and kept her head down, "mean it?"

"I asked you first."

She unbuckled his belt and, loosening it, unbuttoned his trousers to relieve the stricture. Her fingers probed skillfully over the span of his abdomen for signs of internal bleeding. Finding none that she recognized, Cat looked up before he could mask the man's longing on his battered face.

"If you mean, do I love you as in what do I feel when I look at you," she said carefully and precisely, "the answer is yes. But if you mean do I want the pain to both of us of trying to make something work that won't work—not in a thousand years...."

In the pit of his stomach Brad felt her nearness and her intense honesty. She made him feel bound to her. The car seemed to be getting smaller. Her perfume touched him insidiously. The smell of her haunted him now, like a song he couldn't quite recall, and he felt the treacherous lift of desire through all the pain.

But his hand hurt, his head hurt, and now his libido, damn it. His knuckles were swelling. He struggled momentarily to remove his class ring, but his finger was stiffening rapidly.

"Get this thing off, will you?" he said, placing his fingers gingerly into her lap. "They'll cut it off if I don't."

His fingers were long and beautifully crafted but not soft, the flesh at the base of his thumb being as muscular and hard as wood. A fine sheen of blond hair peppered their backs almost invisibly. After a few moments of tedious maneuvering, finally ending up licking it, Cat slipped the band free of the swollen knuckle.

"Harvard," she said with a bland smile as she dropped it neatly into his lap. "You have trodden upon hallowed ground. I'm impressed, Zacharias."

"Yeah—" he chuckled drearily "—I'm really great at treading."

A fine beading of sweat had broken out upon his brow and made Cat again watch him closely for signs of internal injuries. When he grasped her hand and laid it carefully upon his knee, she didn't protest but braced herself as Jerry made a brake-squealing turn.

"Catherine?"

Cat stared as he slipped the loose ring onto her middle finger where it was still several sizes too large, and when her brows lifted to form a question mark, he smiled.

"Repeat after me," he teased, and closed his eyes as he lay back.

Uneasy at joking about such a thing, Cat attempted to withdraw her hand, but he grasped her chin.

"Come on, Cath," he whispered, his expression drifting from agony to happiness and back again, "I just went to war for you. You're supposed to welcome the conquering hero and say the words."

Brad saw immediately that she didn't realize how deeply his underpinning of love went. He could feel her making comparisons with her scars of the past. Her tongue flicked erratically over her lips, and she nervously plucked a lock of hair that had fluttered across one cheek.

"I just said words, Brad," she said breathlessly. "Three of them."

"Then say six more. Say 'With this ring, I thee wed.'"

The moment was too suspended in webbing of silk—a cocoon created of circumstances neither of them had planned on or completely understood, another of those swords cast into the ground, whirring with implications. His career was too vulnerable for a mere affair, and her bruised self couldn't take that last permanent step, not after Wrather.

All or nothing? Cat smiled unhappily. "Don't joke about that. And don't deliver ultimatums."

His lips reached for hers and parted them. His invasion of her mouth was tightly leashed, and he kissed her lightly between each word.

"Who's...joking?" His breath spoke eloquently of his sincerity. "Are...you...going...to...marry...me, Catherine?"

Her practical mind that he admired so much had stymied her, Cat thought. She wouldn't fit into his world, and he would be crippled in hers. She tried to say his name, but couldn't speak.

"Okay, okay," he said, and turned in the seat, stretching himself out as much as possible and nestling his head in her lap.

Cat smiled thoughtfully down at him as he let his breath out in a slow, languid sigh. Her breast was excruciatingly accessible, and he knew that. With tender caresses, she smoothed the front sprigs of his hair.

"Why aren't you asking me about Wrather?" she mused almost absently. "Don't you want to know what he said to me?"

With a matching absence of mind, he drew a circle about the center of her breast and studied the tiny peak as it constricted. "It doesn't matter."

She watched his fingertip making the same pattern again and again. "What?"

"It doesn't matter, what he said."

"You and he talked about me. Of course it matters."

"But I thought he and I were talking about McGrath."

His thumb was poised at the apex of her whole body. The name exploded out of nowhere, and Cat felt as if the shrapnel of it were burying deep into her flesh. Blinking, she pushed his hand away, pushed him away.

"McGrath?" She shook her head. "Why on earth would you think we were talking about McGrath? What do I have to do with McGrath? I don't even *like* McGrath. How could you get such an impression?"

Brad pulled himself up to sit and looked where his head had been, feeling unjustly cast out of the nest. "It wasn't an impression, darling," he drawled. "Wrather told me. Before I ever came down here."

Cat suddenly felt disassociated from reality, lost forever. Wanting fiercely to hold to some clinging lifeline, she wrapped her arms about herself.

"You misunderstood, Brad," she said, shaking her head back and forth. "Wrather couldn't make a mistake like that. He knew how I felt about him. About *him*, Wrather. I only told him a hundred times. He kissed me, and we talked, and...I can't *believe* how you got that misconception. McGrath is married, for pity's sake!"

At great cost to parts of his body that he didn't know by name, Brad swiveled around to face her on the seat. He captured her eyes and held them, driving home the point. "He *told* me it was McGrath, Catherine. He stopped the plane I was on, which probably cost him a fortune in called-in favors, and he made a big point of telling me that Mc-Grath had had an affair with you."

"And you believed him?"

Cat was shrieking at him, and she lunged away from him, as if separating herself from him would make the grotesqueness disappear. Springing up and grabbing her, forcing her to listen, he shook her as hard as he was able.

"Look at me, damn it! What else was I to do? I didn't know you from anything. And I have never had reason to doubt his word before. Lowell trusts the man, Catherine, and I trust Lowell."

"Then you're trusting the wrong people!" she raged.

"Why would he tell such a heinous lie about his very own son?"

Beneath them, the tires of the big machine were hurrying them to a place where Brad would find help, but in her heart Cat knew there was no such place for her. Her defeat, her disgrace of having been tricked so horribly, was magnified a hundredfold for having Brad know about it and having drawn his own opinions long before she was there to defend herself. He knew that she'd been made a fool of, he had known it before she did.

In horror, she gasped, "Who else believes this lie?"

"No one. I didn't tell any of my staff."

"Why would you not?"

"I don't know. I just wasn't ready to."

Cat squeezed her eyes tightly shut. Where would it end? What was the reason for it? Why, why?

"Catherine?"

"I'm all right." She twisted her head aside and waved her hand between them. "I'm just ashamed, that's all. Please don't look at me."

"What's there to be ashamed of?"

"I wish that you—"

"That I what?"

"I wish that you didn't know all the bad things about me." She covered her face. "Whether you believe it or not, I've done some good things in my life, Brad. I've accomplished things that most people wouldn't begin to tackle. I know I've been a fool in the past, but..."

Was there a time when the sheer kindness of human understanding outweighed all the love of heaven and earth?

When Brad lifted his arm and hooked it about her neck and, instead of kissing her, which he could have done, simply held her and said, "I think you're the most wonderful thing in the world," Cat knew that something wonderful was happening. She was finding, beneath the lover, a good, good friend.

"I was wrong about you, Catherine," he said. "I came down here expecting you to be weak, but you're the strongest woman I know."

"I'm not strong."

"You're not afraid to try anything, and you have a sense of rightness and fairness that's almost gone from this world, Cath. You know how people are in my world? They make a bunch of claims, then you have to peel through the husks to find out whether they're lying or not. It's the game, and you either play or let someone else play. But you? I don't have your kind of courage, which is why I admire yours so much, I guess. It is, I think—" he sighed "—why I've fallen in love with you."

Cat watched the gray of his eyes turn to smoke and his brows draw together. It was almost as if they had changed roles, that he was Eve and she was Adam. She could hurt him deeply, but it was the last thing she wanted.

"Let me find my way, Brad," she said with tender honesty. "I have a lot farther to come than you, but I do love you. I swear I do."

The big car swung beneath the canopy of the emergency room and parked. The partition between front and back slid open.

"We're here, Mr. Zacharias," Jerry said. "They can fix you up good as new."

Brad looked at the solemnity of Cat's profile and only wished that that was true.

By the time Cat and Brad left St. Jude's Hospital, Brad had been X-rayed, had had one of his fingers reset and a splint put on his hand for two fractured knuckles. A bandage had been placed across the bridge of his nose. Since he couldn't write, the nurse, mistaking Cat for Mrs. Zacharias, brought her the insurance forms to fill out.

Rolling her eyes at Brad while he smiled into his shirt collar, she dragged her chair beside the bed and began to learn all the details of his life.

They hardly spoke as Jerry drove them out to the ranch. In a short while they had shared some of the worst that life could offer. For the time being, it was enough for Cat to know that she was capable of loving him. Where that would take them, she had no idea, but she had to trust that she could deal with it, whatever it was. And Wrather's lie? She had no idea where that would lead.

When Jerry swerved the big car into the long stretch that led to the house, she guessed that all the good feelings had made her greedy. She had overstepped herself, for as she leaned forward and strained for sight of one of the children, she found none—no lights, no Lady running to greet the car, only a great stack of boxes and crates that stood beside the porch and was covered with garish yellow plastic.

"Oh, no," she groaned. Another car was parked before the flower bed—not the borrowed van but a strange sedan. "McGrath?"

The lines on Brad's face were drawn more deeply when she glanced at him. Weariness had taken its toll. Over Cat's head, he signaled Jerry to approach with caution.

Grasping her fingers, he said, "It's all right, darling. Whatever it is, we'll deal with it."

Cat clung to him more feverishly than she meant to. When they got out and walked up the stone-bordered walk, she drew his sound arm about her shoulders so that her side was fitted safely to his.

"Oh, Brad," she kept repeating. "Oh, Brad, oh, Brad."

"Easy."

Donna Hessing and Travis Tanner met them at the door and, opening it, motioned them inside.

"My God," Donna exclaimed, looking from the splint to his nose and the myriad bruises and split skin.

Brad held up his hand. "I don't want to talk about this. For the record, I tangled with the Incredible Hulk. What's happened here?"

Without a word, Donna moved forward and took Cat by her hand. All superficialities were stripped away to leave nothing but an offer of understanding between two women who, though they didn't know each other, had a mutual respect for the strength each possessed.

"There isn't an easy way to tell you this, Catherine," she said simply.

Brad exchanged a grim look with his friend, and Travis shook his head. Travis explained, "The social services woman took them right from the cemetery, Brad. I tried reasoning with her, but she said that she'd lose her job if she let the children sleep on the streets. And since Miss Holmes still has no permanent residence, and since Mary Delaney was hovering to hear every word, I thought it best to let it happen quietly."

"The children were on the streets when I found them," Cat bitterly reminded them. "We could have managed."

Donna said, "My advice, Catherine, for what it's worth, is to accept Wrather Johnson's offer. If it makes you nervous, I'll draw up the papers myself to insure that your future is as secure as possible."

Brad's voice cut through Donna's suggestion like a knife. "That's impossible now."

Confusion was in the lift of the attorney's brows. "But the man made a good offer..."

Brad raised his voice to a biting command. "Let it go, Donna. We'll find another way."

Cat felt as if she were being drawn and quartered. Without abashment Brad opened his arm, and she went gratefully to him. Over the top of her curls, Brad met the questioning looks of his associates and defied them to say a word. Tears welled in Donna's eyes, but she blinked them back. Seeing, Travis Tanner took her hand.

"They left the house unlocked," he told Brad, "but everything's been taken out, except for the old piano. That way we satisfied the judge."

Cat shuddered, grateful for the protection of Brad's shirt. "That's..." Her voice was muffled. "That's all right. The piano was here when Tom and I moved in."

Anxious to leave now, Travis began urging Donna toward the front door. "Why don't we all go back into town? We can get something to eat and have a good night's sleep. Work on this another day."

"I can't," Cat blurted to Brad, then swallowed. "I mean, you all go on, please. I think I need to stay here just a little while. I have the Jeep. I can drive in later. I need to see Elenie and talk to the kids."

Brad asked Travis, "Where'd you get the sedan?"

"Rented."

"Leave it with me. Get Jerry to drive you back to town. Catherine and I'll talk things over and come in later."

Donna opened her mouth to object, but Travis pulled her quickly to the door. "Sure," he said, and tossed Brad the car keys. "See you later."

The empty house was full of ghosts like a lost mariner's ship, drifting upon some haunted, uncharted sea. For Cat, there weren't even the comforting white shrouds of covered furniture to reassure her; only bare, creaking floors and echoing, hollow rooms. As Brad walked silently beside her through the stark interior, she paused occasionally to touch a wall or a door.

"We tied Bingo's tooth to this doorknob," she fragilely recalled.

"Catherine Holmes, D.D.S.," he mused.

She smiled bleakly. "It didn't come out. He cried the whole evening until Crowe finally grabbed him by the hair and pulled it out with his fingers."

Brad chuckled. "He's in love with you, you know?"

Surprised that Brad knew that, she smiled. "Crowe? Are you jealous?"

With a swift shift of direction, he moved in front of her and pushed her back gently to the wall, pressing his length to hers as he kissed her slowly and thoroughly.

"Madly jealous," he muttered against her pale, trembling lips. "I'll challenge him to a duel. With bows and arrows. He can take the arrows. I'll hamstring him with the twine from the bow."

Not wanting to laugh but doing it anyway, Cat pushed at him. "Wow, you're an understanding kinda guy."

"After today, I don't think there's any question about that."

How giving life was, Cat thought, and how terribly stingy. "I'm going to get the children back, you know," she whispered fiercely. "This is only temporary."

"I know that. I'm going to help you."

She flashed him a look Brad was beginning to know well. "I fight my own battles, Brad Zacharias."

He gave a miniature karate chop to her throat. "Of course you do."

Back in the living room, the only furniture left was the old upright piano at the end of the room, beside the fireplace. It was hideously ugly now, and Cat was suddenly unable to bear looking at it. Leaving him, she moved to the window and stared at the mountains in the distance. Presently the silence became unbearable.

She said, "Do you know that there are more Ph.D.'s in Los Alamos, per capita, than anywhere else in the United States?"

Beside her, he stared out as if they might see some of those intellectuals if they looked hard enough. Their breathing fell into sync, and their heartbeats, too, Cat guessed.

"What's the matter?" she asked.

"My hand hurts."

And her own heart hurt. It hurt so bad, Cat thought it would burst inside her breast. She wanted to tell him that she didn't know how she could go on without the children, but he had tried so damnably hard to help her keep them—more than she had a right to expect—she didn't want him to think she was ungrateful.

Turning, capturing her face, he blew lightly into her lashes. "Nothing exists that can't be fixed, Catherine."

She blinked and laughed, then laid her cheek tenderly against his splint. "I buried my father today, Brad. It doesn't seem real. I wish I could cry."

"Did you love him?"

"Not like you love your father, I'm sure. But he was a good friend. Why do you ask?"

He was tracing the curve of her cuticles, one by one. Cat had difficulty connecting such infinite gentleness with the violent rage that had driven him to risk his life for her.

"That wasn't what you wanted to ask, was it?" she prompted.

He didn't answer immediately, then said slowly, "You loved Wrather for a long time. Is it really over?"

When she didn't look at him, he let out his breath. Guessing she had hurt him—again—she raised on tiptoe and touched her fingers to his lips. "I know he lied, Brad. I know he's done some things I don't want to even learn about. But he saved my life. I don't love him, but I can't lash out or try to hurt him back for what he's done. It's just sad, as if *he* were the one I buried today."

She grew suddenly withdrawn and remote, as if part of her had shut a door and no amount of battering on Brad's part could gain him access. The interior was nearly dark now. They had yet to return to the hotel and get something to eat.

Gently, he pulled her back to the present with a gesture toward the old piano. "What happens to that?"

"The piano?" She walked to the old instrument that was pushed against the wall. She didn't draw out the spindle-legged stool but lifted the keyboard cover to strike several out-of-tune chords.

"Do you play?" she asked idly, not turning.

Brad thought the sight of her back was so beautiful his heart would break. He compelled himself to reply lightly, "I've been known to do a mean 'Heart and Soul' on occasion. Do you?"

She lifted one shoulder and pulled out the stool with the toe of her shoe. Sitting, her bloodstained dress swirled in a fragile whisper about her legs, she tapped her forehead. "Ahh...I took lessons when Wrather sent me to college. Let me see if I can remember...."

Fascinated by the new things he was learning every moment, Brad fell in love with the way her slender fingers experimented with the keys. The suggestion of some song was on the tip of his tongue, but before he could open his mouth, she reached into the depths of her memory and began to play what he recognized as Chopin—an étude, very slowly, very sadly, very emotionally and with remarkable accuracy. Even though the old piano was out of tune, she touched it with the skill of an artist, and Brad felt his heart breaking and falling to the floor in pieces.

She stopped and, keeping her hands upon the keys and her head bent, whispered, "You see, it is because of Wrather that I can sit here and play this for you."

The silence bore no echo of Chopin nor recriminations of the past. Brad felt outraged, like a man who has spent his life's savings for a machine only to find that it doesn't work.

He understood what lay behind her fear of marriage. That very hesitance was also what he loved in her, but they had come to the end of the world, and there was no time left, there were no more paths to explore. It was either reach out and take the chance, or look back upon it for the rest of their lives and know the tragedy of their mistake.

"You're not going to marry me, are you?" he grated.

At his exasperation, Cat turned. The desire to wound him was heavy in her throat, in the texture of her words. "You have no right to speak to me like that."

"I have every right. I love you. Does he love you? No, he throws you away like a used napkin that he's wiped his hands on."

Cat could no longer bear to be in the same room with him, and Brad didn't believe the carnage he was strewing around them. Striding across the space, he captured her before she could dart away and, filling his hands with her hair, tipped back her head.

"Wake up, Cath," he said against the tight shutters of her face. "The only thing that kept you from becoming one of his trophies was me. You know, Catherine, I think you're great at giving love, but you're bloody hell when it comes to accepting it."

Cat knew exactly what he was saying because it was a truth she had resisted for a long time. Pushing his hands furiously away, she was momentarily shocked when he moaned and cradled his hand to his waist.

"Oh, Brad," she whispered, returning and drawing him against her strength that was, by circumstance, more powerful than his own now. "I'm sorry, I'm sorry. You know I didn't mean to hurt you."

She would have sworn she saw the diamond glitter of tears when he finally opened his eyes. A sudden shiver passed through him as he searched her face. "Sweetheart, I think I must have been born to hurt for you."

"No, no, no."

With a tearful pressure behind her eyes that she hadn't felt since childhood, Cat wrapped her arms about his neck and, rising onto her toes, fit her mouth to his and drew his head down until she was telling him with her tongue about her confusion and the questions that had no answers. With a tiny whimper she sent her hands skimming over his back, thrilling to the way he pulled her closer and dipped her over his arm like a reed.

His kisses became relentless, and her breasts ached to be touched. She ached so deeply inside, no relief was possible.

"You're wrong," she argued against his voracious mouth. "I *can* love."

"But for how long?" His voice was hoarse with frustration.

Tracing his jaw with the tiniest tip of her tongue, she slid her fingers beneath the back of his trousers and filled her hands with the tight, flexing muscles of his hips. Lifting herself, moving against him in that old, old motion, she deliberately drove him over the brink into irretrievable passion.

"How long do you want me?" she said into his mouth.

His reply was thick and guttural. "'For as long as we both shall live.'"

His lips found her ear, and the familiar words sent thrills attacking Cat's knees. He would settle for nothing less than marriage? Knowing how little she understood her own heart?

Their mouths met with hungry ferocity as she pressed herself to him with a grinding invitation. Her kisses were a torment Brad couldn't take much more of, as were the little sounds of need she moaned. She was reaching between them, stroking him, bringing him to an apogee that wasn't fair, and the sound of his zipper was like a rasp that cut him to the quick. Brad knew she would give everything but the one thing he wanted: eternity.

Grabbing her, his hand throbbing with pain, he looked down at her with passion-clouded eyes. "Marry me, Cath."

She could not yet focus her eyes, for passion had caught her in its vast net, too. She tried to smile, to comprehend the unsaid. "I do love you, Brad. You know I do."

"Then marry me. Say it."

Stung by the lack of compromise in his voice, Cat stepped numbly back and drew the sides of her dress together. "What are you afraid of, Brad?" Her voice was soft and low and rough. "Are you afraid that if I come to you I'll turn around and disappear? Do you believe in my love so little?"

Defeated in a way she couldn't possibly understand, Brad shook his head and turned away. His heart was breaking. He had failed. It hadn't been enough.

"It doesn't matter," he muttered. "Forget it."

"You're no different from Wrather, are you? Different, but not different."

Male pride flared suddenly in his eyes, and he stepped forward, his finger coming up to point at her lovely, frozen face. "I won't take," he grated, his lips drawn tightly over his face. "Not even from you, my darling."

Her own pride having reached the flash point, Cat couldn't hold back the words that had been waiting to be shaped into sound—half fears, skeletons of impressions. With her eyes brimming with tears that she had said she had vowed she could never shed, she lashed out. "Well, let me tell you something, Mr. Bradley Zacharias," she cried. "If I did agree to marry you, what makes you think that Wrather would stop at a broken hand next time? Did it ever occur to you that I might just be doing you a favor by wait-ing? I'm hurting right now. I'm hurting for you and for me and for my children. I'm hurting because you're what I want, but I don't know if I can change myself enough. We live in two different worlds, Brad. Are you willing to come and live in mine? No, you want me to come to yours, don't you? Well, I don't know if I can. I don't know if your world will have me. I've spent all of my life having people look over my head or around me, feeling uncomfortable when I walked into a room. It's not marriage I'm scared of, it's that kind of exclusion. I couldn't bear being on the outside of my own husband's life. And that, as God is my witness, is the truth!''

Clapping a hand over her mouth, her heels upon the floor like the percussive roll of a cortege for a love that never drew its first real breath, Cat ran from the room.

Chapter Eleven

Up the stairs and down the hall. The explosion of the door slamming shut. Whirling around in her own empty room that now looked like an outpost of hell, Cat half expected to see the walls come crumbling down like Jericho's and a smoke of plaster rising up to suffocate her. Once, just once, could her heart find peace?

Snatching open the door again, she raced down the hall, not really knowing where she was going—anywhere to escape the hurt in those gray eyes. Running, running, she darted into the bathroom and slammed that door like a criminal.

Defeat was clammy upon her skin. Darting to the shower, she twisted the spigots full force and kicked off her shoes, stripped down her stockings in a frenzy. She ripped off the rest of her clothes as if they represented the totality of everything that was wrong with her life, and leaving her black dress upon the floor like the residue of lost hopes, she climbed beneath the needling spray and sank against the wall.

"Oh, God," she moaned in her misery. "God, why does it hurt so bad? Help me, help me! I'm dying."

Her chest seemed filled with knots as tough as fists that pummeled and battered at her from the inside. The sound that tore from her throat didn't resemble anything human. She was strangling and tears were bursting from behind their dammed boundaries, tears that came as hard and fast as the water that washed her skin for they were the collected tears of a lifetime.

With body-racking spasms, then, she poured out her rage into the stream that was sluicing down the drain and into the earth forever. She howled with a misery that had no beginning and no end. She never truly knew when Brad climbed into the shower. Naked, she had slumped into a beaten huddle upon the old tile floor and somehow she focused her eyes and saw his shoes beside her knee.

Shrinking to the wall to shield her nakedness—for she could not recover, some part of her woman's vanity knowing how horrible she looked—she could only peer over her hands with a face that was ravaged and ugly. His splint was drenched, and his suit was soaked to the skin. Reaching down, he took her hand and pulled her to her feet and into the safe harbor of his arms.

"Oh, Catherine." His own tear-reddened eyes found hers, and his lips searched for the salt of her tears. "I do love you. God, I swear I do. I'll wait for you, Cath, until the end of time. I'll never push you like that again. Please don't be afraid."

For timeless moments they clung to each other—with wordless tears, mingled grief. And slowly, without questions or answers, promises or excuses, as he moved his hands over her with a restraint that was almost a reverence,

Cat closed her eyes and turned her face up to his. Lifting her knee, she placed it at his waist and clung to him.

"Take me," she said against his mouth.

His fingers sank deeply, and his kiss fiercely met hers. Cat thought he said her name, but the water and his hands were shutting out the world. Strange, agonized sounds were trapped in her throat, and her head dropped backward as he touched her. She wanted to tell him a thousand things, but he didn't ask, for he was bending to a knee and bracing her own upon his shoulder, reaching for her and finding her with a sureness and a certainty that telescoped all the years of waiting into a single throb of time.

Accepting his worship, she taught him with the knowledge that only women have about themselves—without modesty, without shame—but eventually the teacher became the learner and she learned about him. She marveled and adored. Time melted into itself as the water ran and ran, and just when Cat thought there was no more to be learned, he loosened his ruined clothes and climbed out of them, soaring with an insatiable hunger.

"I want you to know," he grated hoarsely against her cheek as he filled her with himself, "whatever happens between us from this day forward, you are mine, Cath. Forever."

"Yes," she said, not knowing how it would be, but trusting his love and, more than she dared hope, her own very private, very singular trust for him.

"You do love me," he muttered.

"I love you."

"You want me."

"I want you."

"Hold me very tight, my darling."

* * *

Much later, when they had dressed in their ruined clothes and had left Catherine's past for the movers, Brad took a room at a hotel in Santa Fe separate from his staff. The moment they walked into the darkness and the door locked shut behind them, they went into each other's arms without a word.

Not turning on the lights, just listening to the sound of breathing and the heartbeats of each other and comforted by the happiness of knowing that they, alone, were enough; they were like lovers who were together after a long absence. They had no need to declare their passion or their desires. Presently, as if their minds had traded places, Brad reached behind him for the light switch.

A soft glow filled the room. They undressed each other slowly, and Cat lifted her lips for his.

"My Catherine," he whispered, and kissed her for what seemed an eternity—impetuously, fervently, then seeking her eyes and her ears and her chin and the thickness of her hair with tenderness.

"Do you love me?" they said spontaneously, then laughed.

"Come to bed," he said.

The knowledge that she could drive Brad to the brink of losing control was an aphrodisiac that had Cat giddy with love. His taste, his scent and the heat of him were beneath her hands. She adored every inch of him, and he delighted in her newly found prowess. Laughing, Cat played the wanton and flaunted herself to create a chemical so potent, they had to do it all over again.

And after he'd ordered food and they'd gorged themselves, they made love again, and he turned her and molded himself to her back so that they were petals of the same flower. She slept with innocent soundness, but Brad rose and stood before the window as his hand hurt him.

He smiled at the smell of her on him. For the first time in his life he wondered if he was capable of keeping up with a woman. Cat had depths of herself that she didn't fathom yet—great, steel-riveted strengths—and she could take care of herself in ways she wouldn't have believed had he told her. She was quick-witted and tough. She couldn't be bought, and she couldn't be conned. Compared to the people in his world, she was worth any ten of them. Oh, they would like her, they might even envy her. For his sake they would even tolerate her, but they would always know she was different, and that would be her one great sin in their eyes.

As the room filled with the first smoky pinkness of dawn, he climbed into bed and drew her tenderly into his arms. He drew the inflammatory scent of her deep into his lungs.

"I love you, Catherine Holmes," he whispered into her hair.

She stirred sweetly in her sleep and, turning, slid her hand into the warm hollow between his legs.

Sighing, Brad remembered back to a blond-haired boy of twelve who had known another cat, a great tawny animal whose survival in the wild had been on the strength of his wits alone, for he had never been touched by human hands. Battle scarred, the old warrior prowled closer and closer until one day Brad placed a dish of food upon the windowsill.

Day after day the cat came to eat, but whenever Brad showed himself, the animal would slink back into the shrubs. One day he only backed off a distance and waited. With watchful caution he finally ate. Brad could still thrill to the trust that the big feline gave to him and no one else. The understanding between them was one of mutual need and respected distance, and in the weeks that passed the cat allowed his hunger to drive him near enough to be touched.

The one time Brad reached out his hand, though, he disappeared, never to return.

Brad promised himself not to repeat that mistake. He would not crowd this beloved feline beyond what she could bear. If Cat came to him with the fullness of her love and wanted to marry him as proof of that love, she would come of her own free will.

Tightening his thighs, he held her hand trapped between his legs. Closing his eyes he, too, slept.

Cat's return with Brad to New York was the result of a joint decision. After gathering the children and Elenie Sepulvada together, they discussed Brad's house in Long Island. He described to them in enthusiastic detail its three stories and about how he came to have it, and he was honest enough to admit that he owed a great deal of money on the place and had, in fact, considered selling it.

They immediately selected their own individual rooms and began to squabble about decorations. T. John and Babe were eager to adopt the co-op plan of ownership and informed Brad that there had to be tons of employment opportunities in such a place. Everyone would chip in. They did have their upholstering skills, after all. Diana made draperies as well as any trained professional, and she did her own designs sometimes. They would advertise! They would delegate the expenses and responsibilities and everyone could go to school during the day and work in the evenings and study at night. Just like one of the family programs on TV!

Not wishing to burst their pretty bubble, Cat told Elenie in private that there seemed no other option than to go on ahead. She would get her own job, then she would send for the children.

"You have to remember that you've got a life of your own, Catherine, dear," Elenie reminded as she finished jotting down all the instructions about the children's individual needs. "If something should work out...well, you know." She cast a longing feminine eye at Brad Zacharias that said she wished she were thirty years younger herself.

Cat balanced her handbag upon her knees and tried not to show how fragile her own faith was about the plan. "They are my life, Elenie," she said. "They and this man. I feel as if I could take all the children of the world and keep them forever."

The woman laughed. "We must have mercy on poor Mr. Zacharias. This will be a considerable drain on his pocketbook, I expect."

"No." Cat came decidedly to her feet. "I couldn't allow that to happen. I will find a way."

As Cat sat in the airplane's first-class section with Brad and his staff and sipped champagne later that evening, she became just tipsy enough to be enchanting. Privately, she considered it to be a sinister luxury, what with the attendants smiling and inquiring about the splint on Brad's hand and the Band-Aid on his nose as if he were a prince or some visiting dignitary.

Brad had laughingly lied to Elenie and said that a loft door had fallen down on him at the ranch. Now he smiled at the pretty, pink-cheeked attendant and, affecting a hokey nasal twang, said, "I'll be switched, dahlin', if I didn't get mahself thrown from one of those dude-ranch broncs down in Santa Fe."

"Is that a fact?" one murmured with a touch of her tongue to her cheek. "I would've thought that you were an excellent rider, sir."

"Hmm." Brad refused to get sucked into the double entendre. "I guess that depends upon the bronc."

Indeed! They quickly decided it was best to let the couple tend to their own knitting, and when the lights were turned down, Brad shut out the rest of the cabin with his back and drew Cat low into the seat beside him. Like children, it made perfect sense to them and was quite necessary that they look at each other for hours, noses nearly touching as they stroked each other's hair. They nestled together in the darkness and nibbled the tips of each other's fingers until Cat caught his thumb between her teeth and scandalously seduced it.

"My God, woman," Brad whispered as he attempted to undo a button on her blouse only to give up and place his hand beneath her skirt. "Have you no shame? Let's go in the lav."

"You think *I'm* going to do it in a sink?" Cat locked her knees together. "Kiss me quickly while no one is looking."

"I don't think that's possible. The man behind us is a flaming voyeur."

"Really?" She giggled and tried to aim her gaze through the space in the seats. "Then let's give him his money's worth."

Adoring her, Brad took her mouth in a swift, hard kiss. Her hands were a torment as they made brief excursions into the folds of his suit, caressing his back and the sides of his hip, the span of his chest and his waist.

"Remind me never to take this flight again," he muttered, and captured her hand and laid it upon the part of him that ached the worst.

"Your attitude could use a little work, Brad."

"My attitude's fine. It's my you-know-what that's in trouble."

"Your you-know-what is spoiled. Cheer up, it isn't fatal."

Brad tightened his hand in the tangle of her hair. "Look, the way I've got it figured, I've spent half my life looking for you. That means I'll have to do this every twelve and a half minutes just to break even."

Placing his hand upon her breast, Cat laughed. "We wouldn't want you to mess up the national average now, would we? Think of the paperwork."

"I admire your mind more every day," he said fervently as he kissed her until the captain turned on the No Smoking sign just before they were to land at Kennedy International Airport.

For seven rapturous days Brad and Cat were like children turned loose at the spring fair after a long winter. Cat had seen cities before, but from the wrong side of the street. On the arm of a man to whom doormen deferred and bank clerks and government officials were courteous, and even *waiters* were civil to, she gazed up at New York City's skyline in Alice-like wonder and swore she positively would not gawk like some green little gourd right out of the vegetable patch.

But once she was in downtown Manhattan, sliding out of a yellow cab as Brad tipped the driver, she was hooked. North, south, and west, the skyscrapers stretched away in clumps, growing like a gargantuan metallic garden: the World Trade Center, City Hall Park with its stone-and-mortar arch. In the distance would be the Hudson River, New Jersey, Staten Island.

Brad's apartment was in a four-story limestone-and-brick building set well back from the street and enclosed by a staidly discreet iron fence that was kept locked. To one side was an old-fashioned lamppost, and the flame fluted and purled with iridescent frivolity. His second-floor window, composed of tiny leaded-glass squares, extended out from the facade and was supported by four pillars—the most stunning thing Cat had ever seen.

At his office Brad bustled her through the wilderness of his suite, where Cat was shyly formal as she admired everything from the fresh flowers and genuine antiques and walnut and rosewood to the cameo that his secretary, Genevieve, was wearing. Genevieve was a properly sort-of-pretty, very-much-married woman of forty-five.

They ambled through the side streets of Greenwich Village where they browsed through shops for rare pasta and fresh breadsticks and aged cheese and flasks of Chianti. Hand in hand, they caroused along the huge, glittering honky-tonk of Broadway with its movie marquees and giant advertising billboards. Once they had tea in the booth next to Arnold Schwarzenegger at Radio City Music Hall, then strolled between Eighth and Ninth Avenues where the old stone tenement stoops were cracking under all the layers of cheap enamel, and muscled young men jostled against each other and dreamed of fast cars and faster women.

Brad took her on the shuttle to Washington, D.C., where the humidity was higher than the temperature. They sat in on a session of Congress. They took a room at the Mayflower just to change clothes, but decided to make love, too, just so the privacy wouldn't go to waste. They tiptoed around the subject of marriage as if it were bottled gelignite.

Shopping for her wardrobe, Cat guessed, was a terrifying experience for Brad. She refused to take his credit card and simply walk into Saks or Bergdorf Goodman. She browsed. She wandered. She mused. She found a Delta Air Lines jacket in a secondhand shop and wore it with a pair of black slacks and a cap from Bloomingdale's—very spiff. At a sidewalk sale, she struck a gold mine in an old Oleg Cassini jacket and a huge skirt that looked like something out of Scheherazade. With a fabulous scarf that cost more than everything else together, she could mix and match indefinitely, she vowed.

"Put something great with something hideous," she declared with relish, "and if you wear it with style, everyone thinks you're a genius."

While they were window-shopping at Tiffany's, however, Cat stared mutely at her melancholy reflection—her humble layers of cotton and frayed jeans and an impudent dash of silk superimposed upon priceless diamonds and rubies that were achingly his cup of tea.

Brad touched her hand. "What is it, darling?" he asked, and locked her fingers with his.

A tear dropped from her eye onto his splint, for her tears, once they had started to flow, seemed to come at the drop of a pin these days.

"You're giving everything," she said, and looked at his reflection looking at her reflection. "I'm not bringing anything into this relationship."

Laughing, turning her, folding her into his arms while passersby walked dispassionately around them, he held her with tender awe. "My sweet girl, I am without a doubt the most sensible man you will ever know. I'm so sensible I've missed all the fun. For the first time in my adult life, darling, I'm having fun. I'm doing what I want to do, and the rest of the world be damned. I feel like a man must feel who thought he was dying and found out a mistake had been made, Cath. You've given me back my life when I thought it was gone. I'm the one who is giving nothing to this 'relationship.' You're getting a burned-out old man, sweetheart. You're the loser here. Are you sure you're not doing this just to keep from hurting my feelings?"

Sniffing, trying hard to equate that irony with the inadequacy lining her heart, Cat gave him a captivating frown. "Your name's not Bradley, it's Blarney. Grief, you could charm the fangs from a cobra."

She stiffened in his arms. Over her shoulder she caught the profile of a man slipping just out of sight.

"Crowe!" she yelped, and freed herself to dart around Brad. *"Crowe!"*

"What?" Brad asked, confused.

"I saw Crowe! Over there. Look, look!"

Brad peered in the same direction, but saw nothing, no one. He caught her arm and looked deep into her eyes, placing his hand upon her forehead. "Tell me, Catherine, do you find you're nauseated when you first wake up?"

Ignoring him, she stepped into the stream of pedestrians, straining to see. "I tell you, I saw him, plain as day. I turned around and there was Crowe, standing right in the middle of the sidewalk like Crocodile Dundee, watching us."

Brad was hungry. They had a reservation at the Plaza in half an hour. "It happens to me all the time. You get somebody on your mind, then wham—you're seeing them all the time. Come along."

Glowering, Cat punched him in the side with her fist. "What d'you mean, am I pregnant?"

Laughing, he limped past her into the street. "Gee, I think we're having our first fight." He put his fingers in his mouth and gave an ear-shattering whistle. "Taxi!"

On Friday, when Brad took her to Long Island to see the house, Cat felt like Scarlett O'Hara returning to Tara after the war. They had driven miles and miles from Manhattan into the hill country where, from the road one could see glimpses of the Atlantic and on the other, Gardiners Bay.

"Brad!" she exclaimed with her nose pressed against the window. "When you said island, you weren't kidding!"

Brad had to get a ferry to take them to a spot of land where less than a half-dozen houses glistened scarlet in the misty summer evening.

"Don't get excited," he warned, grinning, and turned on the windshield wipers, "it's a moose. Really. A white elephant."

He was dressed for it in his limp fatigue pants and Bass Weejuns with no socks. For a shirt he'd hacked the sleeves out of a mangy sweat top and slashed the underarms. Everything about him, though, had its own separate seduction for Cat. No man she had ever imagined could challenge her so thoroughly or please her so totally. No man or dream had made her unfold so deeply, turning her to liquid inside until she felt as if anywhere the two of them were was home.

The driveway had lost its way in the grass that had overgrown it. Birds twittered and flew away as they parked, and as they climbed from the car a squirrel, startled from his placid evening meal on the gravel, flashed toward his hideaway and sat cursing them from his limb.

Smiling, they shared the scents of pine and overgrown roses and wet grass. The shadow of trees and shrubs crowded the rolling acres. The stone walls of the great three-story house were actually white, but now they were overgrown with ivy, and the incongruous pillars had long since lost their nobility. The roof was slate, and the many windows, all undraped, stared unblinkingly at their arrival.

The moment Cat saw it, it stole her heart. The steps, she knew, could once again be marble splendor spreading from the drive between arms of black wrought iron. The stained glass in the window of the huge front door could once again be stately, and the grottoes and winding paths, the wooden arches and the old roofed well could be radiant with charm and lovingly hospitable.

"Oh, Brad," she murmured, hugging his arm to the side of her breast. "It's wonderful."

"I've fallen in love with a blind woman," he vowed, but Cat recognized the relief that made his reply husky. How many women did he know who would have looked at such a disaster and seen hope? She had no idea. She was delirious to get working.

"Can't you imagine what it'll look like in September? Look!" she cried, giggling as she dragged him around the corner like a tugboat before he could unlock the front door. "A terrace! Oh, Brad, look."

He did look, and he saw a drab flooring of gray stones where a green film of moss had sprouted. It smelled dank, but she adored it and was moving about, her mind racing a hundred miles an hour as she murmured how she could see garden furniture here, and a rustic swing there, a rocker, perhaps, with a chintz pillow, and sofas in blue and white and rattan tables with iced tea on the trays.

She twirled around. "We'll give great parties. I'll make you look wonderful and brilliant. Aren't you glad I'm so unliberated and don't wear false fingernails?"

Brad's delight was in simply watching her. When he opened up the house, she was everywhere at once, poking and chattering about colors and fabrics and motifs. She had to inspect every single inch from the furnace to the attic. The kitchen was disgraceful, and the bathrooms would have been better not to exist at all. She knew exactly what the children would do and what they would say. She planned projects for them all as if they were there already.

"The paneling is what saves it," she declared with deep earnestness. "This teakwood is absolutely priceless. And the stairway is so *good*. Look at the inlay. This house isn't a moose, it's just undiscovered—'' she flashed him an impish smile and curtsied ''—like me.''

He loved her vibrance, her bright, infectious charm and her ill-behaved hair, which was as much a part of his days now as his own body.

''And it won't cost you but four times as much to fix it as it would to build a new one,'' she quipped.

''*The Money Pit*. I can see it already.''

''Hush. You'll hurt its feelings.''

''That can't be helped, my peppery little puss. All this remodeling has made me hungry. I hope you brought shrimps marinara in that basket of yours.''

''Dream on, Zacharias.''

Darkness had come early with a slight drizzle of rain, and Brad brought in the small basket she had packed. They brushed away the leaves that had blown in and collected before the great fireplace. They spread the tablecloth to sit on, and while Brad found a few logs the previous owners hadn't used, he made a fire.

With the dance of the flames turning them to copper, they foraged through the bread and cheese and olives, and drank wine out of the bottle. They talked with their mouths full and licked their fingers as they planned a hundred thousand things they would never get done in four lifetimes.

When they grew so tired they couldn't plan another plan or spend another dollar, Brad reached for her and leaned back against an aging wooden box, fitting her between his legs and closing his arms about her waist as she laid her head back upon his shoulder.

The silence was broken only by the sound of the rain falling softly against the windows and the hiss of the fire sputtering when the drizzle found its way down the chimney.

When she rose presently and moved to stand before the window, unable to see anything in the rainy darkness, he walked up behind her.

"You miss them," he said.

"Yes, but..."

"But, what?"

Turning, rising ever so slightly on her toes so that she could see through his eyes into his soul, she asked, "Brad, do you want your own children? We talked about marriage, and I pulled back. And now you bring me here, and this isn't the kind of house you fix only to sell to someone else. This is a home that you pass down to your children, Brad."

The gray of Brad's eyes became almost unreadable as he continued to look down at her. Cat thought she detected a faint tremble in his hands, and she wanted to bite her tongue. She had overstepped the line. Those were words for a wife, not for a lover.

But she had gone this far, and she might as well go the rest of the way. Dipping her head, she absentmindedly caught a sprig of her hair and drew it over her right eye.

"And then," she added huskily, "you asked me about morning sickness. Are you afraid I will get pregnant, Brad, or that I won't?"

His hands were definitely shaking when he tipped up her head and brushed the errant hair back from her face. He moistened his lips and drew his tongue across the ledge of his teeth. "I..." His breath was a long, slow inhalation. "I want very much to be a father, Cath, but I want first to be a husband."

Between two people who had been through what they had been through the last weeks, two very well-defined people who had looked at life from a number of angles and deliberately set out to make one of them work, this was something they could not slough off, something they could not joke away, something they could not ignore. They had come too far in that kind of union where giving is a habit and not dividing things into "yours" and "mine" is the rule.

Cat wanted her own child, but she wanted even more to give Brad that one gift that no one else in the universe could give him—*their* child. She had only needed to know if that was what he truly wanted.

She smiled from her heart. "Then I guess you'd better buy me a ring, Bradley Zacharias, and put an announcement in the paper."

Brad thought that her touch, her lips moving over him, would certainly turn him into a volcano. She had no mercy as she seduced him and tormented him and took him to the brink of sanity. Her love was an incomprehensible wave that flowed over him, and she took his hands and placed them upon her and inside her, and she placed herself to his lips and, with her eyes closed and her head dropped back, she said, "I would like a son, Bradley Zacharias, of my very own."

Turning, pulling her to him, Brad poured himself into her. "Then love me," he whispered as he held her fiercely while the tide of the passion reached closer and closer to the rocks of their shore. "Don't ever stop loving me."

Not until his office was vandalized did Brad remember that Cat had thought she saw Crowe on Fifth Avenue. Genevieve called at eight-thirty and gave him the news. "I haven't even called the police, yet," she said, shaken. "I don't know what to do."

It couldn't have happened on a worse day. Tonight was a dreary fund-raiser for McGrath that had been in the works for six months. He had an appointment at the bank at eleven o'clock to cash in some bonds so they could fund the remodeling.

He had just showered and dressed. He pinched the telephone beneath his jaw as he snapped on his wristwatch. Cat was brewing coffee as she picked up bits and pieces of the conversation. It was a week later. The announcement of their engagement had been in the Sunday *Times*.

"Just sit tight, Genevieve, and don't touch anything," Brad told her as a stitch of worry pulled in his neck. "Give me thirty minutes."

He slammed down the receiver as Cat stood prettily before him, warming her hands with a cup of coffee that sent curls of fragrant steam floating beneath his nose.

She put down the cup and followed him as he strode angrily to his closet and, sending the door open with a crash that made her wince, snatched out a coat to his suit and explained what had happened. "You think it's Crowe," she said. "Well, it isn't. I'm telling you, Crowe wouldn't do a thing like that."

He bent until his nose brushed the end of hers. "Did I accuse Crowe?"

"I remember what you thought when you looked at the cabin."

Brad didn't know what he thought at this point. Offices got vandalized every day in New York. Every hour.

"He wouldn't do such a thing," Cat was saying as she hurried after him, dressing as she came, arranging her hair, finding her shoes. "Even if he resented you, he wouldn't do anything that would hurt me." Out of breath, she presented herself to him like a child on her best behavior. "I'm going with you. I'm ready."

When they walked into the rooms behind the door with Consultant printed in gold, Genevieve was standing in the middle of the upheaval looking as if her virginity had been violated instead of the suite.

"Your hand, sir," she gasped, and pointed to the splint. "Not you, too."

"A dog bit it," he said dryly. "What's missing?"

"Nothing."

There was hardly anything from the splintered lock to the back storage room that had not been torn out of its place or destroyed. Books had been hurled out of their cases. Furniture had been ripped to pieces and the stuffing was thrown in every direction as if some alien monster had been inside and burst free. All the filing cabinets containing irreplaceable records were confetti on the floor.

But nothing had been stolen. At first neither of them believed that. Not a burglary? The police kept throwing up suggestions about what or whom could have been the target of such destruction. They asked him about his friends, and then his enemies. They wanted to know who she, Cat, was and who were her friends. Had anything unusual happened in his life lately? Anything out of the ordinary?

"No," Brad said, his jaw knotting as he and Cat made the same connection at the precise same instant: We happened. We are out of the ordinary. We just told the whole city of New York about us.

"How did you get that broken hand, Mr. Zacharias?" an officer asked.

"Slammed it in a car door," Brad growled as Cat was suddenly seized with coughing and began stepping hastily through the scattered papers.

The police didn't keep them long, and when the insurance adjuster was finished with his report, she and Brad went to Chase Manhattan Bank for his appointment.

"I'm sorry, Mr. Zacharias," Brad was told by Elias Bauer, who had been handling his account for the past ten years. "None of us know what to make of it. Your assets have been frozen by order of the Justice Department until further notice. I'm sure it's a mistake and will be cleared up very soon. I have a half-dozen people trying at this very moment to find out what's happened. I'm devastated, simply devastated."

It was no mistake. Brad knew exactly what had happened. He had received a warning, and he knew exactly who had sent it. Well, well, if that's what Wrather wanted, he'd see just how well the old crocodile could play hardball.

He strode out of the bank like a man with demons snapping at his heels. So infuriated was he by the passion of the moment, it didn't occur to him that it might not be logical for Wrather to be so jealously vindictive over a woman he had once gone to great lengths to get rid of.

Chapter Twelve

But it occurred to Cat. All day long, as the hours limped depressingly past and she sat beside her husband-to-be deep in the bowels of the Chase Manhattan, she thought of little else.

For Brad, bucking the Justice Department amounted to a string of terse, snappish telephone conversations that were invariably passed along to Elias Bauer's desk. Bespectacled men with prim, tight mouths, carrying locked attaché cases, entered and left Bauer's office.

Cat thought that if she didn't revert to biting her nails over this, she never would, but Brad seemed amused by the whole thing. He made a production of calling in favors owed him and dropped names in a disgraceful fashion. Lowell sent a friend, and Donna Hessing not only came, she brought Paul Hirshfeld, one of the powerful titans of the law firm.

"Everything will be all right now," Donna reassured in a hallway as she lit a cigarette, took one puff, then shakily stubbed it out. "Brad deals with crises like this all the time. Actually, he thrives on them. Are you two going to get married?"

From the beginning, Cat had sensed the relationship Brad and this woman shared. Donna would be an important person in their lives, whether she liked it or not. She said with a disarming self-effacement and the most honesty she could scrape from the bottom of her heart, "Donna, sometime when you have a spare moment, could you make me look exactly like you?"

Time molded into one of those golden moments that rarely, if ever, breaks. They did not touch, they simply knew they would be good friends for the rest of their lives.

All of which didn't change the fact that Cat was hurting the man she wanted least in all the world to hurt. By the close of the working day, Brad had forced the Justice Department to back off.

"I'm having a nervous breakdown," she told Brad later that evening at eight o'clock as they were climbing the steps of Joseph Lowell's two-story mansion in Bronxville for McGrath's fund-raiser.

"Washington parties serve only one purpose on this earth," he said, laughing as he held her hand tucked more securely in his arm. "They lessen a soul's torment in purgatory. Commit a sin, go to a Washington party."

"Pretty disgusting, if you ask me."

"Free enterprise at its best, darling. The guests have money and no press, we have press and never enough money. Everyone understands the rules, and everyone comes out happy."

"I'm not happy."

"You're not corrupt enough to be happy. For which I love you passionately."

Bronxville was a private enclave of tree-lined streets. The people who lived here were senators and representatives, ambassadors and cabinet members, foreign-affairs officials, successful entrepreneurs and those who had climbed high on the corporate ladder, and a few magazine and newspaper moguls.

Joseph Lowell's castle was more of a monument than a home. Its stately walls weren't concealed by shrubbery and twisting pathways but set on a hill beneath great, noble trees, its proud Norman architecture in competition with the pristine perfection of the Washington Monument or the Jefferson Memorial.

Troopers were on duty directing the scores of Ferraris and BMWs and Rolls-Royces, plus so many Mercedes and Cadillacs that Brad's modest Nissan appeared to belong to a pauper. An invitation to one of Lowell's parties was worth more than money. No serious politician considered achieving an important post without attending them.

At the top of the wide marble steps where light was spilling from the dozens of blazing windows, Cat voiced her true fears for the first time.

"I would tell you that I'm in over my head here," she whispered, gripping his hands tightly, "but I passed that stage so far back, I'd like to just graduate up to drowning status. What if I embarrass you, Brad? I'm not trying to be coy. I don't belong in all this Establishment cliquery."

"That's precisely why you do belong."

Motioning to the doorman that he wasn't ready to enter, Brad gripped Cat's wrist and drew her across the portico and down a series of steps at the side. He steered her through a shrub-bordered passageway to a picture window mounted in one of the dark, first-floor bedrooms.

Taking her by the arms, he positioned himself behind her and pointed to the glass. "Look at that woman, then you tell me."

She attempted to face him. "This has nothing to do with the way I look. What I'm talking about goes deeper than that."

"And that's what I'm telling you. Look, Catherine."

Cat stared at the slim, supple stranger reflected in the glass, at the gown he hadn't trusted her to select herself but had taken her to Priscilla Ford for an emergency fitting. "Knowing you, you'll come back as a Delta Air Lines pilot," he'd said.

Ms. Ford, known to work miracles on the spur of the moment with the most difficult clients, had deftly taken a black taffeta bubble dress and transformed it into a semioriginal in two days. Starkly black—"There couldn't possibly be another color for you, darling"—she had redone the neckline so that it dipped scandalously low and made the most of Cat's lovely bosom. With gloves reaching above her elbows and an evening bag that she didn't want to know the price of, Cat was aware of her beauty. She had let her hair run rampant. Caught up the back in a high pompadour, dozens of tight ringlets fell where they chose. Her lips weren't a bright slash of red but a muted rose, which, when contrasted with her eyes, made the rich violet irises appear more vibrant than ever.

When the fitting was finished, Priscilla had raised her Cruella De Vil brows. "She will be wearing emeralds, of course," she intoned, frowning down her nose at Cat but addressing the query to Brad.

"Of course," Brad said, grinning over Priscilla's shoulder before Cat could squeak out a word.

Now Cat touched the breathtaking pendant about her throat and the stones in her ears and the bracelet fastened around the wrist of her glove.

"I don't see anything," she told Brad, shivering.

"Then you're blind." He smiled. "Trust me." Wrapping his arms around her waist, he found her ear. "The danger of the game we all play up here, Cath, is that some people forget it's a game. Nations play it, people play it, the stakes are very high. The people here tonight are the power brokers of the nation, and everyone wants a piece of the action."

"But why do you play?" Cat shook her head. "Why are you supporting a man like McGrath Johnson?"

"Because—" he thoughtfully lifted the stone that lay deep in her cleavage, his fingertips playing lightly over the creamy tops of her breasts "—I still believe that McGrath will be good for the country. I can't get the things I believe in without playing the game. I'm using you tonight, Cath; I want you to know that."

She bridled prettily. "I'm not sure I like being used, even by you."

"You don't play the game, you see. Your freshness and your honesty show, and they make my statements more credible than ever. Tonight I want money for McGrath, and I want information. Cath, I don't know what's going on, but something is. If I don't find out what, it could destroy everything, including us."

"It would help if I dropped my lawsuit against McGrath, wouldn't it?" She toyed with a button on his shirt.

Brad pondered her for long, tender moments. She would never lose her mystery with time, not that strength of presence. He would eventually become unsuitable for his profession, but she was only just now preparing for hers, whatever that was. Life with her would not be boring.

"I'm not asking you to do that," he said with a shake of his head.

"I already did." She laughed, then dipped her head. "Conflict of interest, or something. Because I love you."

She had caught him by surprise—again. Brad caught her tightly to him, his heart pounding. For a long time their lips and tongues searched for answers from each other.

She broke away and spoke against his cheek. "You're wrong about me not knowing how to play, Brad Zacharias. I just haven't learned *your* rules yet." Breaking the mood with a laugh, she took his arm. "Come on, Professor Higgins. Eliza Doolittle is ready to brave the lions."

He made his eyes wide as a look of sheer terror passed across his face. "God!" he gagged. "I think you're serious."

"Absolutely."

Before he followed her back up the steps and into the mansion, Brad wiggled his brows suggestively at the darkened bedroom. "Ahh, I just happen to know that that window has a broken lock. We could be a few minutes late." He made a tiny inch with his fingers. "We consultants are very quick when we have to be."

It was amazing how the simple tone of his voice could start the machinery of her body working, Cat thought, flushing and growing damp with anticipation. She drilled a hole into his chest with her fingernail.

"Now, how would you know about this bedroom window, Mr. Zacharias?"

He chuckled. "I'm innocent. I swear on a stack of Bibles."

"Since you're in such a pious mood, add patience." She hiked up the neckline of her gown with a vampish wiggle. "I must enter now, and be the woman behind the man and make you look wonderful."

"To hell with the way I look," he growled as he unwillingly allowed himself to be guided up the steps and along the portico toward the waiting doorman.

"That's exactly what I thought the first moment I laid eyes on you."

Brad sighed. "It's going to be a long night."

The press corps wasn't admitted on the grounds immediately. Their orders were explicit: Keep your distance. Any interviews must be initiated by the guest. Anyone breaking the rules will be ousted on the spot.

Just to keep on their good side, the reporters had their own allotted part of the vast lawns behind the mansion. The trees were atwinkle with thousands of tiny lights. A grand buffet had been set up, plus a full bar. It was with the press corps that Crowe resumed the surveillance he had started ever since arriving in New York City a week before.

Finding Cat had been easy for Crowe. He had merely found Bradley A. Zacharias in the phone book. He hadn't followed them to Long Island because he hadn't had a car, but he had seen Brad's office after it had been ransacked. Alarmed, he had taken up watch outside Brad's apartment.

His original intention had not been to crash the party. After he saw a face he recognized, however, he reconsidered. After he noticed a *second* face, there was no question about what he must do.

He watched Cat and Brad when they stepped out of their car and postponed their entrance at the front door by way of a small detour to the side of the house. While they were there he broke into one of the parked cars and found an extra camera stashed beneath the front seat. Picking the pocket of a slightly tipsy cameraman snagged him a press pass.

He draped the camera about his neck and flashed the pass at the guard at the gate to the grounds. He decided he would give the party an hour for the liquor to flow freely. Then he would set about finding Cat.

The party was more dismally boring than even Cat could have imagined. Despite the glittering chandeliers and priceless Chippendale furnishings, Aubusson carpets, vintage champagne, miles of Limoges-set tables and finest sterling and fastidious napery, formal waiters and bowing maids to meet every need, a current of bitter boredom ran through the two hundred indoor guests.

The guest list was heavily male. Husbands and wives separated the moment they arrived. The men kept up their political cross fire in every possible corner and cubby. They shot comments and arguments past bored and sometimes openly offended facial expressions.

No wonder Washington wives had a reputation, Cat thought. Some of the men had already been corralled into Lowell's study, submerged in cigar smoke.

Being a new face, Cat was instantly the center of attention among the women. That she could be upon the arm of Brad Zacharias, whom almost all had tried to seduce at one time or another, marked her immediately as one worthy of subtle cannibalism.

To his credit, Brad kept her at his side as long as he could. Saying hello to McGrath was the worst hurdle, but McGrath didn't allude to Cat's dropping of the lawsuit, or that it had ever existed. A little more gray, a little more fleshy, amazingly cordial, he went out of his way to explain to those nearby that they had known each other for many years.

"Her father and my father were friends," he said, and talked about a couple of incidents from their past that would have made Cat feel at home had those memories not been woven into another tapestry with Wrather.

"Will Wrather be here?" she asked him.

"Later, I believe."

Did he know that she had been in love with his father all those years? Cat thought not. He wouldn't have believed, had she told him, that Wrather had lied about her and McGrath.

He asked about Brad's splint, and Brad told him he had dropped a bowling ball on his hand. McGrath then disappeared with Brad and several of the other men into Lowell's study. Cat quickly found herself trapped in a corner with a glass of wine she didn't want, surrounded by women who were getting drunk and chattering on and on about friends and parties to come, about who was having an affair with whom, and why.

After a half hour, Cat was seriously considering escape to one of the bathrooms when a Chinese man walked stiffly up, bowed precisely from his waist and said with perfect English, "Are you Miss Holmes?"

Surprised, Cat placed her hand upon the jewel at her throat. Every woman turned her head, and the ones who hadn't were obviously eavesdroping.

"Who wants to know?" she asked mildly.

His face revealed nothing. "Would you please come with me, madam? Mr. Lowell would like a word with you."

At the name Lowell, a hush settled upon Cat's side of the room, as if she had dropped her glass or thrown up on the man's white jacket.

Brad was still ensconced with McGrath. Cat could have told them all not to worry about her; anyone who could face down a man like Judge Constanza and defy a county sheriff with an unloaded .22 wasn't about to fall apart because of one old man in a wheelchair.

Placing her glass upon a small table nearby and smiling coolly at the ladies, she said, "Of course. Would you show me the way?"

He didn't touch her arm with his white-gloved hands, he just kept motioning with them as he guided her through the huge downstairs floor into one of the wings where the music was no longer audible and the lights were more muted. The wing's stairway had been replaced with a ramp that could accommodate a wheelchair.

When they reached the appropriate door, the man leaned slightly forward and rapped softly with one knuckle.

There was a muffled response. "Come in, Ling."

Ling opened the door. Cat was ushered into a large, airy room, which was stark in its absence of appointments. No carpets were on the floor, and the rich, aged hardwood gleamed. The ceilings were twelve feet high, and the walls were eggshell white. A bedroom, just as Spartan, flanked the study, and a gentle light shone from the bath. That, Cat noted, was quite modern.

Music was playing on an old-fashioned phonograph—a Mozart concerto, she thought.

"Come in, Miss Holmes," the voice said from the bathroom, and she turned as the whispered hum of the wheelchair brought it through an ever-widening blaze of light into the room.

"I *am* in," she said, wincing from the sharp, shrewd stare of Brad's patron of politics.

No one could accuse Joseph Lowell of being soft. A small, birdlike man who appeared even more shrunken because of the wheelchair, he nonetheless had the glint of nobility in his clear blue eyes. He was the great surviving link to the past. He claimed to be above the petty political ties and quarrels of the day. He was of the nation, and the nation was of him. Cat could see why Brad admired the man so deeply.

"So you are, my dear." He smoothed over his baldness with a graceful hand and invited her to sit. His laugh was charming and put her at ease immediately. "You mustn't mind the wheelchair. I may not get around much anymore, but I can still be a good host. Here, take this chair beside the desk."

The chair beside the desk, Cat noted, was in the full glow of the light while he, positioning himself by the wall, was thrown into shadow.

Not knowing if she liked him quite as much as Brad did, Cat walked smoothly to the chair and drew it across the varnished floor until they would both be in equal shadow.

"Thank you," she said, and smoothing her dress with a carelessness that she hoped conveyed its own message, sat easily and crossed her legs once, placing her hands in her lap. Gently, she said, "What's on your mind, Mr. Lowell?"

He considered her for a moment, frowning, then smiled. "Ah, yes. I see why Brad lost his heart while he was down there in New Mexico."

A bit unnerved but not showing it, Cat said, "Oh, I think Brad is much too smart to lose anything, Mr. Lowell."

When he indicated the phonograph and asked if she would mind taking off the record, Cat thought she had offended him. Heroes liked to be lauded.

"Certainly." She lifted the cover and removed the needle. By replacing the disc into its jacket and slipping it onto a shelf, she stalled a few more seconds.

Now the music from outside drifted inside. "Would you like me to open the French doors?" she asked politely. "Then you can hear your party."

"Thank you very much." He laughed. "Since I can't throw you off guard, we may as well sit on the patio."

"That's a good idea."

His muscles were growing lax with disuse, and the skin along his jaw was sagging. His fingernails had the length of an idle man's. He wore only one ring, encrusted with diamonds. Lowell wasn't a man she would want for an enemy.

He asked if she would pour some sherry, which Cat did, and she took her own glass with her as she went to sit in her appointed chair. He positioned his wheelchair against one of the rosebushes and chatted amiably for a moment about the different species growing around his patio.

Then, just as Cat had known he would, he turned and took a deep breath and let it out. "Are you wondering why I sent for you, my dear?"

"To look me over, I expect, Mr. Lowell."

He smiled a becoming smile. "And what do you think I see?"

"Someone whom Brad loves, someone rather unsophisticated who loves him and will make him happy. Someone I'm hoping who can adapt to this whirlwind life he leads."

"Yes. But I see much more than that. All good things. Fine, strong things."

"Have you and McGrath been talking about me?"

"No, dear. McGrath's father and I have been talking about you."

It really shouldn't have surprised her, but for a moment Cat's mind stopped working. She slipped out of the picture like the piece of a puzzle that doesn't quite fit although it has the color and the shape and the texture. She tried to understand how this man whom she didn't even know existed until a few weeks ago could be in her life, affecting it this way.

Dread coiled in the bottom of her stomach. "You're going to tell me something unpleasant, aren't you?

At least he had the grace to lower his bald head and move his hand over it again, this time in a gesture of distaste for what he was about to do. He didn't look up as he spoke. "All my life I have had power, Miss Holmes. Even as a young man, I had the talent for stripping away the layers of a situation and coming to the heart of it. It was a gift I used well, because with that keenness comes the power. But I'm old now, and not as well as I used to be. I'm afraid my vision is not as keen as it once was."

Why are you telling me this? Why isn't Brad here? "Please call me Catherine," she said with a poise that astonished even herself.

Looking up, he moved his eyes over her with admiration. Cat wanted to lunge at him and grab his collar and shake him.

"Does Brad know that you're talking to me, Mr. Lowell?"

He fondled the ring on his finger. "My dear, if Brad thought we were having this conversation, it would be over."

"What would be over?"

The ring caught the light and shot fire at her. "Everything. Wrather Johnson has...how shall I say this? Wrather Johnson is a shrewd man. McGrath, too. But his father is always seeking an angle for himself in every situation. Wrather has tied my hands in a number of crucial areas, Miss Holmes. He is now in a position to say what he wants and doesn't want concerning his son's future, which affects us all; me more than most, but certainly Brad, whom you tell me you love. If Brad warred with Wrather Johnson, Wrather would destroy him. Never believe for a moment that he isn't capable of it."

Cat felt the approach of a terrible, terrible punch line to the story. She braced herself, steeled herself against her past—a collage of failures—and a future that seemed destined to be the same.

"Please—" she closed her eyes "—just get done with it."

"Wrather wants you to go home, Miss Holmes."

The fight drained out of Cat, and not until she heard the crash of her glass to the floor did she realize that she had dropped it. She was that little girl again, cringing before some strange, tall man who had power, much power.

She made no move to pick up the shattered pieces from the floor. Through her teeth she asked, "Why?"

"I think he fears what you know, my dear."

"What...what I *know*? I don't *know* anything about anything. What're you talking about?"

"You made a mistake, Miss Holmes, when you didn't leave before, back before all this happened."

"Leave? You mean, leave McGrath's ranch?"

"Yes."

With the press of a button, the wheelchair drew nearer. Lowell leaned forward, his eyes small with intensity, the light reflecting from his small, gleaming pate.

"I tell you this with great distaste, for it isn't my style. Times change. I can only say that if you don't want Brad to pay for your folly, please, take the money I'm about to offer you and just *go home*. No questions, no attempts to fight back—such as all that lawyer business. This is one time you can't jump into a Jeep and drive away, Miss Holmes. If you really care about Brad, and I think you do, please, I implore you, go home. Let things rest."

From beneath the coverlet draped across his legs, he withdrew an envelope. Cat felt as if all her bones were disconnected. One saw this on television; it didn't happen to insignificant women who took care of little children.

In horror, Cat recoiled from the proffered packet.

"No melodrama, Miss Holmes." He smiled sadly. "In this envelope is twenty thousand dollars. You will be able to help your children with this. It'll give you a fresh start. Take it with my deepest, deepest apologies and sincerest hope that you will make that new start. I would ask you to please not tell Brad about our conversation, but I have a feeling that he already knows that I have to do this. Now, if you'll excuse me, my dear, I'm quite tired. If you would be so kind, please leave by the patio. If you follow the walk—there, yes—you will find the gate to the street with no trouble. I think the fireworks display will be soon. I hope you enjoy them. Good night, Miss Holmes. I am truly sorry."

With that, he placed the envelope upon the balustrade of the patio and touched a button on his controls. The chair whispered softly as it moved back into the shadows, so far back that he disappeared altogether. The sound ceased, and the French doors shut in Cat's face.

How much simpler it would have been if she hadn't been in love with Brad. That was what love did to a person. Love took away the ownership of a person's life, because things never happened to just one, they happened to two. Brad would be hurt because of her, but if she left now, though he might be hurt, he wouldn't be destroyed.

Numb, disbelieving but having to believe, Cat weaved slightly and stumbled from the rose garden out onto the rolling hillside where the party was getting into full swing. A dance floor had been built beneath the stars. Her heels poked into the moist grass as she walked toward it without really knowing where she was going.

Far in the distance she could see the Washington Monument, and as she gazed up at it, a series of pops appeared in the sky, and a glittering shower of red, white and blue stars exploded to hang in the night sky, defying gravity for a few seconds as they reached their apogee and cascaded to earth.

She was consumed with worry. She migrated toward the people, unclipping the emerald bracelet and dropping it into her bag and pulling off the gloves, blotting her face and the space between her breasts.

What should she do? Her leaving would kill Brad. A sob formed in her lungs and threatened to break her. "You cry now, Catherine Holmes," she told herself with a ruthless inner shake, "and you're off my list forever."

The stars evanescent as blue lights flaired from the pieces of fireworks that fell earthward. Out of those fragments popped more and brighter pieces, shooting skyward yet again and opening into a sparkling spray of sapphires.

The dance floor was just beyond. The band had stopped playing. Couples were standing still, laughing up at the sky. Cat wanted only to find Brad.

She imagined that someone said her name. Spotting the bar, she thought ice water might clear her head. She felt a tap on her shoulder, and she moved reflexively, brushing it off as she would shoo one of the children who was worrying her. It touched her again. With irritation drawing her features and panic drumming a tattoo on her skull, she whirled around and looked straight into the solemn black eyes of Crowe.

Cat was the closest to fainting she'd ever been. Her jaw dropped, and she staggered backward—laughing, sobering, her heels sinking lower into the soil so that she weaved dangerously.

"Crowe!"

The sky was a spectacle now. Crowe took her arm and drew her beyond the din, and Cat found her voice at last.

"It *was* you," she exclaimed. "I saw you before, on the street. I didn't imagine it. What're you doing here? Why aren't you... You stole the Jeep, you cad. How did you get to New York?"

"Hitchhiked."

She touched her temple in confusion. "What're you doing here?" She threw out her arm to include everything.

"Looking for you," he said, and smiled one of his rare smiles, marring his handsomeness a bit, for he was at his best when he was untouchable.

So deeply happy was she to see a friend, Cat's lips began to quiver. He attempted to comfort her, but she shook her head and waved between them.

"Don't mind me. I'm just a June bug. This is an awful party." She took his arm and tried to laugh and cry at the same time. "Let's go somewhere and talk. I'm so glad..."

Without planning to, Cat gripped the Indian by both arms and shook him as a child would fight for the attention of a parent. "Crowe, everything is such a mess. Wrather has done something, I don't even know how to begin to explain it. And Brad—I'm going to marry him, Crowe, or at least I was—but I don't know what's going on, only that Brad's in trouble, and I can't help because I don't know how. It's a mess, just a... a stinking *mess*!"

With the most phenomenally gentle hands, Crowe reached up to smooth back tumbling ringlets of her hair.

"I know," he said in his deep, steady voice. "I've come to help you."

When Crowe explained the situation while they walked, Cat thought its simplicity was why she had not seen it. "I knew when we found the cabin," she told him, "that something was very wrong. People had been going up there to the mountains. I blamed McGrath for it."

"I've seen some of the people who came to the cabin," Crowe said. "Some of those people who met with Wrather Johnson at the cabin are here."

Cat's thoughts refused to connect in any tangible pattern. "Do you think it's bad? That they sneaked in by helicopter for secret meetings? What am I talking about? How do I know they sneaked?"

"They sneaked. And did other things."

She knew he meant the parties, the drugs. "Why didn't you ever tell me what you saw when you went up there?"

He gave her a shrug that Cat guessed she would never understand. "It wasn't any of my business. Wrather Johnson is here, too."

Dismay needled Cat between her ribs. "When did he come?"

"After you and the man came."

She laughed. "You can't continue to call him 'the man,' Crowe. His name is Brad."

At her tease, Crowe shyly ducked his head. "I need to speak to your Brad, I think."

"Yes. We'll have to get you into the house. I want you to point out to Brad the people you saw come to the cabin. Maybe he'll know what's going on."

Of all the daring things Cat had done as a girl, she had never sneaked into a person's house as she did now. Taking Crowe to the bedroom window, she fumbled with the latch. "Brad said this lock was broken."

"Here, let me."

After they climbed in the window, Cat felt her way through the bedroom like a burglar doomed for the penitentiary. "What we need is to get you some different clothes so we won't attract attention."

After a few unsuccessful and hair-raisingly harrowing detours, they found some of Joseph Lowell's older formal wear that had been carefully stored in an unused bedroom closet. Though the tuxedo wasn't a perfect fit, Crowe was remarkably handsome in the snow-white shirt and cummerbund and somber black tails.

Cat laughed. "Crowe, I think you're a little overdressed for this occasion. I wouldn't try to pick up a date or anything. Come on, let's find Brad. God, I hope we don't run into that valet of Lowell's."

They sneaked through the carpeted halls toward the brightly lit rooms until they heard the muted clink of glassware and laughter and music. Outside, the band had resumed playing.

"Wait!" Cat hissed, and jerked on Crowe's sleeve.

She drew on her gloves and fidgeted while he fastened the clasp of the bracelet. A matched pair of the ladies who had had too much to drink passed, giving them a tilted, giggling scrutiny as they did so.

Dinner had not yet been served. Most of the guests had migrated to one of the larger sunken rooms that was slightly below ground level. The small stair was unelaborate as it descended into the room, but it was very wide, the focal point of the whole downstairs.

As Cat and Crowe hesitated at its top, it afforded them a view of the entire room—dozens of black-suited penguins with brightly colored Barbie dolls sprinkled liberally among them. Jewels circling the dolls' necks and twinkled from their ears, flashing on their fingers as glasses were lifted and signals were passed back and forth.

Cat looped her arm lightly through Crowe's and whispered urgently from the side of her mouth, "Do you see the two people you told me about? And please be sure. If we make a mistake about this, the cure will be worse than the illness."

Crowe's black warrior's gaze swept disdainfully over the guests as if they were so many puppets playing their parts. Brad Zacharias wasn't hard to spot in the elite clique of men near the great marble fireplace. As if by prearrangement, he looked up to see Crowe. For Brad it was déjà vu, except that this time the woman was beside the Indian.

Crowe watched as a grave quietness came over the tall, blond man. Communication passed as easily as before. The man read him aright, and he was clever enough not to move too quickly. Turning with a graceful hesitance, he slowly and unobtrusively began weaving his way through the hundred or so guests and made his way across the room.

As he began to ascend the stair, however, the undercurrents spread through the room in a way they could not have done in any other place. Dozens of eyes turned at once, and the voices dropped to a low murmur, then hushed altogether.

Cat saw Wrather standing beside McGrath at the fireplace, and both men exchanged a look she would have given a year of her life to see. Turning, Wrather looked at her as if she were poison, McGrath as if he were as surprised as anyone else.

When Brad reached up his hand, Cat forgot about everyone but him. Oh, yes, it hadn't been a mistake to stay and fight for this man.

"Brad," she said with brimming eyes, "this is Crowe."

With a slow, knowing smile, Brad took the Indian's hand into his splinted one and shook it. "Yes, we've met. Sort of."

Crowe inclined his head.

Moisture had slicked Cat's hands. She moistened her lips. "I'm all right. Brad, Crowe has something to tell you."

Brad was at his best performance level in situations such as this. He listened to everything Crowe told him, and he laid his plans with computer swiftness, cross-referencing pieces of information, juggling details, making judgments that would affect many lives and knowing the fearful responsibility of such acts.

"Crowe," he said softly when the Indian had finished, "I want you to take a walk with me through these people. Take this and put it in your breast pocket. It's a tape recorder, and it's operating right now."

In shock, Cat widened her eyes at the man she was engaged to marry.

A sheepish lift was in his brow. "We'll talk about it later," he murmured. "What I'm going to do, Crowe, is introduce you to many people. These will be very important people, heads of unions, newspaper people, corporate bankers, people who are crucial to the making of a president. But some of them will be judges and federal officials. If you've seen any of them at the cabin, you simply say yes loud enough for the recorder to pick it up. But especially try to remember which ones you've seen together."

"What d'you mean?" Cat asked. "Are these people not supposed to be together?"

"Some of them, no. Not to make deals, not to sell people out. But it would tell me a whole lot of things if I knew a few of them were. Do you understand, Crowe?"

"Perfectly," Crowe said.

Feeling a bit left out of it—it was her shrewdness and her ingenuity that had accomplished this coup, after all!—Cat had to be content simply to follow along in their wake.

In the space of a half hour, Crowe had identified, for the record, some twenty people who had had meetings in McGrath's cabin, one of them the assistant attorney general, which raised an interesting question. Cat knew now, though, that McGrath had none of the answers. McGrath was ambitious, but he wouldn't stoop to bribery or blackmail or drugs or women.

Through it all, Brad kept her in the tight circle of his arm. He made light conversation and exchanged pleasantries. He took the usual joshing about their engagement until they reached Wrather. He told outrageous fabrications about what had happened to his hand.

"Wrather," he said easily as the three of them finally worked their way to where he stood beside McGrath and Monique. "I heard you'd come in late. Pleasure to see you again, sir. You know Catherine, of course. And one of her friends, John Crowe."

Cat gripped Brad's fingers with bone-crushing strength as Crowe met the older man's eyes. In Wrather's face was not the slightest recognition.

"Yes," Crowe said distinctly.

As Wrather rotely performed the ritual that courtesy demanded, to Cat he looked as if his heart had stopped beating. Because of her? Because she hadn't gone running with her tail tucked between her legs?

The past, the dreadful millstone she had carried around her neck for so long was suddenly not there. She didn't owe Wrather Johnson anything. He hadn't gotten her off drugs, she had gotten herself off. The score between them was settled for all time.

"Mr. Lowell has something of yours, Wrather," she said as calmly as if he had left a cigarette lighter on the phonograph.

"Oh?" he said in a thin voice.

Smiling, her chin at a proud angle that came as easily as it had once bowed low, Cat released Brad's hand and glided toward the stunned silver man.

"Wrather," she said demurely, and looped her arm through his, "I've been wanting to talk to you. Goodness, it seems like forever. Tom asked about you not long before he died."

"Talk to me about what?" Some of Wrather's aplomb was fighting to recover.

"Interest due, Wrather," Cat purred, her smile blinding as she left Brad and Crowe frowning at her back. "Interest due."

"What was that all about between Wrather and you?" Brad demanded at three o'clock the next morning when they were in his tousled bed on West Seventieth Street and the lights were out and Crowe was in the guest bedroom and Cat had thought Brad had to be sated enough with love to sleep for a week.

Cat pried open her eyes to find the bedside lamp glaring. She squinted like a wizened little man. "Nothing," she said, and, yawning, snuggled against him. "Turn out the light."

Obliging, Brad lay in the darkness a long time, thinking. Tomorrow he would take Crowe downtown to look at some mug shots, just on the outside chance that some of the people he'd seen going in and out of the cabin weren't on the right side of Mr. Clean. He already knew enough to insure that McGrath's campaign would be a legitimate one from now on.

"I did good, didn't I?" Cat murmured sleepily, and tweaked a curl on his chest.

Chuckling, Brad reached back to slap her on the behind. "Stop bragging."

She pretended to snore lightly, and Brad closed his eyes once more. Presently he turned on the light again and propped on an elbow. He pulled the sheet off her face by inches.

"What *did* you and Wrather talk about?"

Throwing him a weak punch that missed, Cat groaned and pulled the sheet back over her head. "I'll tell you later, Brad. It's three o'clock in the morning!"

The light went out. A long silence ensued. The light came on again, and Brad said, "But you did talk about something, Cat. As your husband, I think I have the right to know."

One violet eye glared at him, hungry for blood—his. "Not for two weeks yet."

"That's only a technicality. Are you going to tell me? 'Interest due,' you said before you sailed off into the sunset. What interest due?"

With a slam of her feet to the floor and a wiggle of her hips beneath the disgraceful scrap of undershirt she called a nightgown, Cat clumped to the dressing table and felt groggily around for her bag. Drawing out a piece of paper that was haphazardly folded in half several times, she plodded back to bed and threw the paper at him and collapsed.

"I was saving it for a wedding present," she said from beneath the ivory-colored tent. "But no, you have to go and hound me to death."

Brad was so fascinated with her sexy dishabille, he could have foregone the paper. As she burrowed into his side, he unfolded the handwritten paragraph. At the bottom was the signature of Wrather Johnson.

"What—" he said, starting.

"Just read it," she commanded. "Aloud."

Brad slowly deciphered the trembling, spidery words.

I, Wrather W. Johnson, do hereby agree, as recompense to Catherine Cecily Holmes for the residence promised to her and her father, Thomas Holmes, the full payment of a property of her choice, to be duly recorded in her name to her and her heirs forever. Upon notification of that property, payment will be delivered within thirty (30) days from that date.

Wrather W. Johnson

With a trembling that came close to honest reverence, Brad folded back the sheet and bent over Cat's scrunched knot of arms and legs canopied by her hair.

"It's from me to you," she said.

Brad shook her shoulder. "I can't take this. Do you realize what this is? This is the deed to just about anything you want it to be."

Giggling, she unfolded and snatched the paper from his hand and tucked it ridiculously down the front of her shirt. "It's the deed, Bradley Brad Zacharias, to the house on Long Island. It's my wedding dowery, so don't go getting maudlin on me. You'll take it or the deal is off. The raising and educating of our children, of course, is your financial responsibility. And by the way—" she craned to peck his cheek in a highly unsatisfactory manner "—thank you for letting me send for them tonight. I'm afraid that when we pick them up at the airport tomorrow, you'll have to extend me a teensy bit of credit." She gave him a dazzling smile from behind her hair. "But I'm good for it."

With that, she reached across him and turned out the light, knocking Brad flat on his back in the process. As she crawled back over him to her side of the bed, Brad, not a man to be outdone by a mere piece of paper, proceeded to hunt for it beneath the old shirt.

"God," he groaned as he succeeded, "I love this job."

Epilogue

Many miles away, Babe Polansky was sitting in the bathroom of the YWCA in Santa Fe. Everyone else was asleep, but she hadn't closed her eyes since the phone call from Washington. They were going home, all of them. Something was happening, something wonderful and frightening. Her old life was being left behind and a new adventure lay beyond. All because of one woman who had come into her life without being invited and who had seen something besides an overweight, loudmouthed girl—one woman, not Cat, not Catherine, but Miss Catherine Holmes, gentlewoman.

Babe drew out her yellow pad and turned over a fresh new sheet, smoothing it for a moment as she put her thoughts together. Maybe nothing would come of what she was about to write. Maybe it was an echo of some lost part of herself that was worthless to anyone.

But the words came anyway, honest words from her heart: *Today I found a picture from my past. When I held it to the light, the images had turned to yellow, but I could make out the blurring figures—children, all of us, all shapes and sizes, boys and girls and one stone-faced Indian who was separate from the rest. A look of grim eagerness played on the faces in the photograph, and I tried to remember what I had felt on that distant day. But I couldn't. And as I looked, the images seemed to grow more faint and yellow, consigning themselves to a past whose pain is but a memory now. I searched for answers in those childish faces before they slipped away. None came. And it was in those moments before I returned the photograph to its box that I shed my tears for what was gone. I wept because someone had cared for me. I wept because what I thought was love wasn't love at all, and because my childhood was running away from me, the rising sun at its back. I watched it go until it was out of sight, and that's why tears ran down my cheeks—tears of joy and loss and redemption and whatever else tears are made of. Today I know I have only begun to learn what love is.*

*   *   *   *   *

Silhouette Desire ®

CHILDREN OF DESTINY

A trilogy by Ann Major

Three power-packed tales of irresistible passion and undeniable fate created by Ann Major to wrap your heart in a legacy of love.

PASSION'S CHILD — September

Years ago, Nick Browning nearly destroyed Amy's life, but now that the child of his passion—the child of her heart—was in danger, Nick was the only one she could trust....

DESTINY'S CHILD — October

Cattle baron Jeb Jackson thought he owned everything and everyone on his ranch, but fiery Megan MacKay's destiny was to prove him wrong!

NIGHT CHILD — November

When little Julia Jackson was kidnapped, young Kirk MacKay blamed himself. Twenty years later, he found her...and discovered that love could shine through even the darkest of nights.

ATTRACTIVE, SPACE SAVING BOOK RACK

Display your most prized novels on this handsome and sturdy book rack. The hand-rubbed walnut finish will blend into your library decor with quiet elegance, providing a practical organizer for your favorite hard-or soft-covered books.

Only $9.95

Approximately 16" x 8" when assembled

Assembles in seconds!

To order, rush your name, address and zip code, along with a check or money order for $10.70* ($9.95 plus 75¢ postage and handling) payable to *Silhouette Books.*

BKR-2A

Silhouette Special Edition

COMING NEXT MONTH

#493 PROOF POSITIVE—Tracy Sinclair
Tough divorce lawyer Kylie O'Connor privately yearned for a happy marriage and bouncing babies. But cynical Adam Ridgeway wasn't offering either, and Kylie's secret couldn't keep for long....

#494 NAVY WIFE—Debbie Macomber
Navy officer Rush Callaghan placed duty above all else. His ship was his home, the sea his true love. Could vulnerable Lindy Kyle prove herself the perfect first mate?

#495 IN HONOR'S SHADOW—Lisa Jackson
Years had passed since young Brenna coveted her sister's boyfriend. But despite recently widowed Warren's advances, Brenna feared some things never changed, and she'd forever be in Honor's shadow.

#496 HEALING SYMPATHY—Gina Ferris
Ex-cop Quinn Gallagher didn't need anyone. Yet sympathetic Laura Sutherland saw suffering in his eyes—and her heart ached. She'd risk rejection if her love could heal his pain.

#497 DIAMOND MOODS—Maggi Charles
Marta thought she was over Josh Smith. But now the twinkling of another man's diamond on her finger seemed mocking... when the fire in her soul burned for Josh alone.

#498 A CHARMED LIFE—Anne Lacey
Sunburned and snakebitten, reckless Ross Stanton needed a physician's care. Cautious Dr. Tessa Fitzgerald was appalled by the death-defying rogue, but while reprimanding Ross, she began feeling lovesick herself!

AVAILABLE THIS MONTH:

Silhouette Intimate Moments

JOIN BESTSELLING AUTHOR
EMILIE RICHARDS
AND SET YOUR COURSE
FOR NEW ZEALAND

This month Silhouette Intimate Moments brings you what no other romance line has—Book Two of Emilie Richards's exciting mini-series Tales of the Pacific. In SMOKE SCREEN Paige Duvall leaves Hawaii behind and journeys to New Zealand, where she unravels the secret of her past and meets Adam Tomoana, the man who holds the key to her future.

In future months look for the other volumes in this exciting series: RAINBOW FIRE (February 1989) and OUT OF THE ASHES (May 1989). They'll be coming your way only from Silhouette Intimate Moments.
